MYSTERY

High Tide

Jude Deveraux

High Tide

WHEELER
PUBLISHING, INC.
ROCKLAND, MA

★ AN AMERICAN COMPANY ★

Published in Large Print by arrangement with Pocket Books, a division of Simon & Schuster Inc. in the United States and Canada.

Wheeler Large Print Book Series.

Set in 16 pt Plantin.

Library of Congress Cataloging-in-Publication Data

Deveraux, Jude.
 High tide / Jude Deveraux.
  p. (large print) cm.(Wheeler large print book series)
 ISBN 1-56895-800-5 (hardcover)
 1. Large type books. 2. Fishing guides—Florida—Everglades—Fiction.
3. Everglades (Fla.)—Fiction. 4. Detective and mystery stories.
5. Love stories.
I. Title. II. Series
[PS3554.E9273 H48 1999]
813'.54—dc21   99-054333
                                 CIP

Prologue

"I won't do it," Fiona said with an icy smile, then refused to say another word as she stared at the man across from her. It was a stare that usually stopped people in their tracks. In heels, Fiona was six feet tall—and when necessary, she used every inch of her height to intimidate.

James Garrett might be several inches shorter than she was, but he *did* own the company. "I did not say *if* you were willing to go," he said quietly, his dark eyes as hard as the obsidian they resembled. "I said that you were going. My secretary has your tickets." With that, he looked down at his desk as though the matter were finished and she was to leave his office.

But Fiona hadn't gotten where she was by being timid. "Kimberly needs me," she stated flatly, her lips set so firmly they were little more than a line below her nose. Her chin was elevated in such a way that she was looking down on top of his head. Were those hair plugs? she wondered.

"Kimberly can—" James Garrett shouted, then calmed himself. He was *not* going to tell her to sit down. He wasn't going to have her or anyone else saying he had a Napoleon complex or that tall women made him feel— "Sit!" he ordered.

But Fiona remained standing. "I need to get back to work. Kimberly needs a few adjustments, and I need to talk to Arthur about projections for the coming season."

James counted to four, then turned his back on Fiona and looked out the window at the dark streets twenty stories below. New York in February, he thought: cold, windswept, bleak. Here he was offering his top executive a trip to Florida, and she was refusing.

Turning back to Fiona, he narrowed his eyes. "Let me put it this way. You go on this fishing excursion with this man or I'll separate you and Kimberly forever. Understand me?"

For a moment Fiona stared at him without comprehension. "But I *am* Kimberly," she said in disbelief. "We can't be separated."

James rubbed his hand over his face. "Three days, Fiona. Three days! That's all I'm asking. You spend three measly days with this man, then you never again have to leave the streets of New York. You can set up housekeeping in the middle of Saks for all I care. Now go! Pack! The plane leaves early tomorrow morning."

Fiona had a few thousand words she wanted to say, but the man was, after all, her boss. And his threat of taking Kimberly away from her was more than she could bear. Kimberly and her family were Fiona's life. She had other friends, other enjoyments, but Kimberly was everything. Kimberly was—

Fiona's thoughts paused as she passed James Garrett's secretary. The odious woman

2

was smiling as she held Fiona's ticket in her bent hand.

"Bon voyage," the woman said, smirking. As usual, she'd heard every word that had gone on in her boss's office. "We'll all see that Kimberly is tucked in every night. I'm sure she'll miss you dreadfully."

As Fiona walked past the woman, her heels clicking, she took the tickets and smiled sweetly. "Get your raise, Babs?" James Garrett was notorious for his penny-pinching.

The secretary tried to snap the tickets back, but Fiona was too fast; she caught them and kept going.

Three days, Fiona thought as her long legs ate up the distance back to her office. Three days amid swamps, crocodiles, and... and some man who was *demanding* her presence.

"Just who the hell does he think he is?" she muttered as she strode into her office.

"Who does who think he is?" Gerald asked as he put Kimberly's new designs on Fiona's desk.

Fiona could hardly stand to look at them. James Garrett might think it was only three days, but to her it was— "Oh, hell!" she said as she glanced at her watch. It was nearly six, and tonight was Diane's birthday dinner.

Looking down at her assistant, Gerald, Fiona started to speak, but he beat her to it.

"No need to say a word; it's all over the office. Do you know *why* this man wants *you?* I mean other than the usual reason a man wants a..." He trailed off.

"I've never met him; I know nothing. But worse, I didn't have time to—"

"Buy Diane a present?" Gerald said, eyes sparkling, as he withdrew a beautifully wrapped gift from behind his back. "Ferragamo shoes, size six and a half," he said. "Hope you don't mind if I snooped a bit in your private file, just to check sizes and—"

Fiona wasn't sure if she should thank him or slap him or just fire him. She kept everything on her computer, including what her friends and her many business associates liked or wore or collected. That Gerald had gone into this private file was certainly overstepping his duties as her executive assistant.

"Don't worry about a thing," Gerald said as he removed her sheared beaver coat from the closet and held it up. "I'll take care of Kimberly and Sean and Warren, and I'll make sure the maps get to production. In fact, why don't you take a vacation and stay a little longer? I hear that Florida is wonderful this time of year."

Reluctantly, Fiona pulled on her coat; then in the doorway, she turned back and smiled at Gerald. He was already standing behind *her* desk, looking at *her* designs.

"You change one hair on Kimberly and I'll bring back a crocodile and lock it in the toilet with you," she said with her very sweetest smile, then turned and walked out.

❧◉❧

"All right, tell me one more time," Diane said just before she threw back her head and downed yet another shot of straight tequila. This was at least her fourth drink—or maybe it was her fifth. "You have to go where when and *why?*"

"I don't know," Fiona said in exasperation as she held up her hand to the waiter to bring her another drink. She knew she was going to regret this in the morning, but today had to be the worst day of her life. But now her four best friends in the world were here, and they wanted to share, so...

She looked at each face with love. They'd been together since they were kids, and—

"Hey! Wake up!" Ashley said. "No getting soppy on us. What is this all about? Is this man in love with you?"

"How could he be? I've never met him," Fiona said. "From what I hear he's sixty-some and has a figure like Santa Claus."

"But he's rich, right?" Jean said as she emptied her glass of iced tea. Long Island iced tea, as in vodka, gin, rum, and tequila mixed together.

"If he isn't rich now, he will be as soon as his show hits the market; then he'll—"

"Excuse me," Susan said, interrupting Fiona as she lifted her triangle-shaped martini glass. Susan didn't really like martinis, but the glasses were so sexy it turned her on just holding one. "Not all of us live here in this fabulous city, and not all of us—"

"Yeah, yeah," Jean said, laughing. "Don't

5

start the I'm-a-poor-little-girl-from-Indiana routine."

"Los Angeles," Susan said, deadpan. It was a running joke of the two who lived in Manhattan about whether anything west of the Hudson was civilized or not.

"All right, calm down," Fiona said, holding her hands up in a sign for peace. "I'll tell you all I know—but it's very little. A man from Texas, by the name of Roy Hudson, created a children's show called *Raphael.* I know nothing about it except that it was such a big hit on his local TV station that it's been bought by one of the national channels."

"Which one?" Jean asked.

"What does it matter?" Ashley asked. She had flown in from her home in Seattle the night before.

"PBS or NBC?"

"I see," Ashley said. "Money."

"Of course. Isn't that always what everything is about?"

"Are you going to let Fiona speak or not?" Susan said.

"There isn't much more," Fiona said as she took another sip of her gin and tonic. "As there always is with these things, there'll be franchising, and Davidson wants the contract to manufacture the toys from the show. Simple."

"*Mmmm,*" Jean said. "So what do you—and Kimberly—have to do with this TV show? What's the name of it again? And what's it about?"

"I didn't see the tapes, so I have no idea what

it's about. It's called *Raphael,* and I imagine it's about... Well, actually I don't know what it's about—I just heard about all this today for the first time." Fiona took a deep drink of her gin and tonic.

"So why—?"

"Why has this man said he'd only sell to Davidson Toys if I personally go on a trip to Florida with him?" Usually Fiona's excellent manners would never allow her to raise her voice in public, but her confrontation with Garrett had nearly sent her over the edge.

"I don't know!" she half shouted, then quieted when Ashley put her red-nailed hand on her wrist. "All I know is that this Texas good ol' boy has requested that I go on a..." She had to swallow before she could say the word. "A three-day *fishing* trip with him and a guide named Ace." At that she downed the last of her drink then raised her hand to the waiter for a refill.

Susan was the first to laugh. It escaped out of the corners of her mouth in a way that was familiar to the other women. They'd often said that Susan's sense of humor had saved their sanity.

" 'Ace'?" Susan said, the corners of her mouth twitching. "Do you think he's one of those men who carry photos of his first wife, his second wife, and the third one in his wallet? And photos of all the kids from each marriage?"

"And each photo is at least twenty years old?" Jean said, laughing.

"Little Leroy in the photo is now serving five to nine for grand theft auto."

They were all laughing now, and Diane ordered a high calorie cheesy thing to dip into with fried chips. So far they hadn't gotten around to ordering dinner.

"No, Ace flew a plane during World War Two," Jean said. "He'll show Fiona his war medals."

"Really, girls," Ashley said. "It's Florida. He'll have skin rougher than the alligators he wrestles. And he'll call all women 'honey' and 'babe.' "

"And *his* tattoos were done before they were fashionable," Diana said.

Fiona leaned forward. "As always, you're all off base. Ace is gorgeous: tall, dark, and handsome. He has everything except one little bitty thing."

At that all the women laughed suggestively. "If it's little, I don't want it."

"Oh, not that..." Fiona practically purred. *"That* is developed to the size of—Oh! here's the food," she said, grinning, her green eyes sparkling.

Jean laughed. "Then the little part must be his—" Breaking off, she looked around the table. "All together now, ladies, one, two, three." Lifting her arms in imitation of a bandleader, she directed the chorus.

"His *brain,* " they said in unison.

"You know, Fee," Ashley said, her mouth full of chip and dip, "I could stand three days with some bronzed Adonis named Ace."

8

"Puh-lease," Fiona said. "I like a man to have something besides pectorals."

"Not me," Susan said, mouth full. "I never cared whether a man had a brain or not."

"You'll care after the newness wears off—so to speak," Fiona said seriously. "Then you'll be left with nothing. He'll run off with some blonde bimbo, and you'll be left—"

"Give me a break!" Diane said. "It's my birthday."

"Right," Fiona said apologetically. "It's your birthday, and all we're doing is talking about *my* problems."

"Some problems," Ashley said. "Three days in sunny Florida alone with a beautiful body with no brain and—"

"And good ol' boy Roy and another guy who cleans the fish," Fiona said with a dry chuckle. "Meanwhile, Kimberly—"

"*Aaaargh,*" came the collective groan.

"Okay, okay. I know. No talk of Kimberly allowed."

"Yeah," Susan said, "let's talk about something else altogether."

"I agree," Jean said.

For a few moments all the women were silent.

"So what's this Ace's last name? Or does he just go by 'Ace'?" Ashley asked, running her fingertip around the rim of her glass.

With a sigh of reluctance, Fiona reached down to her briefcase, removed a paper, and scanned it.

"Montgomery. His name is Paul "Ace" Montgomery."

One

❦❦

"I refuse to accept it in that condition," Ace said, glaring at the man who was holding out a clipboard and expecting him to sign the acceptance papers.

"Look, mister, I'm just the deliveryman, and nobody said anything about busted crates. So just sign it so I can get out of here."

Ace kept his hands at his side. "Maybe you can't read, but I can," he said. "The fine print on that contract says that once I accept shipment, it's my responsibility. That means that if it's broken, then it's my problem. But if I find out that it's broken before I sign, then it's your problem. Got it?"

For a moment the man stood there opening and closing his mouth. "Do you know what's in that thing?"

"I most certainly do, since I'm the one who ordered it. And paid for it, I might add."

The man still didn't seem to understand. "So let's get it out of here so we can—"

"No," Ace said. "We open it here and now."

At that the man looked about him pointedly, as though Ace didn't understand exactly where they were. They were in the baggage claim area of the Fort Lauderdale airport. Right now there were only a few porters removing unclaimed bags from the carousels, but any minute the escalator to the left might start delivering a plane full of people. "You want me to uncrate the thing here? Now?" the man said quietly.

"Now," Ace said firmly. "You put it in my truck, it's mine, so I have to pay for it if it's damaged, and I paid too much for it to—"

"Yeah, yeah," the man said, bored, then turned to a skinny kid standing next to Ace. The kid was wearing the same gray uniform that the guy giving the orders was wearing. "He always like that?"

"Naw, sometimes he's a real pain in the neck."

"I hope you're gettin' paid well."

"Actually..." he began, but a bark from Ace stopped him.

"Tim! You want to get away from that end of the crate? I don't want one of my guys touching it until I see that it's working."

With his back to Ace, the deliveryman grimaced. He was tired and hungry, and worse, he was alone. He'd have to uncrate the damned thing by himself all because of a little dent in one corner. Using a crowbar, he pried up one side of the fifteen-foot-long crate, and there, lying in a bed of Styrofoam pellets was the remote control. With a wicked little smile that he made sure no one saw, he pocketed the control, then kept on uncrating. When he got to the other end, Ace was bent over the opposite end, peering inside, a frown of concentration on his face.

12

"Psst," the deliveryman said to the kid in the uniform. The label on his pocket said, Tim, Kendrick Park. "Tim," the deliveryman said, then handed him the remote control.

"Is that what—"

"Quiet," the man ordered. "Don't let him see it."

"Yeah, sure," Tim said, his eyes wide, looking like a kid with the world's biggest Nintendo game in his hands.

"Just don't push the buttons," the deliveryman said, "because the thing will start moving and it'll scare everybody."

"Yeah?" Tim said, somehow managing to open his eyes even wider. But Tim could no more resist the temptation than Adam could. The minute the crate was opened enough to see inside the near end, Tim pushed the buttons—then was extremely satisfied when a woman behind him gave a yelp of fear.

"It's all right," Ace said to the crowd as he looked at the first of what was probably a planeload of travelers arriving in the baggage claim. "It's not real. It's just a fiberglass alligator sent here from California, and we're checking it for damages."

At his words the fear left their faces, but they showed no signs of moving closer to the baggage carousel. What some of them had just seen was what looked to be the enormous head of an alligator lift out of a wooden crate and snap its jaws at the man who was fearlessly putting his hands into the long box.

When no one so much as moved even an inch

in the direction of the luggage, Ace shook his head in exasperation, then turned and snatched the remote from Tim. "Would you help rather than hinder?"

"Sorry, boss," Tim said, but he didn't look sorry. "I couldn't resist it. That thing sure does look real."

"That's why it cost me every penny I had," Ace muttered. "Now get on that end and check its tail. See if there's so much as a scratch."

Now that Ace and Tim had taken over, the deliveryman was leaning against the back wall and using a pocket knife to trim his nails. "So how come you don't have a real alligator?" he asked. "You runnin' out of real ones down here?" He laughed at his own joke. "Too many handbags and shoes?"

Ace had to nearly push a woman aside as she leaned so far over to see inside the crate that she was in the way. "Kendrick Park is a bird sanctuary," he said, as if that explained everything.

When the man looked puzzled, Tim said quietly, "He doesn't like to put things in cages, but alligators draw crowds."

The man pondered that for a minute. "I see. So you thought that if you get a fake alligator you'll get tourists, but ol' Ivan here won't cry crocodile tears of loneliness. Right?" He was grinning at his little witticism.

When Ace didn't bother to answer, Tim said, "Exactly."

"You about through with your inspection, Mr. Birdman?" the deliveryman asked.

"The damage on the crate is on the bottom. To do a proper inspection, we're going to have to take it out and look at its belly."

"Just what my wife says to me every night," the man said under his breath to Tim, who turned red and choked on his laughter. At the moment his boss didn't look as though he was in the mood for jokes.

"Okay, Tim, get the tail. Careful. I don't want it hurt. Okay," Ace said a moment later as he looked at the huge alligator replica stretched out full length on the floor. "It looks undamaged."

"So you want to sign this now, so I can go get something to eat?"

"All right," Ace said, stretching out his hand; then he took a deep breath before he signed the paper saying the terrifically expensive replica was now his responsibility. For a moment he glanced up at the plane passengers that were now surrounding them. They were silent, tired after their flight from New York, or maybe they were just awed at seeing what they had hoped to see on their trip to Florida. Whatever, they were just standing there watching this free show while suitcases went unnoticed, round and round on the carousel.

"Okay, so let's get him back in his box," Ace said. "Tim, you get the tail, and I'll get the head."

For a moment, Ace hesitated as he tried to figure out how best to get a grip on the beast. In the next second he inserted his hand, then his arm up to his armpit down the alligator's mouth. When a collective *"Ooooh"* went up from the watching crowd, he smiled. This was going to work, he thought. Over on the other side of the state, Disney was making a fortune with his fake animals, while farms here in Fort Lauderdale were barely able to feed their 450-pound 'gators. And getting ma, pa, and the kids to want to go see a flock of flamingos was a losing proposition—and he had the empty bank account to prove it.

As Ace and Tim were putting the giant fiberglass alligator back into the box, neither of them saw the inquisitive toddler slip between the suitcases and pick up the remote control that Ace had carefully set on top of his toolbox. The little boy, at eighteen months, just loved to push buttons.

⚬⟋⟍⟍⟍⟋⟍⟍⟍⟍⟍⟍

"Bloody hell," Fiona muttered as she disembarked the plane. She'd had a couple of hangovers in her life, mostly while in college, but nothing like this. Not only did her head hurt, but she could feel even the tiny bones in her ankles. She'd fallen asleep on the plane, and the attendant had had to wake her, which made her the last one off the plane.

Dragging her backpack on over her shoulder sent more pain through her. She and the rest of The Five, as they'd dubbed themselves as kids, had stayed out until two A.M., laughing riotously over everything in their lives, but most

16

especially over Fiona's having to go on a *fishing* trip.

"You?" Jean had said. "I can't imagine you more than two miles from a manicurist." Jean was a sculptor and her hands always looked scraped and worn. But all four of the women knew that Jean didn't need to do anything to make a living; she had a trust fund.

As Fiona walked into the airport, the bright light coming through the huge windows made her hide her eyes while she fumbled in her bag for the sunglasses she'd bought at LaGuardia Airport. In New York they'd seemed so dark she could hardly see through them. But now the glare made them seem like clear glass.

The airport seemed empty as she trudged ahead, her aching head filled with nothing but bad thoughts. How was she going to survive the next three days? Would this man require *her* to clean fish?

When she stepped onto the escalator leading down to the baggage carousels, the movement almost made her retch. Quickly, she fumbled in her bag for a tissue, then held it to her mouth. Why was she here and what did this man Roy Hudson want with her? And why Florida? And if Florida, why not some nice clean, private beach? Why was he insisting on going into the swamps or whatever to look for—

Because Fiona had a tissue to her mouth and her eyes closed, she had descended the escalator without seeing the silent, watching crowd at the bottom. But when she stepped off, she nearly fell on top of a man with a paunch and not much hair.

"Pardon me," she said in a voice as husky as her brain was feeling.

The man looked up at her and his face softened. "Any time," he said, then stepped aside so she could see what they were all watching.

Later, Fiona said that she didn't think, she just *moved*. What she saw—her eyes blinking behind the dark glasses, her mind full of swamps and alligators and the treachery of the state of Florida—was a man with his arm being eaten off by an enormous alligator. As the alligator started to thrash its tail, then move its head from side to side, the man shouted something incomprehensible as he tried to free himself from the attacking reptile.

In school Fiona had been the girl with the fastest reaction time in any game, whether it was soccer or pickup sticks, and now she lost no time. Next to her was a woman with an airport luggage cart, and on top of it was a pink bowling ball bag with the name *Dixie* embroidered on it.

Without a thought, Fiona picked up the bag and threw it with all her might at the midsection of the alligator.

She wasn't prepared for what happened next. The alligator exploded! It didn't open its mouth and release its victim. Instead, there was a terrific noise, then the whole nasty green thing seemed to fly into thousands of pieces that went flying around the airport.

While Fiona stood there in stunned silence, the rest of the people in the airport seemed to go crazy. Instantly there was screaming and shouts of, "Bomb, bomb!"; then sirens went off and people started running.

Unmoving, still not understanding what had happened, Fiona removed her sunglasses and looked at what she thought had been an alligator. A man came toward her and there seemed to be a double row of teeth attached to his upper arm. Her eyes were on the oddity of the teeth, but when she looked up at the man to ask why he was wearing teeth, she saw that he was furious and he was coming after *her*.

Instinctively, Fiona took a step backward, whereupon she tripped over the luggage cart of the woman who had had the bowling ball bag. But now the woman was gone, probably to join all the many people who were screaming and running frantically for the exits.

"Lady, I'm going to kill you," the man said as his hands made for Fiona's neck.

But the alligator teeth, and what looked to be a detached eyeball, slipped down his hands so that both teeth and murderous hands were coming for her throat. Fiona opened her mouth to scream, but no sound came out.

But then, just before the man reached her, two security guards and a boy with red hair grabbed the man, teeth and all, and pulled him away.

"Thank you so much," Fiona said when a third and fourth security guard helped her to stand up. "That man should be locked away.

19

He's a danger to society, and if you don't—Wait a minute! What do you think you're doing?"

The guard was pulling Fiona's hands behind her back and snapping handcuffs on her wrists. "We're holding you for the police, that's what. The man says you're the one that threw the bomb." She could hardly hear him over the cacophony of the people in the airport, running every which way, screaming names of people they couldn't find.

"Bomb?" she shouted. "I threw a bowling ball bag at an alligator that was eating a man's arm."

"Yeah, right," one of the guards said. "We got alligators crawling all over the airports here in Fort Lauderdale. It entertains the tourists to no end."

"But you can ask—"

"Save it for the police," the second guard said as the two of them pulled her toward the exit door.

"What about my luggage? You have to call my boss in New York. He can—"

"Ah. New York," the first guard said as though that explained everything.

Before Fiona could say another word, she was pulled along by the men and led to a car marked Airport Security. Just like on TV, the man shielded her head from getting banged on the top of the doorframe as he forcibly helped her inside the car.

Shaking with fatigue, Fiona sat down on the dirty bedspread and looked at the telephone on the cheap, battered bedside cabinet. The beautiful hotel where she was supposed to stay had canceled her reservation when she didn't show up before six. At first she'd politely tried to explain that she'd been in jail for the last six hours, but when she saw the young female clerk back away as though Fiona were a criminal, she tried threatening. This got her nowhere fast, and the manager soon came out and asked her to leave.

So now she was in what had to be the sleaziest motel in all of Florida. It was four A.M. and she had to meet Roy Hudson in two hours.

With her hands protected with a tissue (because who knew what type of person had used this phone last?), she punched the buttons to call Jeremy.

When his sleepy voice answered, Fiona burst into tears.

"Who is this? Is this a prank call? You'd better speak up!" Jeremy loudly demanded while Fiona tried to get herself together.

"It's me," she managed to whisper. "Oh, Jeremy, I've just had—"

"Fiona, do you know what time it is? I have to get up and go to work in three hours."

"I haven't been to bed at all. Oh, Jeremy, I've been in *jail.*"

That got his attention, and she could

imagine his sitting up and reaching for a cigarette. She waited a moment until she heard his lighter click, then heard him inhale.

"All right, I'm listening," he said in his lawyer voice.

Maybe he didn't like a girlfriend calling him before dawn, but a client in trouble was a whole other matter. After about ten minutes of listening to Fiona's semihysterical telling of her outrageous story, Jeremy interrupted.

"They let you go? No charges?"

"What could they charge me with?" Fiona's voice was rising. "I thought I was saving the man's *life*. Not that it was worth much. Did I tell you that the ungrateful jerk tried to *murder* me? I ought to *sue* him."

"Ah. There's the word. Is he planning to sue *you*? What about the people at the airport? Did anyone have any accidents during the panic you caused? Heart attacks? Were any ambulances called?"

"Jeremy! Whose side are you on?"

"Yours of course," he said in a tone of dismissal, "but money is money. Did the man say he was going to sue you for destroying his alligator?"

"I don't know. I don't remember. They kept us separated after we got to the police station. Oh, Jeremy, it was so horrible, and I wish you were here to hold me. That man—"

He cut her off. "Did anyone else mention a lawsuit? What about the airport personnel? You caused mass hysteria, so I doubt if they'll take that lightly."

Fiona ran her hand over her face. There was no longer any hope that she still wore makeup. "Jeremy, I called you as my *friend,* not as a lawyer."

"Maybe you'll need both, so would you please answer my questions?"

Part of her wanted to be babied, hugged and cuddled as best he could over the telephone, but another part of her was sane and sensible. She took a deep breath. "The woman whose bowling ball bag I used came to the police station and said I had to buy her a new bag. And her ball was dented too."

Jeremy let out smoke so fast he nearly choked. "You dented her bowling ball?"

"Don't start on me," Fiona snapped. "I've heard it all from those horrible policemen. I guess I must have put a lot of my anger into that throw because I hit that... that... thing pretty hard."

"Enough to dent a bowling ball," Jeremy said in wonder. "Remind me never to make you angry at me. So, what did you do about the woman's bag and ball? And, by the way, why didn't you call me from the station?"

"Because they said I wasn't under arrest, that I was their 'guest' until this thing was cleared up, therefore I didn't need any fancy-smancy New York lawyer."

"You need to document this. You might have a case for a lawsuit against them."

"I never want to see them again. I gave the woman a check for three hundred dollars and—"

"You what!?"

"Paid for the ball I dented," Fiona half shouted into the phone. "Isn't that what you just asked me?"

Jeremy didn't speak for a moment. "You want to calm down?"

"How can I calm down? I didn't want to leave Kimberly in the first place; Garrett made me go. Now, *there's* someone I'd like to sue. He threatened me that if I didn't go on this trip he'd separate me from Kimberly forever. Can he do that?"

"He's your boss," Jeremy said, stubbing out his cigarette. Privately, he thought that it would be a great relief if Fiona were separated from Kimberly. "Look, Fee, honey, I need to get some more sleep. It doesn't sound as though you're in serious trouble, but I'll call a friend of mine down there in the morning and have him call you. I'll have him make sure that nothing bad is going to happen to you." His voice softened. "Now I want you to take a long, hot bath, then get into bed and dream about me."

Finally, Fiona smiled. It seemed that she hadn't smiled in days, maybe even in years. "I'd like that," she said softly, leaning back against the headboard. But the creaky thing almost came off its cheap frame, so she had to sit up quickly to keep from falling, and the movement broke the spell.

"I can't," she said in a little-girl whine. "I have to meet this old man, this Roy Hudson, in just over an hour."

24

"Can't you call and delay the meeting?"

"It's for"—she swallowed—"fishing. You have to go out in the boat very early for fishing. Maybe the slimy little things take afternoon naps; I don't know. But I have to be there very soon."

"All right, calm down. This man Hudson is rich, so I'm sure he'll have a boat with a crew. A yacht probably. Think you could handle a yacht? Have yourself a few drinks? Lie in the sun?"

"Drinking is what got me in this mess in the first place, and sun is *not* going to touch my skin and make me look sixty at forty, and—"

"Okay, have it your way. Be miserable if you want to. Just tell me where you'll be, so my friend can reach you."

"I'll be at Kendrick Park until we get on the boat. I think it's a bird sanctuary, and get this, as if I didn't have enough problems, one of the men on the boat is named Ace."

When Jeremy was silent, Fiona spoke again. "You don't think that's funny?"

"Not particularly. What's wrong with that name?"

She thought about telling him of what she and The Five had come up with about the man, but Jeremy liked The Five as much as he liked Kimberly. "I think it might be a woman thing."

"I'm sure it is. Look, honey…"

"Yes, I know, you need your beauty sleep. Did I tell you that when I didn't claim my suitcase, they put it into an incinerator? After all, they'd already had one bomb scare that day, so they didn't need another one. I am here with the clothes on my back and what's in my pack."

Jeremy yawned. "If I know women, that thing is full of everything you need for a week on a deserted island."

Tightening her lips, Fiona glared at the phone. His chauvinistic comment was one of dismissal, and all his care and concern had been about legal matters. He hadn't offered her a word of sympathy for all that she'd been through. So much for a shoulder to cry on! "At least your photo was in the bag that got burned up," she said, then hung up. But the gesture didn't make her feel any better. She had an hour and a half to get ready to meet Roy Hudson.

Two

It was six o'clock on a winter morning, and already it was bright enough for Fiona to need her sunglasses. Of course a night spent in a police station, while recovering from a hangover that would have killed a lesser person, didn't help any.

It seemed that James Garrett's secretary had "forgotten" to give Fiona the name and number of the car service that was to take her to this Kendrick Park, so Fiona had taken a taxi. Just one more item to add to the list of indignities she'd already suffered on this trip-in-hell, she thought.

The taxi let her off in front of what seemed to be impenetrable jungle. "I think there's a mistake. This place is supposed to be a park."

The cab driver shrugged. "This is the address," he said, pointing to a small, sun-bleached sign near what was possibly an opening in the jungle mass.

Reluctantly, Fiona paid him then got out of the car.

"Better watch your shoes," he said as he drove off, laughing.

Upon closer inspection there was a four-foot-wide path meandering through the shrubs, but deep sand covered the walkway. "Of course," she muttered. "What did I expect? A sidewalk? Oh, Fiona, you do have a sense of humor."

She was wearing her New York uniform: black wool jacket, white silk blouse, short black skirt, black hose, and black high heels. In her suitcase had been some lovely outfits perfect for wearing on a boat, but they were now ashes, she thought with a grimace. But maybe this place had a gift shop and she could at least purchase a pair of sneakers.

But the further she walked, the more run-down the place seemed. Not exactly Disney, she thought. There was a little kiosk that seemed to be a ticket-taking booth, but no one was there this early in the morning. Further on was another building that looked as though a good wind could knock it over.

What a dreary place, she thought, picking her way across the sand, but still getting it in her shoes. Cupping her hand, she looked inside the window of the larger building. On one side was an old-fashioned juice bar with stools covered in worn red plastic and what had to be the gift shop on the other side.

Fiona rubbed the dust from the glass and looked closer. Inside all she could see were things about birds. There were bird photos, plastic birds, huge bird kites, bird posters, birds made of stone. Even the cash register had birds painted on it.

Turning away, for a moment she leaned against the building, removed her shoe, and poured a couple of pounds of sand out. The only shoes a place like that was going to carry were for webbed feet.

With a glance at her watch she saw that it was nearly six-thirty. So where was everyone? At that thought she almost cried because *they* were probably all still in bed. Sleeping.

Suddenly, she thought she saw movement through the abundant greenery. "If it's an alligator, I'll throw myself on it," she said aloud, then cautiously moved toward what looked like something in human clothes.

A man was bent over something. She couldn't see much of him, just his back and one corner of his right ear.

"Excuse me," she said softly, but the man

didn't seem to hear her. "Excuse me!" she said louder.

"I'm not deaf!" the man said as he turned partway around, then swung back again. "Damnation! Look what you made me do. Don't you know better than to sneak up on people? What are you doing here this early anyway? We don't open until nine."

With that he turned back toward her, and there was a tall, long-legged white bird in his hand. For a split second it registered with Fiona that the man was as tall as, if not taller than, she was, which was a welcome treat.

"Hello, I'm—" she said, and had her hand extended when she recognized him.

"You!" they shouted in unison.

He recovered first. "If you've come here to apologize, I won't accept it. The only thing I'll accept from *you* is a check."

"Apologize? Are you out of your mind?" Fiona said, her anger instantly at the boiling point. "I saved your worthless *life.*"

"From what? Death by plastic? Look, lady, I don't know why you came here, but I want you to leave *now.*"

"For your information, not that it's any of your business, I'm meeting someone. Are you killing that bird?"

He dropped the bird, and it went running into the plants. "And who would you be meeting?"

"Roy Hudson," she said, and hoped with all her might that Hudson owned this place so she could do what she could to get this creep fired. "And Ace."

"Ace?" the man said, his face softening.

Now she had him. Maybe Ace would beat him up. "Yes Ace. He and Roy are meeting me, and we're going fishing."

"Really. So what are you doing here? Planning to use the cormorants?"

At that she could only blink at him. Was that a private Florida joke?

"You are certainly dressed for fishing," he said, looking her up and down.

She badly wanted to zap him with a put-down that would set him on his ear. "At least today you're wearing something other than a set of teeth." At that retort, which made no real sense, she happened to look at his shirt. Embroidered on the pocket was, Ace, Kendrick Park.

"That's it," she said, then threw up her hands and started walking back to the entrance. "I have had it. I have reached the limit of my endurance. I am going back to New York where people are *safe*."

"Fiona," came another voice from behind her, this one older and friendly, but she didn't stop walking toward the entrance.

"Honey, I'd recognize you anywhere," the man said as he caught her arm and prevented her from moving.

"Let me guess," she said with heavy sarcasm. "Roy Hudson."

"Right you are, little lady. Now come over here and meet the rest of the crew."

Roy Hudson was in his early sixties and looked to be as cuddly as Winnie the Pooh, whom he somewhat resembled. Fiona felt like asking him if he had a penchant for honey and a friend who loved to bounce.

"This is Ace Montgomery, and he owns this little ol' place."

"And he deserves every square inch of it," Fiona said as she smiled across Roy's outstretched hand into the eyes of the owner of the dilapidated Kendrick Park. But she didn't extend her hand to shake Ace's.

"We've met," Ace said, his upper lip curled into a sneer as he again looked Fiona up and down. "Miss Burkenhalter and I had a... a confrontation at the airport."

"How wonderful," Roy said, then slapped Fiona on the back so hard she nearly fell forward onto Ace. "You all ready to go? I gotta car waitin', and the boat's all packed."

"Mr. Hudson," Fiona said firmly. "I think there's been a mistake. I know that you talked to Garrett about me and that you requested me, but I really don't know anything about the merchandising of action figures. Or stuffed animals or whatever it is you want to sell. And I also don't know anything about fishing. So, if you don't mind, I think I'll excuse myself from this excursion and return to town."

Putting her hand into the outside pocket of her backpack, she pulled out her cell phone. Truthfully, she was dying to tell The Five that she'd been right: Ace was gorgeous beyond belief: black hair, black eyes, a body... And he was as big a loser as she'd predicted, she thought as she glanced back at the crumbling gift shop.

31

As she lifted her finger to push the buttons, she looked at Ace. "Don't worry, it's real, not a plastic fake."

Before Ace could reply to that gibe, Roy started laughing. "That must have been some meetin' the two of you had yesterday. But we got days for you two to tell me all about it." With that he put his arm around Fiona's shoulders and firmly turned her away from the entrance and just as firmly held her arm in a way to prevent her using the telephone. "Now, honey, why I asked for you is somethin' we gotta talk about. But not yet. First we need to have some fun."

Throughout this exchange, Ace had been glaring at Fiona with so much hostility that, had the circumstances been different, she might have been afraid of him. But right now her mind was too full of plans to be afraid of anything. She stepped away from Roy as she realized she *had* to get out of this situation. Even Garrett would understand if she left after what she'd been through. All she'd have to do is mention "lawsuit" to Garrett and he'd forgive anything.

"I think we need to get this lady some different clothes, don't you, Roy?" Ace said in a voice that dripped with kind consideration. But the steel grip he put on Fiona's upper arm was anything but kind.

"I'm not staying here," she hissed at him, then turned back to smile at Roy. She'd better not anger the man who owned *Raphael,* not when Garrett wanted the franchise rights so much. She'd just explain to Roy that they'd have to take their little trip at another time—preferably after this man Ace was rotting in the ground.

"I have clothes for her," Ace said loudly to Roy; then into Fiona's ear, he said, "You either come with me or we spend this afternoon with lawyers talking about how you're going to pay for the property you destroyed."

Jeremy wouldn't like that, she thought, then tears came to her eyes as the man's hands bit harder into her flesh. "I, ah, think I should wear something different," she mumbled to Roy, then tried to keep up with the stride of the maniac parkman.

Once they were out of sight of Roy—out of sight of civilization, she thought as the plants closed about them—she halted and jerked her arm out of his grip.

"There are laws against this," she hissed at him so Roy wouldn't hear.

Ace closed the one step that separated them and put his nose to hers. "There are laws against destruction of property, too. My lawyer said I was a fool for not suing you. Do you have any idea how much that alligator cost me?"

"Trade price or retail?"

Obviously, the man had *no* sense of humor. At the look of rage on his face, she stepped backward.

With the muscles in his jaw working frantically, Ace grabbed her wrist and half dragged her down what could have been called a path. As it was only about six inches wide, the plants scraped her arms, and she was sure they were snagging her hose. She'd been walking on sand for so long that it was beginning to feel normal to have grit between her toes.

"Where are you taking me?" she demanded, but he just kept pulling her along, saying nothing.

Finally they came to a clearing in the "jungle," and there was a tiny house, the front of it fitted with screens from the roof to halfway to the ground. Ace threw open a screen door, pulled her through the long narrow room, then opened another door and shoved her down onto a bed.

For a moment Fiona felt real fear. If she were to scream, no one would hear her, and she was utterly alone with a raving madman.

"Don't flatter yourself," Ace said with a sneer. "You're not my type. I like women to be *women,*" he said, then disappeared into a closet.

Fiona recovered instantly. Nothing like having your femininity attacked to dispel fear. "And what the hell is *that* supposed to mean?" she asked as she came off the bed.

"Here," he said as he tossed a pair of jeans and a white cotton shirt on the bed. "Put those on."

She looked down at the two garments. "Your clothes? You want me to wear *your* clothes?" Her tone said that she'd rather wear poison paint.

She wasn't prepared for his reaction. As fast as a snake's tongue, he grabbed her by the shoulders and pinned her against the wall. "Listen to me, Miss Snooty New Yorker, I've had all I can take from you. You destroyed something that took me and everyone else in this park three years to earn enough money to buy. And you don't care one damned bit that you did it. All I've heard is that *you* don't like it here, that this place is not up to *your* New York standards."

Though it didn't seem possible, he leaned even closer to her, and he had to bend down somewhat to put his nose so close to hers. "I want you to listen to me and listen well. I don't care why you're here or what Roy Hudson wants from you. All I care is that in the next three days—*on this boat trip*—he's going to decide if he wants to invest some of the profits of his TV show into this park. This place may not look like much to you—you've made that abundantly clear—but this place is *my* life."

His voice lowered. "So help me, if you screw up this trip with your snot-nosed arrogance, I will sue you for everything you have, everything you will earn, and for what you plan to leave your children. Am I making myself clear?"

He paused a moment, but when Fiona didn't reply, he pressed her harder against the wall.

She could feel the pressure of his big hands, and she could feel the power of his huge body so close to her own. She'd had intimate contact only with Jeremy, and Jeremy was about half the size of this man.

"Yes," she managed to say from dry lips. "I understand."

"All right," he said, then stepped away from her as though he couldn't move fast enough, then turned away. "Get into those clothes," he said, his voice somewhat softer. "I'm going to try to find you some shoes." At the door he turned back, strode across the room, picked up her cell phone off the bed, then put it into his pocket. "Don't try to leave," he said at the door. "There are some nasty creatures out there."

"Out *there?*" she managed to gasp, but he was already out the door.

Fiona took the three steps across the room to the bed then collapsed, trembling. She didn't know if she was afraid or angry. She had never been talked to the way that man had just addressed her, and she'd certainly never been shoved up against a wall.

Survive, she thought, that's what she had to do over the next three days—survive. She had no doubt whatever that the man's threats were genuine. Hadn't even Jeremy thought that the man had a right to sue her?

It was amazing how a person's life could change in seconds. Had she left the plane earlier, she might have seen that the alligator was fake, then she wouldn't have...

"Strength," she said aloud, then made herself get off the bed and look at the clothes. What had he meant when he'd said that he liked women to be *women?* She'd never before had any complaints about her appearance.

After a quick look around to see if there were spying eyes, she stripped down to her underwear, then quickly put on the man's clothes. The jeans were too big in the hips and in the waist; the shirt was too long in the sleeves. But she wasn't a New Yorker for nothing, she thought as she went into the closet to look for a belt. Fashion was her forte.

It was a big walk-in closet, but it was mostly filled with bird books and bird... things. She had no idea what most of the stuff was, but she was sure it all had to do with birds. In one corner hung three pairs of trousers and four shirts. There were two of those gray uniforms, like the one he had on today, folded on a shelf. Whatever else he was, he wasn't a clotheshorse.

Fiona found a cowboy belt with a fancy silver buckle hidden under a pile of brown file boxes. Peeking inside one of the boxes, she saw folders labeled with the names of different birds. She tried the belt around her, kept her nail on the place where she needed a new hole, then found a Phillips screwdriver and jammed it into the leather. Actually, it felt good to hit something owned by "him" with a sharp instrument.

When the hole was made, she threaded the belt through the loops in the jeans and pulled it tight. With the shirt tucked into the pants, she rolled up the cuffs and stood the collar up at the back of her neck.

When she was dressed and he still hadn't returned, she went into the only other room, the bathroom, with her backpack. Looking in the mirror, she regarded her face. At work she wore little makeup, and she slicked back her hair with a spray that made it as stiff as pipe cleaners. She knew that Garrett thought that women in business was going against nature, so any woman who worked for him toned herself down. Plus, there was his vice president, who tended to put his hands on the prettiest of the female employees.

Now, Fiona filled the basin with water, then dipped her head into it and loosened the spray that she had put on her hair this morning out of habit. When her hair was thoroughly wet, she grabbed a towel and rubbed it dry. When she looked back in the mirror, she smiled to herself as her short, sleek hair sprang into fat curls. Her makeup was now running down her face, so she fixed it, but she used a heavier hand on her eyes.

When she stepped back, she looked at herself and again smiled. She was now emphasizing what she had spent years trying to underplay: she was a dead ringer for the fifties movie star Ava Gardner.

The next moment, she heard the door open, and she left the bathroom. When Ace stepped inside the room, a pair of sneakers in his hand, he did a tiny double take at the sight of her. It was a subtle movement, and he recovered himself quickly, but she saw it.

However, the anger did not leave his face. "Try these. I'll wait for you outside," he said, then slammed the door behind him—and Fiona smiled. Maybe next time he'd think twice before saying she wasn't "a woman."

The shoes fit perfectly. They were well-worn, old-fashioned sneakers, and she wondered where he'd got them. It was while she was bent over, tying the laces, that she saw something silver sticking out from under the bed. Except for the inside of the closet, the rest of the house was extremely neat. There were very few items in the house, but what was there was tidy and dusted. The bathroom had been very clean. In the corner were a couple of cabinets with a hot plate and a tiny under-counter refrigerator. The only picture on the wall was a black-and-white print of a man.

Other than all the bird things in the closet, there wasn't one personal item in the house, so she was curious when she touched the silver object hidden under the plain gray bedspread. It was a picture frame and the smiling woman in the photo was beautiful. She looked like every prom queen/beauty queen/cheerleader in the world: long blonde hair, big blue eyes, perfectly pink cheeks, and a baby doll mouth.

Not even Kimberly is this pretty, Fiona thought as she turned the frame over. It was Tiffany sterling and written on the back was, "Lisa Rene Honeycutt."

Fiona slipped the picture back under the bed, finished tying her shoes, put her pack over her shoulder, then turned to go outside. On second thought, with a one-sided smile, she turned back, pulled back the bedspread, and emptied her high heel shoes of sand onto Ace Montgomery's clean white sheets. She then arranged her New York clothes as though they had been removed hurriedly. Still smiling, she went outside where Ace was waiting and scowling.

"It's a beautiful morning, isn't it?" she said as she sailed past him, acting as though she lived in the house and he was just passing by. She came to a fork in the path and went right.

Three minutes later she was standing in front of a couple of shacks that had big locks on the doors.

"Are you finished showing off?" came Ace's voice from behind her. "Because if you're going with us, then this is the way. Unless of course you want to repay all of us in work. We have a swamp that needs to be mucked out. With all the animals it gets full of—"

"Very funny," she said, then moved past him so close that her shirtsleeve grazed his chest.

Two steps later he grabbed both her upper arms, then swung her around so she was headed back toward the shacks.

"Keep your hands off of me!" she shouted.

"All right, then go ahead. Be my guest." With that he moved back, his arm outstretched, and she saw that she had almost stepped into what looked like the foundation of yet another shack. Whatever had been there, it was now only a deep hole barely covered with vines.

"That's dangerous," she breathed. "Some kid could—"

"Right. There are lots of places of danger around here, but it takes man power to fix them. And man power costs money. And we get money from tourists who might come to see a mechanical alligator or from investors. Yesterday I had both of those, but today I have only one left."

He said all of this in a tone that implied that she was an imbecile.

"You know," she said quietly, "I don't think I've ever disliked a man as much as I dislike you."

"I can assure you that the feeling is mutual. So now, shall we go before Roy packs up and returns to Texas?"

Three

❧☙❧

The boat was no yacht. No, it was a beat-up old fishing boat that Roy said he'd had for twenty years. To Fiona's tired eyes, it was an exact duplicate of Robert Shaw's boat in *Jaws*—the one the fish ate. "Caught a lot of fish in this baby," he said.

"And I can smell every one of them," Fiona said under her breath. When Ace gave her a look of warning, she coldly smiled back at him. After she'd walked out of that ruin that was laughingly called a park, Roy had been so overwhelmed by her resemblance to a woman he declared to be his all-time favorite movie star that thereafter Fiona could do no wrong.

"They don't make women like her today," Roy had declared as he ushered Fiona along, leaving Ace to come or go as he pleased, since Roy seemed to have forgotten all about him. "Back then women looked like *women*. Today the actresses are just girls. Julia Roberts. That Guinevere girl. What's her name?"

"Gwyneth Paltrow?" Fiona said. "But you like women who look like women, right?" She said this last over her shoulder loud enough to awaken any birds that were still sleeping, but, gathering from the growing racket around the three of them, they were all awake.

Roy didn't seem to miss anything. "You're just gonna have to tell me all about that first meetin' you and Ace had. He say somethin' you didn't like?"

"Horrible things," she said, batting her lashes at Roy. Considering that he was at least four inches shorter than she was, this wasn't easy. "I do so hope you'll beat him up for me."

With a roar of laughter, Roy tried to put his arm around Fiona's shoulders and pull her close. But his attempt was not successful because he had to lift his arm up, and besides, his arm wasn't quite as long as his belly was wide. Easily, she escaped his grasp.

There was a car waiting for them, and when Fiona bent to get inside, Ace said into her ear, "You want to stop playing the simpering maiden and behave yourself?"

"What was that?" Roy said when she was inside.

42

"What was what?" Fiona asked innocently.

Ace got in the front seat next to the driver, while she and Roy were together in the back.

"Ace, my boy, are you all right? I thought I heard you give a holler."

"He banged his shin against a hard object," Fiona said, refusing to give in to her need to rub her heel that she'd used to give him a good swift kick.

During the twenty-minute ride to the boat, Fiona had done little but ease Roy's hands off various parts of her body. He would point out things along the highway, then lay his hand on her knee when she leaned forward to look. Next there was something on the other side of the car, so he'd leaned across her that way.

Each time, Fiona would twist around in such a way that she eluded his many hands. And the one time when the car unexpectedly turned a sharp curve and Fiona went plowing into Roy, Ace had to turn around and see it. He gave Fiona a scowl that was meant to tell her to stop enticing the old man. She had no way to defend herself. What could she do, yell that the dirty ol' man couldn't keep his hands off of her? No, she thought as she tried to remember why she was there.

Because she had been threatened and black-mailed, she thought. Her entire career was on the line. And probably everything she owned, if Ace was to be believed.

"You sure are pretty," Roy said under his breath, and Fiona could have kicked herself for "revealing" her resemblance to an old-time movie star. In her late teens, she'd loved being told that she looked like a glamorous movie star, so she'd studied Ava Gardner's movies and her looks. She'd learned to make what was a strong resemblance into an impersonation that a drag queen would envy.

But by the time Fiona hit twenty-four, she was tired of receiving attention because of looking like someone else, so she'd started playing down the resemblance. People didn't realize that movie stars didn't look like themselves when they first stepped out of the shower. It took work to look great. And when Fiona didn't work at looking like someone else, she didn't look like her. No one at Davidson Toys had ever said she looked like anyone else.

And with this randy old man pawing her and trying to relive his youth when he'd lusted after a dark-eyed beauty, she wished she hadn't played up the resemblance. But that odious man Ace had accused her of not being a woman so—

By the time they reached the boat, she was sick of good ol' boy Roy, sick of the black looks she was constantly receiving from the Birdman, and, all in all, sick of being blackmailed. In the last forty-eight hours she'd been blackmailed by two men, first by her boss, Garrett, then by a man who would step over anyone to get money.

So when Ace gave her one of his quelling looks because she'd made an innocent comment about her concern about the safety on the old boat, she was tempted to push him overboard. In fact, she lifted her hands to do just that. But he sidestepped her.

"Do you always solve everything with violence?" he asked, a curl to his upper lip. "Do you always strike first, then find out what you've done later?"

"Me?" she managed to gasp. "You're the one who held me against a wall and—"

She broke off because Roy had called her to come admire his scaling knife—or some other thing he had in his possession.

"If you mess this up for me, I'll make you sorry," Ace hissed as Fiona started toward the end of the boat, where Roy was beckoning her.

"You're going to have to cheer me up before you can make me sorry," she snapped back at him, then kept going. Maybe if she found out *why* Roy had requested her presence (other than the fact that he lusted after women half his age and a head taller than he, that is), then she could leave earlier. As it was, three whole days of this and she'd be a blithering idiot.

Roy was still calling her, but as she walked down the rotting old deck, for the first time she noticed the only other person on board. Eric was probably in his early thirties, short and not someone you'd notice or remember after you'd seen him. Even looking at him, she couldn't describe him.

"Hi," Fiona said, giving him her most dazzling smile. Thanks to exorbitant dental bills paid by her father, her teeth were perfect.

Eric looked up from where he was tying a

rope to a shiny metal hook with an expression of, Are you talking to me?

Fiona didn't have time for chitchat. "Have you worked for Roy long?"

"Long enough," he said cautiously.

I'm in a bad private-eye movie, she nearly said aloud, then took a deep breath. "I'm trying to find out why he wanted me to come on this trip."

The man pulled the rope tighter. "You'll have to ask him. I just do the work; he doesn't confide in me."

"But you drive a car for him, and now you're on a boat with him, so you must have heard something."

He gave her a little smile as he looked her up and down in a way that let her know that if she wanted to visit his cabin, he was willing, but he wasn't going to *talk* to her.

For the second—or was it the third?—time that day Fiona threw her hands up in frustration, then started walking again. "And people say that New Yorkers are crazy," she muttered. "I've got an old man panting after me, the guy who swabs the decks is leering at me, and a bird freak tells me I'm sexless. If this keeps up I'm going to jump overboard and those crocs wouldn't *dare* tangle with me. Yes, yes, Roy, I'm coming," she yelled. "Keep your shirt on." She lowered her voice. *"Pllleeeaaaasssseee* keep your shirt on."

"Fiona, honey, you're not eatin' enough to keep a bird alive," Roy said, then seemed to think that was the funniest joke he'd ever heard. " 'Keep a bird alive' and Ace here is an expert on birds, get it?" he said as he nearly exploded in adoring laughter over his own witticism. "I tell you, sometimes I just plain crack myself up."

They were sitting at the table in the inside of the boat. You couldn't really call it a cabin, but when you were in a country that had weather that ranged from hot to hotter to hell, what did you need with a back wall? Fiona thought. Roy took up the end of the table, while she was sitting across from Ace. Heaven help her, but he was *laughing* at Roy's asinine jokes.

"Roy," Fiona said loudly so she could be heard over his self-induced chuckles, "why did you call me here? If you'd wanted someone from my company to go fishing with, I'm sure someone else would have been more suitable. No, thank you," she said loudly, and pointedly, to Ace, who'd just poured himself more wine from the jug but hadn't offered to fill her glass.

This exchange made Roy put his hand over his mouth to hide his mirth. "You two wanta tell me how you met before today?"

"No!" Fiona and Ace said in unison, then refused to look at each other.

"Roy," Fiona said firmly. "I'd like to know why you asked *me* to come here."

"Honey," Roy said as he reached for her

hand, but Fiona moved to pick up her full wine-glass and drank some of the awful stuff.

"More?" Ace asked when he saw her grimace. "It's a good vintage, at least three months old."

"By golly," Roy said as he slapped the table. "I sure do wanta hear what went on between you two."

"You like a good story, don't you, Roy?" Fiona said, still trying to direct the man's mind. "After all, you created *Raphael*, didn't you?"

"Ah," Roy said, and he instantly sobered. "I didn't think it would be so popular." His voice was soft, as though he regretted something.

"But that's good," she said, leaning a bit forward and for the first time thinking that there might be a person inside the teddy bear body.

"Not every person in this world thinks that success is everything, Miss Burkenhalter," Ace said loudly.

"No one asked you," she fairly hissed at him, then turned back to Roy. But Ace's interruption had broken the man's mood.

"Now, now, don't you two spat," Roy said, his face once again looking as though he wanted to throw a party. "Why don't you two tell me about yourselves? What have you done since you were kids?"

The last thing Fiona wanted to do was stay up all night telling Roy and the scowling raven across from her all about her uneventful childhood. Besides, she'd had no sleep for a couple of days now, plus a great deal to drink, not to mention a stint in a Fort Lauderdale police station and...

When she stood up, she staggered a bit in fatigue. "Is there a place to sleep on this boat, or do we jump in the mouth of the nearest whale?"

"I swear you're a lot like—" Roy broke off, then smiled. "You're a lot like a friend I used to know." Standing, he took her arm and looked at her in a way that made Fiona hope that he wasn't going to bury his face in her chest. She didn't think she'd have the strength to fight him off.

Still stumbling, she followed him into the back of the smelly old boat, and when he showed her two sets of bunk beds, she didn't think about the lack of privacy, she just fell into the nearest one and went to sleep, a smile on her face because she thought that the worst day of her life was finally over.

She was very, very wrong.

Four

ॐ

Fiona had had the dream before. She was suffocating as she was being held down by something huge. But in the past she'd awakened to find that it was just the covers wrapped too tightly about her. And once when she was staying at Diane's house, she awakened to find herself underneath the family's Irish setter. "You're sleeping in his bed," Diane had said without the merest trace of humor.

So now Fiona was reluctant to wake fully. Her head hurt, and she was tired beyond description, so she didn't want to wake up. "Go away," she said and tried to elbow whatever was on her off. But the big thing didn't move, and she found that it was so heavy that she couldn't move. Also, there was something warm on her stomach. "If that damned dog has peed on me..." she muttered, then gave a good sharp kick, but the thing was too big to allow her to move.

It took her a moment, but she began to wake more fully, and it slowly dawned on her that it was a *man* on top of her. As her mind began to clear, she remembered where she was (the smell brought that memory back), so she knew that the big man motionless on top of her had to be Roy.

"Listen, mister," she said as she pushed against him. "I may be here at your request, but that doesn't mean—" She kept pushing, but the man wasn't moving. "He's passed out," she whispered. "All three hundred pounds of him has passed out on top of me." And worse, she was definitely getting wetter around the middle. "An incontinent drunk!" she hissed, then tried to get her legs up so she could use her larger muscles to push against him. Her personal trainer said she had great quads. "So let's use those babies," she said, then braced her hands against the sides of the bed to get a good grip in preparation for the push, but her hand grasped something cold and wet.

"Can't a man even sleep," came a voice she had heard too often in the last few days. In the next moment the room was flooded by an overhead light, and she looked over Roy's big body on top of her into Ace's handsome face, a face that was now twisted in shock and horror.

For a moment Fiona didn't understand anything, not until she followed Ace's eyes and saw that the thing in her hand was a knife, and when she glanced downward, she saw that she and the bed were covered with blood.

She didn't scream. She didn't make any sound at all, just held the knife up and looked at it. She was vaguely aware that there was activity going on around her. Since there were only four people on the boat—correction, three live people, one dead one—she knew that the people moving were Ace and Eric.

Minutes later, Roy's big body was rolled off of her, but Fiona still didn't move. The cool night air made the blood that was soaking her clothes feel cold, but she didn't move. It was almost as though her spirit had left her body and she was looking down at herself. She heard a man's voice say, "...going into shock..." but she didn't relate it to herself.

She heard a voice, the deeper one, giving orders to start the engine and head for shore. Then she seemed to hear water running, as though a teakettle were being filled. Oh, goody, a tea party.

It wasn't until she could feel the teeth-shaking vibration of the engine that someone threw a blanket over her and tried to help her out of the bed. But her legs collapsed under her, so the man lifted her in his arms. "Trainer wrong," she whispered. "Quads no good."

Moments after he set her on a chair at the table, he handed her a hot cup of something.

"Listen to me," he said, leaning toward her. "Can you hear me?"

"Of course I can. What is this? Darjeeling? Or is it Earl Grey?"

"I want you to tell me what happened. Why did you kill him? Did he have something on you? Or did he just try to rape you and you let him have it?"

Fiona looked at him over her mug of hot something or other. "What?"

"What did he do to you? I'm a good listener, and we need to get our stories straight to tell the police."

Fiona's head was beginning to clear enough that a few thoughts were coming into it. Gradually, she was beginning to realize what had happened. She had been in bed with...

She looked up at Ace with his face twisted in an expression of sincerity and sympathy. For all the world he looked like an actor playing a rape counselor.

She set the mug down. "You think I *killed* someone," she managed to breathe. "Murder?"

Ace sat back in the chair, and his face hardened. "Look, I'm trying to help, but maybe you should save everything for the police." With that he got up and walked to the back of the boat, where she knew the body was.

Fiona wasn't going to let him get away with what he'd just said. Instantly, she stood up, and when she did, the blanket that was wrapped around her fell to the floor. She looked down at herself and saw that she was covered in blood from her neck to her knees, and when she looked back up, she saw Ace bending over the bloody body of a man she'd had dinner with just hours before.

Fiona had no idea that she made a sound, but the next minute Ace grabbed her and was holding her head over the side of the boat as she heaved again and again, until there was nothing left inside her.

Gently, Ace set her down on a wooden seat at the side of the boat. "Better?"

She was trembling, shaking so hard her teeth were chattering. Ace disappeared for a moment, then returned with something in a small water glass.

"Drink this," he said in a way that made her obey without question. After she'd drunk the whiskey, he pulled her up to stand in front of him. "Look, I know that I'm destroying evidence, but..."

She didn't understand what he was talking about. But then, nothing in the last two days made sense to her. Holding her wrist in a gentle way, he pulled her into the back of the boat, but he was careful to place his own body between hers and Roy's so she couldn't see him stretched out on the floor.

"Get in the shower," he said, but when she didn't move, he leaned over, and turned on the water. "Now peel off and get in there."

She couldn't think about what was making her clothes stick to her skin, couldn't think about the cold, wet stuff on her skin that was beginning to dry. When she didn't move, Ace reached out both his hands and tore open the front of her shirt—his shirt.

"Get it off! You hear me!" he shouted at her.

It was as though he thought she was about to leave her body again, which she was, but his voice brought her back to reality. In the next moment he was tearing at her clothes in a way someone would remove burning rags from a human body, as though it was her very life to get out of them.

When she was naked, he pushed her into the shower. The warm water woke her up and made her mind focus on one thing: getting out—out of the shower, off the boat. OUT. But when her way was blocked by the big body of Ace Montgomery, she did her best to get past him.

"Oh, no you don't," he said, and pushed her back inside, trying to close the door against her. "You need to wake up, to return to reality."

"I have to get out, you bastard," she shouted as she tried to push past him.

At the moment she didn't think of the

embarrassment of being naked in a shower while fighting a clothed stranger who stood just outside the door. All she thought about was getting away from this place. "Let me out of here!" she shouted at him, trying to open the shower door, but he was too strong for her.

When she kept pushing against the door, he opened it and got into the shower with her. At first she fought him. He stood with his back to the shower pipes and held her about the waist as she fought him with all her might. He held her hands so she couldn't claw his face, but she managed to rake quite a lot of skin off the back of his hands, and she pounded his chest hard.

After long minutes of fighting and not being able to move him, she started sobbing. And when she started to cry, her body went limp against his. Both his arms were around her back, the warm water cascading over both of them, he fully clothed, she naked, and he held her against him while she cried.

Five

"Where are you taking me?" Fiona asked as she looked across the dark car at Ace. It had been only hours since she'd found Roy's bloody body on top of her, but it seemed like a lifetime ago. After the shower—and cry—with Ace, she had, surprisingly, felt better. If angry and wanting to cut the head off the nearest person is better, that is. Once again, she was wearing Ace's clothes, this time gray sweatpants and a thick green sweater that had the name of some Ivy League school embroidered over her left breast.

In the time since the... finding, as she was calling it in her mind, Ace and Eric had done a lot of whispering. They seemed to agree on everything because they had done a lot of nodding and looking at Fiona as she sat on the edge of the boat and watched the moonlit water. As far as she could tell, they seemed to think that she might throw herself overboard at any moment. But Fiona looked at the water and at the stars and tried to direct her mind to her real purpose in life: Kimberly. What was going on with her now? Fiona wondered. Who was handling her? Did her assistant Gerald send the maps to production or had he left them on the floor in the Saks bag?

"You ready?" Ace finally asked; he was treating her as though she were a mental case about to flip out again. What did she expect, right now he had every reason to think she was a murderer.

When he'd finally shut off the shower, opened the door, and stepped out, he'd handed her a blanket, then kept on walking. He'd disappeared somewhere on the boat, and when he'd reappeared later, he'd been dry and composed—and he had looked at Fiona with the cool disdain he always wore when he looked at her. No one would have guessed the intimacy that had recently happened between them.

But Fiona remembered the scene too well. "Florida doesn't agree with me," she said, making a feeble attempt at a joke—and some human contact—as he helped her off the boat.

But he didn't smile or acknowledge her attempt at levity in any way. His face was grim.

If he could forget the scene, so could she, she thought. Once on shore she looked about. She had no idea where they were, but there was a Jeep waiting for them, so one of the two men must have called ahead from the boat. Ace put his hand under her elbow to help her into the car, but she jerked away.

"I am not an invalid," she snapped as she propelled herself into the car. He tossed his duffel bag and her backpack onto the backseat, slammed the door, then got into the driver's side, and the next moment they were on the highway.

"Is it too much to ask where you're taking me?"

"To the police," he said tersely.

"Ah, yes. Since I'm a criminal, right?"

He didn't answer but just kept driving.

"Would it do any good to tell you that I didn't kill a man who is twice my size and probably twice my strength?"

"I've seen your strength," he said.

"I thought you were being eaten alive!"

she screamed at him. "Why can't you understand that? I didn't stop and think about whether or not that creature was real or not, I just reacted."

Ace was very calm, exaggeratedly calm, as though he knew he was dealing with an insane person. "I know. And I'm sure that when Roy attacked you, you didn't stop and think either; you just pulled his knife out of its case and stabbed him."

"I was hard asleep. I hadn't slept in two days, remember? And the knife I had in my hand was lying on the bed beside me. It wasn't in a case."

"His knife was always in the case he wore about his waist. I'm sure you saw it."

"No, I did not," she said through her teeth. "How could anyone see anything underneath that belly of his? And I didn't look anyway."

Ace turned the steering wheel sharply as he made a right turn. "Look, why don't you have some coffee? Eric made a fresh pot for us."

"Wasn't that kind of him? Did he make it before or after he killed Roy?"

Ace gave her a sharp look before looking back at the road, but he said nothing.

"Why am I to presume that *you* are innocent? Or that the other man is? If *I* didn't kill him, then one of you two did."

Ace didn't seem perturbed by what she was saying. "It's a matter of motive. I lose any possibility of getting money for Kendrick Park with Roy's death, and Eric no longer has a job."

When he said no more, Fiona had to think about what he was saying. "You think that I killed the man just to get out of a fishing trip?" She was incredulous.

"You were awfully unhappy about being there, so maybe you had deeper reasons."

At that Fiona looked out the window and tried to judge how fast they were going. At least sixty. If she jumped out of a car going this fast, she'd break every bone in her body.

With a sigh, she picked up the big silver Thermos at her feet and poured herself a cup of coffee, drank it, then poured Ace one and handed the cup to him. What the hell? she thought as she put her hand on the door latch. If the police were as stupid and as implacable as this man, this was her last night of freedom forever.

But at Fiona's first movement, Ace put his hand on her forearm, the empty coffee cup falling to the floor. "Don't do anything stupid."

"Stupider than what's already happened to me, you mean? Stupider than the last two days? Stupider than—" Breaking off, she put her hand to her forehead. She was still so tired that she couldn't seem to keep her eyes open. In fact, she was dizzy with fatigue. "I, ah..." she began but couldn't remember what it was that she was going to say. She put her head back and closed her eyes.

Minutes later, she was vaguely aware of a garish pink motel sign flashing on and off over her head and the car pulling to a halt. She thought that Ace got out, and she even thought that she should try to run for it, but her body wouldn't move. Instead, she kept her head resting against the back of the seat, her body limp with fatigue. Someone could have cut her feet off with a chain saw and she wasn't sure she'd notice.

But as though she were in a dream, she seemed to feel strong arms lift her and carry her through a doorway, then place her in the heavenly comfort of a real bed—a bed that didn't undulate with the whimsy of the waves. As she lay there, sinking even deeper into what was surely more a coma than sleep, she seemed to hear someone stumbling about. Drunk, she thought, then smiled and gave herself up to sleep. She didn't feel the bed sag as a heavy body got between her and the door.

❦

A terrific headache woke Fiona. It was that kind of groggy, empty headache brought on by too little food, too little sleep, and too much to drink. With every muscle in her body aching, she swung her legs off the bed and sat up. For a moment she didn't know where she was and especially not why she was there. She had a vague feeling that something was wrong, but she wasn't sure what it was. But she was sure it had to do with Kimberly, so she'd better get to work and sort it out.

A noise behind her made her turn. There was a man sound asleep in the bed beside her. What was Jeremy doing here? she wondered, but as the man turned over, his face toward her, she knew that Jeremy had never had a head of hair that thick in his life. Nor lips that full, or a nose that strong, that aquiline, or—

"Holy—!" Fiona said aloud as memory came back to her with the force of a tsunami hitting a beach.

In the next second, she'd grabbed her backpack from the rickety chair by what passed for a desk and she had her hand on the doorknob. But in the following second, a larger, darker hand covered hers.

"I don't think you should leave," Ace said; then he rubbed his hand over his face. "And please don't hit me or kick me. I'm not in the mood for one of your assaults this morning."

"My—" she began, then calmed herself. "You are not my keeper, and you have no right to hold me here."

Ace didn't seem to hear her. Yawning, he stepped back from the door but not far enough to give her space to flee. "You think that diner over there delivers?"

"How would I know? I was drugged and carried in here against my will, remember? What do you think they give you in this state for kidnapping?"

"You weren't drugged, and you weren't held against your will. You were asleep," he said without emotion. The truth was, Fiona was beginning to wonder if he had any emotion except anger. "Do you want the bathroom first or me?"

At that Fiona looked toward the cheap wooden bathroom door speculatively.

Ace yawned again. "Don't worry. It doesn't have a window. I asked for a windowless bathroom."

"You're sick, you know that? And I *was* drugged; I know the feeling too well."

"Oh? Personally, I don't do drugs, but if you—"

She didn't bother to listen to the rest of his sentence but slammed into the bathroom, her pack over her shoulder. Twenty minutes later she emerged, showered and made up.

"Ah," Ace said as he looked up at her. "You're wearing your mask again." He was sitting on the single chair in the room and looking at a magazine. Lying on the table in front of him was a long piece of what looked to be curtain cord. The moment Fiona saw it, she started backing up. *Someone* had killed Roy Hudson, and if it wasn't her, then it could have been him.

"Look," she said softly, "maybe we should go to the police. Maybe you should call them now, and—"

"We'll go in a while, but if I've learned nothing else in the last days, the police don't give you time to eat, much less shower. I need to be prepared for what's ahead."

When he left the cord where it was, seemingly unaware of its existence, she said, "Sure," then smiled at him. "You go ahead and shower and shave. I'll wait for you here."

For a moment he blinked at her. "I need to

make sure that you don't run out the door while I shower and..."

Looking at her, he kept blinking, and it took Fiona a moment to realize that he was perplexed—and embarrassed. How was he going to use the bathroom and shower while keeping watch over her?

The memory of their shower together came back to her. At the time all she'd thought of was the trauma of Roy's dead body and Roy's blood all over her, but now she remembered her nudity and his wet clothes.

He hadn't been embarrassed when *she* was the naked one, but now that the tables were turned, he... What? Thought she would jump on him?

"Go on, get in the shower. I promise I won't look." Her tone was that of a mother talking to a nine-year-old who'd newly turned modest.

He seemed to hesitate for a moment, but then he turned away from the bathroom. Some tough guy, she thought, chuckling to herself.

"If I let you walk out the door, I'm an accessory to murder," he said as he walked to the big window and looked out between the drapes.

"Right, and you have to protect your own skin," she said.

"Look," he said as he dropped the curtain and looked back at her, "I know that right now you want to run, but where would you go? You can't very well fly back to New York and walk into work tomorrow as though nothing

63

happened. Roy was a prominent man, and his murder will make the news."

"I didn't kill him."

"Probably not," Ace said as he pulled out a shaving case from his duffel bag. "Come in the bathroom and sit."

"I will not—" she began, but then thought, Why not? She went into the bathroom with him and sat on the toilet while he shaved.

"The way I see it, I'm doing you a favor," he said, foam on his face, a safety razor at his throat.

Fiona was looking about the room for something heavy to hit him over the head with. But the room had long ago had everything stolen from it that could be carried away. Maybe the razor would slip...

"And how are you doing me a favor?" she said. If she could get him to turn his back when he returned to the bedroom, maybe she could hit him with the chair.

"If you ran, you'd be a fugitive from justice, and—"

She forgot about killing him. "Justice? You can say that word to me? What do you know about justice? I was taken away from Kimberly to go on a slimy fishing trip, and—"

"Who is Kimberly?" he asked as he dried his face.

"Really," Fiona said with the heaviest sarcasm she could muster. "Bird feathers in your ears and eyes? Do you actually *live* in America?"

As he picked up the phone, he gave her a puzzled look, but the next moment he was talking to someone. "Ham and eggs, hash browns, toast, coffee, the works. Yeah, and that too. Sure. You can deliver it to—You don't deliver? But I'm in the motel just across—Oh, I see." Ace waited a moment before he spoke again, then he lowered his voice and spoke in honeyed tones. "But couldn't you make an exception just this once? For me?" He was obviously talking to a woman.

"I'm going to be ill," Fiona muttered, then took one long step toward Ace, snatched the phone from his hands, and said into the receiver, "There's a twenty tip in it for you."

"Be there in a tick," a woman's voice said; then the phone went silent.

Fiona dangled the receiver from her fingertips while looking Ace straight in the eyes, an I-told-you-so smile curving her lips. "You're out of high school now... Ace." She said his name with contempt. "Not all women are cheerleaders lusting after the football captain."

Turning her back on him, she walked away, at least as far as the small room would allow. Truthfully, the longer she spent with this man the more ready she was to turn herself in to the police. Now that she was fully awake, she was thinking of the seriousness of murder and that if she didn't kill Roy, either this man or the fish cleaner did.

Or maybe the two men had done it together.

For a moment neither Fiona nor Ace said a word.

"Soccer," Ace said. "I played soccer in high school, not football."

Fiona almost said, "So did I," but she conquered herself. Right now she was concentrating on springing out the door the second the waitress appeared. If she could escape him, maybe the best thing to do would be to turn herself in to protective custody.

Minutes later there was a knock on the door. After all, how long did it take to fry perfectly good food into the greasy mass that was sloshing about on the tray the woman held out?

"That'll be sixteen fifty, plus tip of course," she said, beaming up at Ace with so much concentration that she didn't notice Fiona edging toward the door. "I even brought you this morning's paper. It's all about those two killers from..."

She had glanced down at the newspaper, then back up at Ace, but she quickly looked back at the paper again, and her eyes widened. The next instant she looked up and saw Fiona in a position as though she were about to spring.

With a quick scream of pure terror, the plump waitress dropped the tray and began running across the parking lot to the diner.

"What the hell was that all about?" Ace said, standing there watching the woman run.

Stooping, Fiona grabbed the paper.

It took both of them precious moments to comprehend what they were seeing. Photographs of Ace and Fiona were on the front page, and the headlines said that they were killers on the run. Below their picture was a shot of Eric lying on a hospital bed, one eye swollen shut, his face a mass of bruises, and the caption said he'd been left for dead by Ace and Fiona after the brutal slaying of Roy Hudson.

Ace grabbed their two bags, the car keys, and as he went out the door, he grabbed Fiona's arm and pulled her toward the Jeep. Within seconds they were screeching by the windows of the diner. Every patron in the place was standing at the window watching and pointing.

"Bonnie and Clyde," Fiona shouted over the sound of the tires tearing out of the parking lot. "I feel like Bonnie and Clyde."

"Yeah," Ace yelled back, "and look how they ended up."

Six

She had to give it to him: he could drive. He wasn't reckless, and she doubted if he even once exceeded the speed limit, but he moved in and out of traffic with quick efficiency. He wove the car down side streets in residential areas, always with his eyes on all three mirrors as he watched to see if anyone was following them. She didn't ask him if he had a place for them to go because she was afraid that he would have a negative answer.

Once he mumbled something.

"What?!" she asked in fear.

"Redheaded woodpecker," he said. "Rare in this area."

Given their circumstances, she could only blink at this remark.

After about forty minutes he pulled the sun visor down and removed a little black remote control, pushed a red button, and the next minute they glided into a garage and the door closed behind them. "Come on," he said without looking at her, then disappeared inside a door, leaving her in the car.

Slowly, Fiona got out of the car, her backpack on her shoulder. When she stepped through the door, she was in a small kitchen, very plain, clean, but with a feeling that no one actually used it. She could hear a voice through the doorway. Cautiously, she stepped into a living room that had a white Berber carpet and black leather furniture. There were three big watercolors of local Florida scenes on the walls. Hotel rooms were more personal than this place.

Ace was sitting on the couch talking into a telephone.

Fiona thought that she should put her finger on the button and cut him off, but she didn't. Common sense overrode her fear. If the police didn't know where they were, why did she have to fear a telephone tap?

"You have the names?" Ace was saying. "Right." "Yes, I understand." "Yeah, here at Joe's." "No, I'll stay here as long as I can." "Yes, she's here with me."

At that Ace leaned back against the couch and looked at Fiona sitting on the matching black leather chair. "No, no, of course not," he said into the phone, then smiled. "She's as tall as me, so she's wearing my clothes."

At that Fiona sat upright and glared at him.

The reply of the person on the other end made him smile broader. "Yeah, okay, tell her not to worry, I have it under control. I'll wait for your fax." He paused. "Yeah, okay, and you too."

When he put down the receiver, Fiona was still glaring at him, but he ignored her. "Are you hungry? I'm not sure what there is to eat here."

Fiona came off the couch in one motion and planted herself in front of him. "I want to know what's going on. What do you have under control? Where are we? Who were you calling, and what was so funny about your... about these clothes? Except that I'm sick of them, that is."

He was wrong, she thought, he was at least two inches taller than she was. They'd be equal if she had on heels, but in the old tennis shoes, she had to look up to him, ever so slightly, but she was looking up.

As he often did, he ignored her; he stepped around her and went into the kitchen. Fiona was inches behind him, so close in fact that he almost hit her in the face with the freezer door of the side-by-side.

"Ah, here we have a variety of frozen grease. So what's your poison?" He held up two pack-ages—one of eggs wrapped around ham and another of eggs wrapped around cheese.

She took a deep breath. "I want to know what's going on," she said as calmly as she could. "I am wanted for murder. The newspaper—"

"No, *we* are wanted for murder." He'd put the frozen packages back into the freezer and was now looking in the cupboards. "You know how to make pancakes?"

At that Fiona put her arms straight down to her sides, her hands in fists, opened her mouth, and let out a scream.

Ace had his hand over her mouth before she'd let an ounce of air escape her lungs. "What the hell do you think you're doing?" he demanded. "If someone heard you, they might investigate." Slowly, he removed his hand and nodded toward the countertop in the kitchen. "Now sit down while I make breakfast."

She didn't move. "So help me, if you don't tell me what's going on, I'll scream my head off."

"You really do have trouble with anger, don't you? Have you thought of seeing a counselor?"

At that Fiona opened her mouth again, but this time he didn't move. Instead, he just looked at her speculatively.

Closing her mouth, Fiona narrowed her eyes at him. "So why aren't we at the police station, Mr. Do-Gooder? Just hours ago you were telling me that I couldn't be a fugitive from justice, that I had to turn myself over to the police. But now that you're also accused, we're hiding."

"You want blueberries in your pancakes?"

70

"I want some answers!" she shouted at him.

"All right," he said, "but sit while you ask me what you want to know."

"No," she said calmly as she took a seat on a barstool on the far side of the counter, "I don't play that game. I don't beg you for information. You start talking."

"I guess it would be too much to ask that *you* would cook while I explain."

Fiona gave a snort of derision. She had no idea how to turn on a stove, much less make food with one of the things.

"Thought not. All right, as you know, Eric killed Roy Hudson last night so we—"

"Wait a minute," Fiona said slowly, her hands on either side of her head. "I thought you believed that *I* killed the man."

Ace was at the stove, his back to her, but he turned around, a look of astonishment on his face. "How could you have killed a man twice your size?"

"This is not funny," she said, "and I don't appreciate your levity."

"Okay," he said with a sigh as he turned back to the griddle on the stove. "I had to get you out of there last night, so I pretended to Eric that I believed you were the killer. For all I knew he had a couple of stowaways on the boat ready to attack us." He placed the first stack of pancakes in front of her.

Since it was more than she usually ate in two days, she got up, found another plate, then lifted all but one of the pancakes and put

71

them on the empty plate. During this she was thinking about what he was saying and doing her best to remember all that had happened last night.

"But later when we were alone, why did you keep saying that you thought I was a murderer?"

"To keep you angry so you wouldn't think about what had just happened." He had a spatula laden with yet more pancakes. "Is that all you're eating?"

"Yeah," she said with a cold look at him. "We unwomanly women don't eat too much." But the pancakes were quite good.

He put two more on her plate, put three pats of butter on each pancake, then slathered the whole stack in syrup.

"You were going to turn me in to the police," she said as she looked at the pancakes and decided to take just one more bite.

"Protective custody. Seemed to me that Eric had it in for you. Or maybe it was just that you were the weaker of the two of us." At that he held up his hands as though to prevent her attacking him for his non-p.c. reply, and she saw that the backs of his hands were deeply scratched. It must have been painful for him to drive.

"I'm sorry," she mumbled, her mouth full, her eyes on her plate, her face red in memory of his holding her in the shower.

"What did you say? I couldn't hear you." He cupped his hand to his ear.

"I said that you had no right to treat me as

though I were a child. You could have told me what was going on," she said loudly.

"Right. Before or after you went into shock over finding a bleeding corpse on top of you?"

At that Fiona pushed her now-empty plate away. "So what now? Where are we, by the way?"

"This house belongs to a friend of mine. It's my getaway when he's not here and I've had too much of..." When he paused, Fiona got the impression that he didn't want to reveal too much about himself. "Anyway, no one in Florida knows about this place, so we won't be found here. I called my brother to find out what he can about Eric and your Roy Hudson."

"*My* Roy Hudson?" She almost exploded. "What is that supposed to mean? At least you met him before when you hit him up for money for that bird farm of yours."

"No," Ace said thoughtfully, "I hadn't met him, and I never asked him for money. Oddly enough he came to me. I received a badly typed, misspelled letter saying that he thought he was about to come into some money and he wanted to give some to Kendrick Park. He said that if this was all right with me, we'd meet at the park and leave from there to go on a fishing trip; then he gave a date and time."

He looked back down at his huge stack of pancakes. "I didn't know anything about you until the day we left. Even then I was only told your name."

"Okay, so now what do we do? Or am I not to ask that? You seem to like the caveman role, where all women just obey and don't ask too many questions."

"You have a sharp tongue on you," he said, looking at her from across the counter.

"Some men like my tongue," she snapped back, then regretted her words.

He didn't reply to that but kept his head down for a moment before looking back at her. "I want to wait until I see what my brother can find on Eric and Roy. There has to be a motive. Unless Eric just likes to kill for the fun of it, which I doubt."

"Why? Why doubt something like that? Lots of people kill just because they enjoy it."

Ace picked up her plate and his, then walked with them to the sink. "I don't know. It's just a feeling I have. I think this thing was planned, and I think it has something to do with you."

"Me?" Fiona said, then started to defend herself but stopped. "I don't know anything or anyone involved in this."

"Even if the police dig deeply," he said softly, "they won't find something that could be construed as a motive?"

"You mean like he had photos of me naked and he would have published them on the Internet if I didn't pay him, what was it you said?: 'Everything you have, everything you will earn, and for what you plan to leave your children.' Is that about right?"

"You have some memory on you. So?"

74

"So what?" she asked, staring at him.

"Do you have those photos or not?"

"Very funny. No, I don't have any nudes of myself, and where have you been for the last decade? It's fashionable to be photographed naked. But it doesn't matter anyway. I haven't done anything that anyone could blackmail me for."

"Surely you have some secrets."

She narrowed her eyes at him. "Not that I would tell you and not that Roy Hudson could know." Her voice rose before he could speak. "Any secrets I have might cause me embarrassment, but there's not much that couldn't be printed in the church bulletin. What about you?"

"Me?" he asked as though he were a bystander and not part of this.

"Yes, you! That newspaper said that you were my accomplice."

"Oh that," he said in dismissal as he put the dishes in the dishwasher. "I'm sure that was an afterthought. What I want to know is who beat up Eric? Was that part of the plan, or did he anger someone else?"

"Maybe he beat himself up."

"Saw that on TV, did you?" he said, obviously laughing at her.

At that Fiona got up and went into the living room. She really didn't like his attitude of flippancy. He was treating all of this as some great joke and just as soon as his brother sent a fax, all would be cleared up. She heard him doing whatever it is that people do in a kitchen, and when he finally returned to the living room, he didn't seem in the least perturbed. "Doesn't any of this bother you?" she snapped. "Don't you want to get back to your birds?"

At that he turned to glare down at her. "You think I want to stay cooped up inside this place? You think I want to be here with someone who has made my life a living hell since she stepped off a plane? No, I don't. But, unlike you, I'm trying to make the best of it. I'm trying to save us some time in jail, because that's where they'd put us until this thing is figured out. So, if you don't mind, I'd like a little appreciation, if not thanks."

"Sorry," she muttered.

"I didn't hear you."

"I apologize," she shouted. "Did you hear that?"

"Yes, and I'm sure the neighbors did too," he said. She watched as he opened a desk drawer and took out a cell phone.

"Who are you going to call?" she asked suspiciously.

"Not that it's any of your business, but I plan to call my fiancée. I'm sure she's worried sick."

"But the police—"

"Won't be trying to trace calls from this phone—it belongs to the owner of this house."

"Well, I'll just..." she said, and nodded toward the bathroom. But the truth was that she had no intention of getting out of earshot of him and his call. Was his fiancée the perky little blonde in the photo she'd found under his bed? And, for that matter, what was the photo doing under his bed?

Fiona stepped into the bathroom and turned on the water, but she left the door open. Miss Perky must have been sitting by the phone because she answered it instantly.

"Yes, honey, I'm fine," Ace said in a voice she'd never before heard from him. It was an almost fatherly voice, very tender and soothing. "Yes, yes. I know. I saw the papers. No, of course none of it's true. It was just a misunderstanding, that's all."

At that Fiona made a sound in her throat that caused Ace to get up and walk around the corner where he could see her.

Close the door, Fiona thought, but she couldn't make herself do it. This man's private conversation was none of her business, but, still, she couldn't seem to work up the command to close the door.

"Yes, she's here with me," Ace said softly into the receiver.

After that remark, Fiona knew that she'd die before she moved an inch.

Ace laughed in a seductive way, then said, "Very tall, very skinny," then paused. "Oh, that. Flat." He held the telephone an inch away from his mouth. "Lisa wants to know how old you are."

"Thirty-two," Fiona said before she thought.

"See, I told you," Ace said. "Now stop worrying. Mike has Frank working on this. By this evening we'll know everything there is to know about both of them, especially *why* Eric killed Roy. That's the key to everything. And after we find out the reason, then Miss Burkenhalter and I will go to the police and it'll all be over with."

Pausing as he listened, Fiona watched him in the mirror. He had the softest, sweetest smile on his face, as though he were ice cream sitting in the sun.

"Come on, now, sweetheart, stop crying. I'm fine. No, I can't tell you where I am, and you can't visit me." He smiled broader. "Yes, I know she's here, but she's also been accused of murder. No, of course she didn't kill anyone." "Yes. You can tell the police I said so. Look, why don't you take a couple of pills and go to bed? There's nothing you can do to help me."

He paused for several long moments, then turned his back so Fiona couldn't see his face. "Yes, me too," she heard him say, then, "Okay, I'll call you when I can"; then he turned the phone off and handed it to Fiona without making a comment on her eavesdropping.

"You want to call someone, do," he said over his shoulder as he headed for the kitchen.

Jeremy, was Fiona's first thought. He must be frantic with worry over her. Quickly she pushed the buttons for his number as she walked into the living room.

Like Lisa, Jeremy must have been waiting for her call.

"Where the hell are you?" he exploded. "Do you have any idea how much trouble you're in? Fiona, I don't know if I can get you out of this. You *must* turn yourself in and *immediately.*"

"Ace has some relatives looking into why Eric killed Roy, and—"

"Fiona, are you out of your mind? Are you insane? As far as I can tell, this guy Eric is in the hospital with a battered face and a ruptured spleen. He says that you and this guy Ace beat him after you killed Roy."

"Oh," Fiona said, and her body began to tremble. "I haven't really heard all of it. We didn't see the papers, and—"

"It seems to me that you didn't really think about anything. Do you know how your case is going to look when you're reported as flaunting your flight in front of a diner full of people? They say that you and that man nearly ran down a busload of children in your wild escape."

"We did no such thing. Jeremy, do you think I'm too skinny? And old?"

"Merciful heavens, Fiona, have you lost your mind? Wait, wait, later I can testify that you were in shock and incoherent."

Maybe he was trying to be helpful and maybe she should be grateful that he was thinking like a lawyer, but she didn't like being called "incoherent," for any reason, and she wanted to get him back. "Did you see the photo in the paper of Ace?" she practically purred. "He's really quite beautiful. I never saw such thick hair in my life, and—"

"Fiona," Jeremy said coldly, "if this is an

attempt to make me jealous, I don't think this is the time or place, do you?"

When Fiona heard a step by the doorway into the living room, she mumbled, "I gotta go," then hung up on Jeremy's loud protests. She didn't want to be chastised by Jeremy—even if she did deserve his anger at her ingratitude.

Ace entered the room with a tall glass of iced tea. "He upset about the mess you're in?"

"Oh, yes," Fiona said as lightly as she could manage. "He was very worried about me. He always worries about me. And your girlfriend? Lena?"

"Lisa. Fiancée. The wedding date is set for three weeks from now. You want something to drink?"

"No thanks. So, you told her I'm tall and skinny and old, not to mention..." She glanced down at her chest. It was true that she wasn't going to win a wet T-shirt contest, but clothes hung better on her than on...

Oh, hell, what did she care what this man's girlfriend thought of her?

"Sorry about that," Ace said, his mouth full. "She thinks that every woman I meet is after me, so I have to tell her that all of them are real dogs."

"Sounds like a mature relationship."

"It works. And you? Boyfriend missing you?"

"Sure." She tried to give a smile of insouciance. "And he's terribly jealous of you, too. So at last we have something in common. I think I'll call my office and just see what's going on."

Before he could reply, she had dialed the number of her office. Gerald answered.

"Fiona, darling, where in the world are you? No, don't tell me. If I know, I'll have to tell the police. They've been here all morning. It's been awful."

Not as awful as finding a dead man on top of you, Fiona thought but didn't say. "Any problems at work?" she asked, trying to get her current situation out of her mind.

"Well," Gerald said, "I had to change Kimberly just a tiny bit, but the launch this morning was a great success."

Fiona could feel hysteria rising in her throat. "You launched Kimberly early? Without *me?*"

"Considering what was going on with you, Garrett thought we should go ahead and get her out there, and besides, he said that since you'd killed Roy, our chances of getting the *Raphael* franchise were now greatly reduced, so we need everything we can get from Kimberly."

Fiona was sputtering. "I—did—not—kill—anyone."

"Oh, sure. I know that. And in the pool, I bet on your side."

"Pool." Her voice was flat, emotionless.

"Oh, Fee, by the way, the maps in the trunks look divine. Listen I gotta go. *Soooo* much to do. If the police call again, what should I tell them?"

"That Kimberly and I are—Oh, the hell with it," she snapped, then hung up.

Fiona tossed the phone onto the top of her

backpack and plopped down onto the black leather chair. If possible, she felt worse than she had. When was this nightmare going to be over? She had to get back to work before that treacherous Gerald did something dreadful to Kimberly.

"If you don't mind my asking," Ace said, "who is Kimberly?"

"Mine, mine, mine!" Fiona half shouted. "And if that little pink-eared swivel-hipped Gerald thinks he can take her from me, he'd better be prepared to fight to the death."

Ace blinked at her for a moment. "You want a drink? How about a little TV? Maybe something on the Disney Channel?"

Fiona was smoldering, furious, as she glared at him. "You think this place has any paper in it? And a pen? Or a pencil?"

Immediately, Ace stood up, left the room, and moments later returned with a legal pad in a plastic folder and a roller-ball pen. "Best I could do. Will it be okay?"

"Fine." She snatched the pad and pen from him.

Minutes later they had both settled down to do the only thing they could do: wait. Ace watched TV while Fiona drew. A couple of times she looked up at him, and each time she marveled that the man could find so many bird shows on TV.

Phrases from the TV show came to her.

"One hundred and sixteen species of birds breed in the Everglades."

"One ounce of feathers was worth two ounces

of pure gold to the people who made ladies' hats."

Minutes later she looked up to see a picture of the man whose portrait she'd seen in Ace's house.

"In 1905, Guy Bradley was killed trying to protect a rookery at Oyster Key. It was the day conservation was born in America."

But she didn't have time to think much about what Ace was doing as her own mind was going fast and furiously and she was sketching her ideas as quickly as she could move the pen. Drawing and designing for Kimberly soothed her. She didn't plan to use anything that she was drawing now, but in the way professional chefs cooked to relax and race car drivers took a Sunday drive, Fiona calmed down with a pen and a pad of paper.

She didn't look up again until she heard the music for the show's credits, and there the name "Dr. Paul Montgomery" appeared again and again. For a moment, Fiona stared, transfixed. He had written, produced, and researched the show. He'd even supplied "additional photography" and "consultations."

For the rest of the day she drew while he flipped through ninety-some channels and watched TV, and he managed to find one show after another about birds. Bird names, phrases, and sounds floated about her head.

"The stately sandhill crane..."
"The great egret..."
"The blue-winged teal stays here year round...."
"Roseate spoonbill..."
"Black-bellied plover..."

But she always looked at the TV when she heard the music for the ending credits for a show, and she always saw the name "Dr. Paul Montgomery" roll over and over on the screen.

When it grew dark outside and Ace said he was going to bed, she barely heard him.

"If you want the bed, I'll take the couch," he said.

"No, no," she said absently, not lifting her eyes from the paper. "Take the bed. I'm staying here."

After a moment of watching her, Ace shrugged, then went to bed and was asleep instantly. But later he awoke, saw the light still on in the living room, and got up to investigate. Fiona had fallen asleep, the notebook on her lap, pages falling all about her. Carefully, he pushed the pages off of her, carried her into the bedroom, and placed her on the bed.

As he pulled the light spread over her, he said, "I don't know who Kimberly is, but I don't think she's worth all this."

Turning, he went back into the living room, turned off the light, and stretched out on the sofa. He was tempted to look at her drawings, but there was something in him that held back. He didn't want to know more about her than he already did. No, he just wanted to get out of this absurd situation and return to Kendrick Park and the life he loved.

Two minutes later, he was asleep.

Seven

⚜

I get to go home today, was Fiona's first thought upon waking. This nightmare of hiding from the police, of finding dead bodies, of hearing that Kimberly had been launched without her, was about to end. Stretching, she thought of all that home meant: her own clothes, seeing her facialist again, having a massage.

"Coffee?" came a voice from the doorway, then Ace's head came into view. "There are some bagels, but they've been frozen."

Fiona grimaced, then forced a small smile. "Sure. Anything. What did the fax say?"

"It hasn't come yet," he said as he entered the bedroom as though it were his right. "Look, don't worry. It takes time for these things. My brother and my cousins know a lot of people, and they'll find out things."

She took the steaming mug from him and sipped. He could drive and he could make coffee. "I don't think I want to know what kind of business your relatives are in. Do they have names like 'Bugsy' and 'Scarface'?"

For a moment Ace blinked at her as though trying to understand what she was implying, then he gave her a crooked grin. "Sure. And I got a brother named 'Deuce.' What about you?"

"No brothers, no sisters. Just me."

"Lonely childhood, huh?"

"Not quite. I spent most of my life in boarding schools and had a wonderful time. Can you call someone and see what they've found out?"

"Already did. So far no one's heard back from anyone. That could be good or bad."

"Would you explain please? I'm not up to the jargon of criminals or the Mafia."

Again Ace blinked at her before he spoke. "If none of the people doing the searching have reported back yet, it could be bad, meaning that they've found nothing. On the other hand maybe they stepped on so many toes that they were wiped out."

"I don't like your sense of humor," Fiona said as she handed the empty mug back to him. "All I want to do is get out of here and back to New York."

"And to your beloved Kimberly," Ace said, looking at her as though he hoped she'd explain.

"Would you give me some privacy? I want to take a shower."

"Sure. There are eggs, so I'll make a couple of omelettes." As he stood up, he nodded toward the bedroom closet. "There're clothes in there."

"Men's?" she asked with a grimace.

"What else? At least this way you won't give Lisa anything to be jealous about."

"Oh? How tall is this Lisa?"

"Five four," Ace said from the doorway. "Why?"

"When I meet her, I want to be wearing the tiniest skirt this side of the children's department. My *legs* are five foot four inches long. Now get out of here!"

He left, but Fiona had the sweetest sense of revenge when she thought of the look on his face. It was almost too bad that this whole escapade was going to be over so soon; after all, it might be nice to have someone to use to make Jeremy jealous. He altogether took her too much for granted.

Fiona stayed under the shower until the hot, hot water washed away some of her fatigue and the sense of doom she'd lived with for the last two days. Today she just knew that everything was going to be all right. Today she was going *home!*

After she'd dressed in yet another pair of men's trousers and another man's shirt, she went into the kitchen, where Ace was making some heavenly smells.

"You don't eat enough," he said as he slid a fat, gooey omelette onto a plate. "You had one meal yesterday and that was it."

"Nerves," she said as she dug into the omelette. "Usually I eat—" She broke off because she was becoming too friendly with this man.

Ace stood there waiting for her to finish her sentence, but when she didn't, he turned away. "Hey! Look what I found." With a flourish, he opened a kitchen cabinet door to reveal a small TV and the controls to a stereo system.

"Oh, great," she said, mouth full. "Birds for breakfast. Did I tell you that I love squab? And roast duck and—"

"Cannibal!" he said with so much disgust that for a moment she thought he was being serious, but a twinkle in his eyes gave him away.

"And pigeon eggs," she said. "And I have a hat with osprey plumes on it."

Ace was smiling as he picked up the remote control and turned on the TV to a national morning show. But his smile vanished instantly as a news reporter came on. Photos of Ace and Fiona were behind her head.

"And now we have an update on the brutal slaying of *Raphael* creator Roy Hudson in Fort Lauderdale. In an attempt to find a motive for the murder, police had Mr. Hudson's will read. It seems that the sole and only heirs of what could be a vast estate are Fiona Burkenhalter and Paul, better known as 'Ace,' Montgomery.

"Through an anonymous tip, police have also found out that Burkenhalter and Montgomery were in the same hotel in different states three times in the last fourteen months. Police are speculating that this murder of Roy Hudson has been in the planning for quite some time.

"And yesterday it was revealed that Burkenhalter and Montgomery were the cause of the bombing scare at the Fort Lauderdale airport on the day before the murder. Deliveryman Arnold Sacwin told police that he believed that the two alleged killers were working together in an insurance-fraud plot to destroy an expensive mechanical alligator manufactured in Hollywood.”

The news reporter paused a moment to allow a film clip to be shown. Arnold Sacwin, the man who had delivered the alligator, was on camera saying that he’d known from the beginning that there was something fishy about the “whole operation.” “This woman comes out of nowhere and knows just where to throw that bomb so the ’gator explodes,” he was saying into the microphone. “Then that guy Ace had the... well, you know, to try to make me think that he’d never met this broad before. Didn’t fool me for a minute.”

After that, the picture switched back to the woman in the newsroom. “Police are investigating every possible lead on the whereabouts of the two alleged killers, and all citizens are asked to call the police if they are spotted. And the police ask, please, don’t get near them. They are believed to be armed and dangerous.”

Ace pushed the button to turn the TV off, and the next minute he grabbed Fiona’s shoulders and was pulling her upright. “Don’t you pass out on me now!” he shouted into her face. “We don’t have time for this. You hear me?”

All she could do was nod. Her mind was too horror-struck to comprehend what she’d just heard.

“Listen to me,” Ace said, his nose close to hers. “I’m going to give you a choice, but I’m also going to give you some advice. Are you hearing me?”

Fiona looked at him, and she could hear his voice as though it were a long, long way away.

"Someone has gone to a lot of trouble to set this up. This person has spent a lot of time on this, so it's my guess that if we went to the police now when we're as innocent as we are, they'd..." Pausing, he looked at her white face, her eyes huge in her face. Sheer, stark terror was what he was looking at.

He had to readjust his hold on her because she was sinking further down. "Listen to me! We have to get out of here. If we go to the police now, we'll never be able to clear ourselves. Are you understanding me?"

"I want to go home," she whispered. "I want to get Kimberly ready and..."

"Don't give up on me now." He took a breath, then moved her to sit on the stool. "You and I know something," he said. "Do you understand me?"

"No," she said honestly. She didn't understand anything at all.

"Look, I'm not going to lie to you. I don't know what's going on either, but yesterday I kept seeing things that didn't make sense, and now hearing that Roy made out his will to you and me seems to pull it all together."

"Pull what together?" she said, looking up at him. Her brain was fuzzy and not working properly.

"You and me. I knew that Roy had something to say to us, but I had no idea what it was. He was going to tell us that he was leaving everything to us. To you and me. That's what that fishing trip was all about."

"He wanted Davidson Toys to manufacture the... the little..."

"I know. Like *Star Wars,* those things."

"Yes."

"But don't you see? He was killed to keep him from telling us about his will."

"So we got to hear it on national news?" she asked.

At her tone of sarcasm, Ace gave her a blinding smile. "That's my girl. Yesterday I kept asking myself why Roy demanded that both you and I go on that trip with him. What was the connection? What do toys have to do with birds? New York with Florida?"

"Am I supposed to reply to that?" Fiona wanted to give her mind to what he was saying, because if she didn't, she'd think about the reality of what was being done to them.

"You don't know the connection between you and me, and I don't either." He bent so he was nearer her face. "But someone does, and that person was willing to kill to keep us from finding out."

"So how do we tell the police what the connection is if we don't know it ourselves?"

"We tell them when we know it," Ace said quietly.

"No," Fiona whispered, then grew louder. "No, I'm no detective. I don't know anything about sleuthing."

At that he grabbed the phone off the kitchen wall and held it out to her. "Then call the police and give yourself up. Tell them that you didn't know anything about the will. Tell them that you had no idea that I was in the same hotel as you were three times in the last fourteen months. Tell them that it was just a coincidence of cosmic proportions that you destroyed the alligator of your fellow inheritor. Tell them that you liked Roy and had no self-interest in his giving the toy franchise to the company you work for. Go on. Why are you hesitating?"

"I don't like you," she whispered. "I don't like you at all."

"And I'm not crazy about you and your bad temper either," he snapped back at her. "But I don't want to spend the rest of my life in prison, especially not for something I didn't do. Now, with or without you, I'm going to try to find out who and why. But, quite honestly, I'm sure I'll fail because the key to this is what's between us, and we can only find that out together."

"You want me to run away with you?"

"Basically, yes. I want you to help me fight this for as long as we can."

"We're wanted by the police. We're fugitives."

"Better that than to be put in a jail cell," Ace said, then turned on his heel and walked out of the room.

For a moment Fiona sat on the stool and looked about the room with unseeing eyes. She didn't want to be here. For that matter, she hadn't wanted to go on the whole trip. For that matter...

But hindsight wasn't going to get her anywhere, was it? she thought.

"There are lambs and there are bulls," her father used to say. "And bulls have *all* the fun." So maybe she wasn't her father's daughter for nothing. He'd been the one to push her to take on Kimberly's account, and he'd been the one—

Fiona got off the stool and took a deep breath. Her head was filled with every movie she'd ever seen about prison, about jailbreaks, and filled with every bloody end that all movie and TV criminals seemed to come to.

With her head up and her shoulders back, she went into the bedroom, where Ace was packing a bag.

"Do you think your friend would mind if I took more of his clothes?" she said, but she couldn't keep the trembling out of her voice.

Eight

"I don't know. I don't know," Fiona said as she put her hands over her ears. "I've told you everything there is to tell. I don't know any more."

"But we haven't found the connection," Ace said. "There must be something or someone who connects us."

"Maybe Roy chose me for one reason and you for another. Maybe—"

"Then what connects you to him and me to him?"

"I don't know," Fiona said, then turned on her heel and went outside to sit on the porch. They had been in the cabin all day long, and Ace had done nothing but ask her questions and try to make her come up with a reason why Roy Hudson should leave both of them all his money.

"Guilt," Ace said early on. "I think he felt guilty for what he'd done to us or to someone close to us. We just have to figure out what and who it was."

But, try as they might, they couldn't come up with any tragic thing that had been done to them that could have been someone else's fault.

And heaven knows that they'd tried.

This morning Ace had said that they had to leave the house and go somewhere where no one could find them. At the time Fiona had been glad because the house was so barren that it had depressed her just being there. Little did she know that in comparison to where he was taking her, the house was a palace.

Where Ace was taking her was to his "childhood home." The place where he'd grown up.

While she was packing, shoving the clothes of a man she'd never met into a suitcase, she didn't know what was waiting for them.

But one thing she'd already learned on this

94

trip: they couldn't call a deli and have food sent up.

"So how do we eat?" she'd asked as she slipped three cotton shirts into the case.

Ace shrugged. "Off the land, I guess."

Fiona wasn't going to go hysterical. She'd read *The Yearling* and had seen the movie *Cross Creek*. "Does that mean"—she swallowed—"fishing?"

Ace paused in packing long enough to glare at her. "If you think the two most-wanted people in America can walk into a grocery, I want to hear about it." Then he looked her up and down, all six feet of her. "You especially are easily recognizable."

Fiona knew that there was truth in his words, for all that he made her feel as though her height were a physical defect. She bit her tongue to keep from saying that all women couldn't be overdeveloped dwarfs such as he seemed to like. Now was the time to think with her head and not her emotions.

"Are you going to pack?" Ace snapped at her. Ever since he'd seen the TV show that had destroyed his theory that lack of motive would clear them, he'd been a monster.

"I was thinking," she said softly. "Two years ago Kimberly was in such a jam that she had to use a disguise to get herself out. She had to wear a fake mustache and men's clothes so she wouldn't be recognized."

"What kind of friends do you have?" he asked.

She ignored his question as she looked

toward the chest of drawers across from the bed. After a moment's searching she withdrew a black rayon scarf that was the size of a small tablecloth.

"Now what?" he snapped. "We don't have time—"

He broke off when he saw Fiona drape the scarf over her head, then pull it across her face. She was the picture of a veiled Muslim woman.

Ace stood there blinking for a few moments, then disappeared into the bathroom, reappeared with a large container of bronzing gel and started smearing the lotion on his face and hands. "You're not stupid, are you?" he said softly, and Fiona was glad the veiling hid the enormous grin on her face. She didn't know when a compliment had pleased her more.

After that Ace took over. Since the scarf could only be made to cover the upper half of her and they had no long black skirt, her trousers and old sneakers showed below. "We'll take my friend's car," he said as he went into the kitchen, Fiona behind him. He started pulling supplies out of the cupboards and putting them into paper bags. "We'll take what we can from here because we'll need to conserve all our money. How much do you have with you?" He began emptying a broom closet of cleaning supplies.

Incongruously, as she watched him, she thought, Wherever we're going doesn't have maid service. "About fifty dollars. I was going to use my NYCE card down here, but I never had a chance."

"Great. I have about twenty for the same reason. It'll have to last us for"—he glanced up at her, then back down—"for as long as we can hold out. Are you ready?"

"I guess so," she said, but instead of moving, she sat down on a barstool. "I have to admit that I'm—"

She was going to say that she was frightened, but Ace didn't give her a chance. Instead, he put his hand behind her head and gave her a hard, hard kiss. It wasn't a kiss of passion. It was a kiss of courage, and it told her that he was just as afraid as she was but that it would be better if neither of them actually said the word.

It worked. When Ace moved away, he stood there looking at her, and she knew that he was again asking her to decide what she wanted to do. He wasn't forcing her into this; he was letting her make up her mind of her own free will.

Standing, she put her shoulders back and took a deep breath. "Ready when you are, sahib."

Ace laughed. "I think that's Hindi, not Arabic."

"Whatever. Let's go."

Their disguise worked. In the garage, Ace took the dark blue Chevrolet of the house's owner and left the Jeep behind. Fiona draped the black scarf over her upper half and used a pin she'd found in the bathroom to hold the veil in place.

As soon as they pulled out of the garage, Ace said, "Damn! I meant to put on more of that bronzing stuff. I want to be as dark as possible."

For a few moments Fiona watched him as he fumbled with the bottle and the steering wheel; then she took the bottle from him and put lotion on his face. He had nice skin, and the warmth of his body flowed down her fingertips, up her arm, and seemed to land on her lips.

After a moment, he glanced at her out of the corner of his eyes, and she said, "Turning you on?" in such a way that he laughed.

"Not quite. Ow! Watch the fingernails."

"Sorry," she said; then when she felt Ace's face go rigid, she stopped and looked at what he was staring at.

There was a roadblock in front of them, six state police cars, and at least a dozen men with rifles in their hands.

Fiona sat back down on her seat.

"What would your friend Kimberly do now?" Ace asked quietly.

"Brazen it out," Fiona said, then looked at him. "Unless you want to throw open the car doors and make a run for it."

Ace looked at her as though she were stupid, for there was no cover along the sides of the road. If they ran, they'd be mowed down in seconds... Which, of course, was her point.

"Brazen it is," he said, then inched the car forward.

A big blond state trooper looked into the car. "You folks just passin' through?"

"My English is no so good," Ace said to the man; then he heard Fiona's sharp intake of breath and realized he was doing a bad Italian accent. But what did an Arabic accent sound like?

"*Ooooh*," Fiona groaned, and both men looked at her.

To Ace's great delight, he saw that Fiona's belly had increased by a foot and a half. Obviously, she'd shoved her backpack up under the tail end of her veil. And the bulge hid her trouser-clad legs.

"My wife is not well," Ace said. "The baby will be born soon."

Fiona leaned toward the window and batted her lashes at the man. "In my country we have heard that American policemen can deliver babies. This is true?"

The man stepped back so suddenly he almost tripped; then he banged the top of the car twice. "Out of here," he said, and Ace lost no time driving through the roadblock.

Ten minutes later Ace pulled off the main highway and stopped at a small grocery with a large produce stand next to it. Fiona waited in the car while he purchased three bags full of fresh produce, then went into the store and came out with more bags of unknown contents.

It was during this time, while sitting alone in the car under a shady tree, that she was able to catch her breath and think. And the first thing she thought was: He's not what he seems.

For the last few days she had been under so much stress, so much turmoil, that her senses had gone into hiding and she hadn't thought about what she was seeing or feeling. But now, watching Ace choose fruit from the outdoor stand, the words screamed in her head: He's not what he seems.

From the first she'd prejudged him based solely on his name—Ace. She'd assumed he was a redneck or—what was it they called them in Florida?—a cracker. Where he lived, in that run-down place on a derelict bird farm, seemed to fit her prejudgment of him, but, try as she might, she couldn't seem to fit him into that cracker pattern.

First of all, there was his education. How many rednecks had advanced degrees in ornithology? For that matter, how many did anything with birds except shoot and eat them? But Ace watched one TV show after another about birds, birds, and more birds.

And then there was his accent. It was slight, but now and then he pronounced a word in that rare, distinctive New England accent. Maybe he originally came from Rhode Island or Boston or Maine, she thought. Wherever, he hadn't always lived in backwater Florida.

Besides his words, there were his movements and the way he wore clothes. She had a feeling that he could sleep in his clothes and get up looking smooth and unrumpled. And bed head would never dare afflict that thick black hair of his.

As she watched Ace pick up fat red tomatoes and smell them before putting them into a bag, she thought, What redneck cooked for a woman? And when he paused and looked up into a tree, she knew he'd sighted some bird.

So who was this man she'd turned her life over to? she wondered. He was poor, that was true, she'd seen that, yet he had relatives he could fax to do detective work. He drove like he was a professional race car driver, yet his apartment had been filled with books.

The only thing Fiona was absolutely sure of was that he wasn't what he seemed and he was not telling her the whole story. In fact, now that she thought of it, he was telling her next to nothing. He was demanding that Fiona tell him lots and lots about herself, but in return he was keeping himself a secret.

As she watched him go into the store, she thought, Two can play this game. If he was going to keep secrets, so could she. First of all, she sure as hell was not going to explain Kimberly to him. And second, she was going to use any method she could think of to find out as much about him as she could. Remember, she thought, knowledge is power.

When Ace got back into the car, he told her that the police had been there, but no one thought that the two murderers would be able to get through the roadblocks. "They think we've gone south to Miami," Ace said as he swung back onto the road. "It seems that the police received three anonymous tips that we'd been seen that far south."

"So they won't be looking for us here?"

"Not for a while yet, and I'd be willing to bet that the tippers were named Taggert."

"Are they relatives or birds?"

"Cousins," Ace said with a quick grin as he got back on the highway, only this time they were heading back the way they came.

"Please tell me we're *not* following whatever bird you saw back there."

"Blue-gray gnatcatcher," he said. "I'd like to see the nest—it's held together with spider silk—but, no, I just wanted to make sure that no one was following us. If the policeman tells anyone about the woman about to give birth, someone else might be suspicious."

"Right," Fiona said, and for minutes she didn't breathe, but, as far as they could tell, they were safe and no one was following them.

But when Fiona saw the house where Ace had grown up, she almost said that she'd rather turn herself in to the police. Jail couldn't be as bad as that cabin.

It had a rusted metal roof that was peeled up in places, and in others the metal was missing altogether. But she doubted if too much rain got inside as thick piles of Spanish moss covered the big holes. There was a sort of porch on the place, but one of the columns had collapsed, so the roof was hanging down on one side. There was a front door and two windows with missing panes. The upper part of the building was gray wood, and the lower was rotting.

No wonder he liked Kendrick Park, she thought. This building made those at the park seem like the Taj Mahal.

Ace got their bags out of the car, then stood

holding them while Fiona stared at the cabin. "It's a bit rustic," he said under his breath.

What was he up to? she wondered, because she had the feeling that this wasn't real, that he was trying to make her believe he was a poor little boy from the wrong side of the tracks. There were bells ringing in her head that told her that he was doing this for a reason. But what reason?

She didn't know the answer, but she did know that she could play this game too. If he wanted to believe that she thought he was some redneck briar, so be it. She could pretend as well as he could. "So. Do these Taggert relatives of yours wear shoes? Pick their toenails with a Tennessee pig sticker? What about the Montgomerys? Ever seen a bathtub?"

Tension visibly left Ace's body as he opened the front door. Not that it mattered much whether it was open or closed, since it was hanging on one hinge. "Come on, we've electricity," he said, motioning with his head for her to enter.

"Let me guess. Your family knew Edison."

"Sure. He built the house. Wait until you see the woodstove."

Fiona had to close her eyes for a moment to give herself strength, and she vowed that when this mess was over, she was going to give more to charity to help poor people. It was disgusting that anyone in America should live like this.

Some part of her was hoping that the inside of the cabin would be nice, but instead animals had been using it for their own. There was an old couch that should have been discarded twenty or so years ago, and it looked as though something had built a nest in it. She hoped it wasn't a bird or he'd never allow it to be cleaned.

On the other side of the cabin was what passed for a kitchen, with a few battered cabinets, a big woodstove against the wall, and in the middle was a table with a broken leg.

Toward the back was a door.

"Let me guess," Fiona said. "One room and a path, right?"

"Two rooms," Ace said cheerfully as he put a load of groceries down on the table, then had to catch them as they nearly slid off. "We'uns gotta bedroom."

"Tell me again how bad jail is," she said as she tested a chair for sturdiness, then sat down cautiously. Surprisingly, the thing held.

"The point is that you might get out of here, but you won't get out of jail."

She looked about the cabin again. "Let me think about that and get back to you."

Again Ace laughed. "Here," he said, "put these on and let's get busy."

When he handed her a pair of bright yellow rubber gloves, she looked up at him in question.

"This place hasn't been used in a while." He grinned. "Well, okay, maybe in years, and Florida's wet, so it reclaims places quickly, so..."

He seemed to think that she knew what he

was getting at, but she had no idea what was going on inside his mind—not about *anything*.

Putting his hands on the table, he bent over until his nose was close to hers. "We clean while we talk."

"Clean?" she said as though she'd never heard the word before. Behind him something furry ran across the floor. "This place needs a veterinarian and a really hot fire."

"Up!" he said, then grabbed her wrist and pulled her out of the chair.

When Fiona moved, the chair, never sturdy to begin with, broke a leg and nearly sent her sprawling. To keep from falling, she clutched at the nearest thing, which happened to be Ace. He grabbed her to him and held her upright.

"Sorry, I..." She stopped speaking as she looked into his eyes, her body pressed against his, and she saw interest there. But she wasn't about to admit her own interest. She wasn't going to find out any of his secrets if she let his terrific good looks sway her. Why, oh, why couldn't he have been five feet tall and fat?

"Don't get any ideas," she said as she pushed away from him, but carefully keeping her head turned so he couldn't see her face.

But Ace had seen and felt the attraction between them. "I think you're the one who—"

He broke off at the look Fiona gave him. "Okay, peace," he said, then held out his hand to shake hers.

But Fiona turned away and didn't touch him. "Look, abnormal circumstances make for abnormal relationships," she said, "so let's think about the future and other people who are involved in this, and let's not let circumstances..." She turned back to look at him and saw that he had one of those male smirks on his face.

"What?!" she hissed at him.

"You really *must* tell me what you read that makes you live in such a fantasy world."

"Give me that!" she said then snatched the broom out of his hand.

"Don't tell me *you* know how to use a broom," Ace taunted. "Not Miss Cotillion. So where *did* you go to school? No, no, let me guess. Miss Somebody's School for Young Ladies."

"Oops," Fiona said as she swept a cloud of dirt and couch stuffing and, she hoped, animal droppings in his direction. "Are you going to continue to waste time, or are you going to fill that bucket? I do hope this place has water."

"With or without alligators?"

"If you're fetching it, with."

At that Ace laughed, then went out the front door. In minutes he was back, the bucket full of water, and he was still smiling. "Okay, you first. You now, me later."

She gave him her most wide-eyed, innocent, ingenue look. "How economical—two baths from the same tub of water. A Montgomery family tradition?"

But he didn't take the bait and reveal anything about himself. "No bath for you if you don't start," he said, smiling.

She was truly puzzled and paused in sweeping to look at him. "Start what? Other than doing your dirty work, that is?"

"I want you to tell me everything about yourself. There's a connection between us, and we need to find out what it is. So now you tell me about your life, and later I talk about me."

Fiona hesitated. This was going to be tricky. How did she reveal but not reveal? How did she let him know that she wasn't going to tell him anything unless he told her everything, without sounding like a petulant child? As to that matter, how did she know what to keep hidden?

"Go on, out with it. It couldn't be that bad. Start with where and when you were born, and go on with it from there." He had his hands in a plastic bucket, and he was about to attack the filthy kitchen cabinets.

When she still didn't speak, he looked at her. "Come on, think about Kimberly. Think how much you want to get back to her and have lunch or whatever it is you two do."

For a moment, Fiona had to turn away. New York and Kimberly and her job, Jeremy and The Five, were so clear to her that she could almost touch them. How had she gone from so much happiness to... to this in just a few days?

"Indulging in self-pity?" Ace asked softly, one eyebrow raised. "Remember that the sooner we find out who's behind this the sooner we can both go home."

Fiona hit the floor with the broom and moved a fat clump of debris. "My mother died soon after my birth, leaving me to be raised by my father, except that he was a cartographer and moved around a lot."

Once she started, she got into telling her life's story. And Ace could certainly listen. At first he seemed so absorbed in what he was doing that she wasn't sure he was hearing her, so twice she contradicted herself. Both times he instantly caught the errors, then told her to go on. Each time she had to hide her smile. It was flattering to have someone listen so intently to something that was so personal.

All in all, she'd had an uneventful life, certainly not one that had prepared her for finding a dead man on top of her, or for living in a two room shack while hiding from the police.

She told him that after her mother's death, she'd been sent to live with an ancient aunt and uncle. They were very boring, seldom allowing her to run and play, instead wanting her to sit quietly and color or play with paper dolls. With her head cocked to one side, she looked at him. He had a rusty hammer and a couple of nails and was now refastening the side of the clean cabinet. "I played with dolls a lot," she said.

Without looking at her, he nodded but said nothing.

For a moment, Fiona just looked at him. He had a knee on the bottom cabinet, the other leg stretched back with a foot on a chair. He was reaching up to the top of the upper cabinets, so that his long body was stretched out, his muscles straining against his shirt. For a moment, her mouth went dry and her hands tightened on the broom handle until the thing threatened to break.

"Dolls, right," he said without looking down but encouraging her to continue.

"Yes, dolls," she said and made herself return to sweeping. She told him that at six her father sent her to boarding school, and she had *loved* it. On the first day she met four other little girls who were the same age as she. "We called ourselves The Five, and we've been best friends ever since," Fiona said but refused to allow herself to think about that. What kind of hell of worry must they be going through now, with Fiona falsely accused and in hiding?

"What about your father?" Ace asked as he stepped back to the floor. "Ever see him?"

"Oh, yes," Fiona said, and her adoration of her father came through in her voice. "I know that a therapist would probably tell me I was neglected by him, but I never felt so. He was perfect."

Her pace increased and happiness flowed through her as she talked about her father. For several minutes she forgot about where she was and why as she told about her father, John Findlay Burkenhalter. He visited her three times a year, and each visit was more exciting than the last. He always showed up bearing fabulous gifts for her *and* her four friends. "He took us to circuses and fairs and ice cream parlors. Once he took us to a department store and had a woman make up our faces when we were just twelve; then he bought all the makeup for us."

When Ace made no comment to this, she sighed. "You have to be a girl to understand that. The fathers of all the other girls in the school were always telling their daughters no. It was as though the fathers didn't want the girls to grow up. No lipstick, no short skirts, no anything."

Ace was looking at her in impatience. Right, she thought, she was to recount facts, not make this into an essay contest.

"That's it," she said. "I went to college, majored in business, graduated, had a few jobs in New York; then eight years ago I started work at Davidson Toys."

"With Kimberly," he said thoughtfully.

"I didn't meet Kimberly until I'd been at Davidson Toys for a year and a half."

"Do you think Kimberly could be the connection between you and Roy?"

"Not hardly," Fiona said, then stepped back to look at the room. She had removed enough debris to fill half a New York elevator.

But, obviously, no compliment was going to come from him. Instead, he was deep in thought.

"Did you ever go to Texas? Even as a kid?"

"Never," Fiona said. "Could you point me toward the, uh, you know."

"Out back," he said without much concern. "But watch where you walk."

She didn't want to think about what danger there could be as she tiptoed out the door. There was an overgrown path cut through the plants, and she followed it, expecting at any moment to be jumped on by some creature that no civilized person had ever seen before.

But her trip was uneventful, and when she returned to the cabin, Ace had taken a toaster oven from the back of the car.

"Your friend is going to hate you when he returns to his house and finds all his things gone. You didn't by chance pack sheets and towels, did you?"

"Two sets of each," he said, and for just a second his eyes met hers, but she looked away. She had no idea what the sleeping accommodations were.

"So what's for dinner? I'm starving."

"Shrimp, which you get to peel while I talk."

At that Fiona let out a groan, a genuine groan about the shrimp but a pretend groan about hearing his life story. So now maybe she'd find out some truth, and not his Beverly Hillbilly act.

But Ace didn't tell much about himself. He was one of four children, he told her, and a bit of a misfit in a gregarious family. When he was seven, his mother's odd, quiet younger brother broke his leg and came to stay with Ace's family.

"We formed a bond," Ace said as he peeled

oranges for the sauce. "When I was eight, I spent my first summer with my uncle here in this place. By the time I was ten, I was living here full-time." As he said the words, he looked about the horrible old house with love.

She had to turn away to hide her grim expression. He may have lived here, but there was more to his life than this ramshackle old cabin. But he wasn't volunteering that info, was he?

"What about school?" Fiona asked as she slipped her fingernail under the thin membrane of a shrimp.

"Here, let me show you," Ace said impatiently as he bent over her, then put his arms around her as he showed her how to peel the shrimp.

For a moment Fiona held her breath. His chin was on her hair and his big, tanned hands were covering her own much smaller, much whiter hands. It was the situation, she thought. She was alone in a paradise wilderness... Well, maybe not a paradise, but they were certainly alone... And Ace was a fantastically good looking man, so it was to be expected that she'd feel some attraction to him.

To get herself under control, for a second she closed her eyes and remembered New York and her office and her cool, clean apartment. She'd had it professionally decorated, and it was beautiful, and now she could see it vividly. But when would she get back to it?

Abruptly, his hands stopped on hers. Obviously, he was as affected by her nearness as she was by his.

With her heart pounding, she turned her face to look at him, knowing that her lips would be very near his. She'd said that unusual circumstances make for unusual—

But he wasn't looking at her. Instead, he had that faraway look that she knew meant he was listening. Did he hear a car? Distant police sirens? Was danger imminent?

It was then that she heard a bird call in the distance and knew that that was what had his attention.

"Ow!" he said when the knife blade scraped his thumb.

"Let me see it," she said as she grabbed his hand. "The skin isn't even broken."

Moving away from her, Ace sucked his thumb. "I should remember about you and knives," he said, then frowned when Fiona smiled at him.

"When you get through suffering, you want to go on with your story?" She was smiling to cover her annoyance. She'd been attracted to him, but his only interest was—

Stepping back, he wiped his hands on a paper towel, then turned back to the now-clean kitchen sink.

"My uncle Gil had a Ph.D. in ornithology, so I was home-schooled until I was thirteen; then we moved closer to the main road so I could go to high school."

"Where you played soccer and fell for the lovely Lisa."

"Actually, I met her later, when I was lecturing at her college."

113

Then Lisa is much younger than he is, she thought, but she didn't say so. "Ah, college. Imagine growing up here yet going to college. You wouldn't think someone who lived in this place could afford college. Or even that such a person would want to go on to higher education."

Ace took a long while before he answered, as though he were thinking about every word before he said it and considering just how much he wanted to reveal. "I put myself through college by running a tour boat for bored, rich people. And after my uncle died and left me Kendrick Park, I tried to make a go of it. I was doing all right until the 'gator got destroyed." He said this without the least animosity in his voice, and he didn't mention that *she* had done the destroying.

"I'll pay for your plastic alligator," she said quietly. "I have some money in an IRA, and I can mortgage my apartment. How much did your green glass monster cost?" she said, trying to make light of the situation.

He turned away from her. "Women don't pay for things."

"What?" Fiona asked, not sure of what she was hearing.

He turned back around. "I said that women don't pay for things. Not my things, anyway. This is getting us nowhere. Have you finished with those shrimp yet? Do you think you could assemble a salad? Can you see any connection between us?"

She threw up her hands in defeat. "You

are a throwback to a Neanderthal, you know that? And, yes, I finished the damned shrimp, and the only connection I can see between us is that we were raised by people other than our parents."

"What about the salad?"

She didn't bother to answer him, just held out her hand for him to give her a knife and ingredients. She chopped vegetables on paper towels, and for a while they were silent.

"All right," Ace said finally. "Let's compare notes about who was where when. The news said that you and I had been in three hotels at the same time. Where did you go last year?"

It took Fiona a while to remember all the places she'd been in a whole year because she traveled a lot—always on business that had to do with Kimberly. "That's why this trip to Florida was so strange," she said. "I have nothing to do with anything at Davidson except Kimberly. Just Kimberly. What do I know about some kids' show in Texas? *Why* did that man demand that *I* go with him?"

"You sure it was you and no one else? He asked for you by name?"

"Yes. And you?"

"The same. But it made sense in my case because Roy said he was thinking about donating money to Kendrick Park."

"He should have mentioned that you'd get the money over his dead body," Fiona said with a grimace.

Ace didn't laugh. "As for travel, I made five short trips in the last eighteen months, and three of them had to do with raising money. I hate the blasted trips because they take me away from the park, and the birds need me more than the fund-raisers do."

"So why not hire a PR person so you can stay at the park?"

When Ace didn't answer, she looked up from the carrot she was chopping. He had his back to her, his head was down, and he was studiously mixing something in a bowl.

Suddenly, enlightenment hit Fiona. "They're women," she said under her breath. "The people donating the money are women, and they demand that you and you alone talk to them about the money."

Ace didn't say anything, so she got up from the chair and walked to the counter to look at him. His face was deep red.

Fiona gave a ladylike laugh; then she threw back her head and really laughed. "What puzzles you about Roy isn't that he asked for you in person but that he was a *man.*"

Turning his head to one side, Ace gave her a sheepish grin. "It was a bit unusual."

Still laughing, she sat back down at the table and continued chopping. "So tell me, Rapunzel, did you hide out here in the outback with your uncle to get away from the girls?"

"You have a smart mouth on you," he said; but he was smiling. "This is getting us nowhere, and the day is fading fast. Look under the third floorboard from the wall behind you and get out the candles."

"Sure thing, Abner," she said. "And where do you keep the chawin' tobaccy?"

"If I remember correctly, it's near the Bordeaux hidden under the sixth floorboard. Or is it the Chardonnay under six and the port is under eight?"

"Get me a crowbar, Pa," she said, and Ace's smile changed to laughter.

"Sit down and we'll eat. We have work to do if we're going to figure this out."

Ten minutes later they were seated on the two unbroken chairs and eating shrimp marinated in fresh orange juice, then broiled in the toaster oven, and a green salad that was a meal in itself. The year listed on the wine's damp, moldy label showed that the wine had grown years older than when Ace's uncle had put it under the floor, and it was delicious.

But as Ace and Fiona ate by candlelight and tried to figure out what connected them to each other and why Roy Hudson would make them his heirs, outside, someone was watching them.

Nine

At nightfall both of them were still sitting at the table finishing the bottle of wine. Unspoken between them was the fact that they had found nothing that would link them together. They had talked all through dinner but could discover not even one small thing that could link them.

"Why?" Fiona asked, tipping her wineglass back and finishing it. "I can't figure anything out. Why would Roy Hudson leave his money to *me?*"

"Or me," Ace said thoughtfully. In the store he'd bought a newspaper, and by candlelight he had read it aloud to her. Both of them had yelped when Ace read that Hudson's will had been made out four years previously. Four whole years!

Ace said he had a hunch that the connection between them was from longer ago than four years, so he'd asked Fiona to tell him more about her childhood.

She had told him all she could think of that might be pertinent. In spite of their lengthy separations due to her father's endless travel, they exchanged letters every week. "And I had every one of them until last summer," she said. "Someone broke into my apartment building, came down from the roof, and went into three apartments. Mine was one of them. One of the things the creep stole was a box of letters from my father. I don't know what he thought was in the box, but what he got was letters written to an eleven-year-old with a broken leg. Those letters meant nothing to anyone except me."

Ace looked at his empty wineglass. "We know something. You and I know something that we don't know we know."

"And how do we find out what it is?" Fiona said angrily. "And what if we never figure out what it is that we know? Do we hide out in this shack forever? The police are bound to find us sooner or later; then we'll go on trial for... for *murder!*"

Through these last days she'd tried not to think about the reality of the situation she was in right now but—

"Quiet!" Ace said as he blew out the two candles, leaving them sitting in absolute blackness.

"What are you doing?" she hissed.

"I heard someone."

"How can you hear anything over that noise?" she said, referring to the calls of the birds and heaven only knew what other animals that were outside. But Ace didn't answer, and as she listened, she heard him move quietly about the cabin, and his stealth sent the hairs on the back of her neck rising.

Her heart was in her throat as she listened. Any moment she expected a bullhorn to sound and to hear a voice saying that she was to come out with her hands up. "I don't want to play this game anymore," she whispered.

"Sssssh!" Ace said, and she could tell that he was by the window.

The next moment something touched her shoulder, and when she started to scream, a big hand covered her mouth instantly. Instinctively, she began to fight as she was pulled upward out of the chair.

"Will you hold still?" Ace said into her ear. "And stop wiggling."

To remind him that he still had his hand over her mouth, she kicked backward with her heel, and when she heard a grunt of pain, he released her.

"You are the most violent woman I have ever encountered," he said, his mouth close to her ear. "If I take your hand and lead you into the bedroom, are you going to hurt me?"

"It depends on what you plan to do with me in the bedroom," she whispered back to him.

For a moment Ace was silent, as though he was trying to figure out what she meant; then he gave a little guffaw of laughter. "That's my girl," he said softly. "If you can make jokes, you're okay."

He put his hand on her shoulder, then felt all the way down her arm to her hand. When he took it, Fiona said, "I'm glad you didn't ask to hold my foot."

"Be quiet," he ordered, "and stay close by me."

Obediently, she followed him into the bedroom, their soft-soled shoes barely making a sound on the worn wooden floor.

When they were in the bedroom, Ace put his lips close to her ear. "Look, I'd like to be a hero and stay awake and on guard all night, but I've got to get some sleep."

Fiona wasn't sure what he was leading up to. This afternoon she'd helped him put sheets on the two ratty old beds in the bedroom, so she knew that he planned to sleep. So what was he trying to tell her now?

"We're sleeping together," he said. "We

can't risk being apart in case… in case someone is out there."

"You mean the police? Wouldn't we have heard them? I mean, don't they arrive in a fleet of white cars with lights and—"

"Did you kill Hudson?"

"Of course I didn't!"

"Neither did I," Ace said. "So that means that whoever did is still out there somewhere. In the morning we get out of here, but now we both need sleep and we need to stay together. We are each other's alibi."

"Great. I can hardly wait to tell the court that I couldn't have killed Roy because I was in bed with Roy's other heir."

"Why don't you use that razor tongue of yours on someone else for a while? For now, I want you to get into bed, and we're both going to get as much sleep as possible. Who knows what tomorrow brings?"

"It couldn't be worse than the last two days," she said as she sat on the edge of the bed, then turned and stretched out. And a Frozen Charlotte doll, with its porcelain torso, arms and legs all one piece, could not have been stiffer than she was.

When Ace lay down beside her, she didn't relax one muscle. The bed was narrow and there was one deep dip toward the middle, so their bodies were pressed together along one side.

"I have a confession to make," Ace said softly from beside her.

"What is that?" she asked, and she could hear how nervous her voice sounded.

"I *did* kill Roy Hudson."

At that Fiona drew her breath in sharply and thought about how she could run. To where? For that matter, from where, since she hadn't any idea where the hell she was.

"I killed him just so I could get into bed with you."

"What?" Fiona asked as she brought her mind back to the current situation. "You did what?"

"I planned everything. I planned going to the motel, then the house, then to my uncle's cabin, all of it, just so I could pounce on you."

"*Aaaarrrgh,*" Fiona groaned. "You are a real jerk, did you know that?" she said; but his joking had made her relax. "The first thing I do when I get out of here is send Miss Lisa Rene Honeycutt a sympathy card."

"And I'm sending ol' Jeremy the lawyer congratulations on finding the last virgin in the country."

"Virgin? I'll have you know that I—" She broke off because she could feel his suppressed laughter; it was shaking his body. "If you think you're going to get any info out of me about *that* side of my life, you are mistaken. Now, give me that pillow."

For a moment Ace rolled off the bed, and Fiona almost asked if he was coming back. But in seconds he returned, with the pillow from the other bed. "Okay, now let's get comfortable. In what position do you sleep?"

The way he asked made it sound almost scientific. "Left side," she said.

"Perfect. Me too. Turn over."

She did, and the next moment he had snuggled up against the back side of her and his arms went around her. Maybe she should worry, she thought. Maybe she should consider that this man actually had murdered Roy Hudson. But she didn't think of anything bad, because for the first time in days she felt safe. She snuggled back against him, her head on his arm, and closed her eyes.

"Not so much wiggling, if you don't mind," Ace said sleepily into her hair. "I am human, and you may be skinny, but..." His voice was fading into sleep.

"But I do have other assets," she said, and smiling, she drifted into sleep too.

∽◈◈∾

When Fiona awoke, it was daylight, and at first she couldn't tell if it was very early or a cloudy day, and for a moment she had no idea where she was. She was lying on her side, and as her eyes began to focus, she saw something scurry across the floor.

But she didn't jump. Two days ago she would have leaped up and started screaming, but now she turned onto her other side and tried to go back to sleep. But there was a second pillow beside her, and it had a smell on it that was familiar and strange at the same time.

Abruptly, her eyes opened, and she lifted her head enough to look about the room. It was not a room that one should look at in daylight. By candlelight it was bad enough, but full morning showed the holes and the dirt and the rot and...

Where was he? she wondered, frowning, then told herself to calm down. Just because her entire existence depended on this man who was a stranger to her and now he'd disappeared was no reason to panic.

But in spite of her good intentions, she leaped from the bed, ran through the living room, out the front door and into the Florida wilderness. She was surrounded by palms and vines and more palms and things that looked as though they were just waiting for a human to step into them.

"What happened to dear ol' concrete?" she whispered as she looked about her. If there had ever been a path around the horrible old shack, it was gone now. And looking at the vegetation in front of her, she was sure that if she stepped into it and stood still for the length of time that it took for a crossing light to change, she would be enveloped. Or maybe eaten, she thought with a grimace.

"Over here, and be quiet," she heard a whisper; then when she looked toward the sound, she could barely make out the shape of a human form.

"I will not run toward him and throw my arms around him," she said aloud as she forced herself to walk slowly toward the shadowy outline. In New York, three times she'd walked through scuffles that could have been bad. In

124

one there were a couple of knives being brandished. But nothing that had happened in the city was as frightening to her as walking through those bushes.

"Do you always talk to yourself?" Ace asked, annoyed. He was sitting on a tree stump, his profile to her, as he stared out at something that Fiona couldn't see. There was a little opening between the trees that almost allowed what one could call a view.

"And good morning to you, too," she said. "And, yes, I slept very well; thanks for asking."

He didn't stop frowning, and he didn't look at her. "Sit down and be quiet. There's fruit and bread over there, and since you ran out of the house in terror, you can use the bushes back there."

"Terror?" she said, annoyed with herself for showing her fear and with him for seeing it. "I live in New York City, and I'll have you know—"

"Quiet!" he said as he lifted a pair of binoculars to his eyes.

It took Fiona a few minutes to relax, to get over the sense of panic she'd felt when she'd awakened alone in this wilderness. She stepped a few feet away, took care of necessities, then went back to where he was sitting.

So they'd slept together, she thought as she sat down a few feet away and picked up a slice of melon from the plate near him. So what? What did that mean in this day and age? Even if they'd had sex, it wouldn't have been any big deal.

So why was she feeling so warm and cozy toward him? Because she'd not slept so well in years? Was that why? She'd read about that Ann Landers survey in which women said they'd rather cuddle than have sex, but Fiona had never believed it. She liked sex.

But then, Jeremy wasn't much of one for cuddling. No, he was more of a wham, bam, I've-got-to-go-back-to-work sort of guy. But then, so was Fiona. She'd always had a thousand things to do for Kimberly and time to do only twenty of them.

"Sleep well?" she said, looking at him but pretending not to.

"Yeah, sure," he said, but it was more of a grunt than words.

"So what's made you so bad-tempered this morning?"

Putting down his binoculars, he glared at her. "Have you forgotten why we're here? We're the objects of a major manhunt because we're accused of murder. By now, I'd hoped to have found out what it is that connects you and me and the answer to why Hudson left his money to us, but I've found out nothing. Zilch."

The truth was, Fiona couldn't really grasp the reality of why they were there. Finding Roy's dead body seemed to be something that she'd seen in a movie or maybe dreamed about. Perhaps it was the way a person's mind had of coping with intolerable situations: She couldn't really believe that it had happened. At least not to her, anyway.

"What are you looking at?" she asked as she picked up a piece of buttered bread. There was a single, chipped glass full of orange juice near him, and she drank from that. Why not? If they could share a bed, they could share a glass.

"Birds," he said flatly. "Remember? I'm the bird man. I was trying to make a go of this place before you destroyed my tourist attraction."

She ignored his snide remark; she wasn't going to let him draw her into an argument. "This place? You mean we're on your property? Your park?"

"Of course. Where did you think we were?"

"Had no idea," she said, her mouth full. "My father was a brilliant cartographer, but he used to say that I had inherited none of his ability to ascertain direction. I can get lost inside a closet."

When Ace didn't say anything, she said, "What's that bird? The little green one?" She was pointing above her head, but Ace didn't bother to put his binoculars down to look.

"Parakeet," he said tersely.

"You mean like you buy in a pet shop? That kind of parakeet?"

"That kind exactly."

"No kidding? I didn't know those things came from Florida. I figured they came from someplace exotic, like... like Borneo, maybe."

"That particular budgie escaped from somebody's cage, but the species originally came from Australia."

It took her a moment to decode what he was saying. When it came to birds, he seemed to talk in shorthand. "You mean the poor little thing escaped from some kid's cage and now lives out in the open?"

Turning, he gave her a look that said he thought she was an idiot. "It was a poor little thing when it was in the cage, but now it's better off. There are thousands of them around, and they breed and live naturally, in the 'open' as you call it." With that he turned back and put the binoculars up to his eyes again.

"So. Are you going to be in this bad mood all day?"

"I'm going to be in a bad mood until we find out why we were named as some dead man's heirs."

"Maybe you and I aren't connected. Maybe Roy just liked us."

"And when did you meet him?" Ace asked sarcastically.

She was not going to allow him to draw her into his snippy manner. Maybe a change of subject was better. "My father died in Florida," she said softly. "Because of that I never wanted to visit this place. I had to get rip-roaring drunk the night before this trip to give myself courage to get on a plane."

When Ace said nothing, just kept looking through his binoculars, she continued. "Just before my father died, he and I made plans for me to visit him in this state. I'd never done that before; he always came to me. He said that his map-making jobs were too rough for me, that

I was a city girl and wouldn't like to go traipsing across alligator country. Or cannibal country. Or through tribes of natives that carried poison blowguns."

"How did he die?" Ace asked, this time his tone gentle, no more snapping at her.

"A heart attack. He was in the wilds doing some work for a man when his heart gave out. I was told that the end was very quick." For a moment she was silent, looking out across the narrow open space that seemed to fascinate him.

"He was everything to me," she said, then sighed and tried to smile. "My father was a very happy man, and he wouldn't like for me to get maudlin." For a second she closed her eyes, and she could almost see her father. "He was a beautiful man, very distinguished looking. I never saw him in anything but the most beautiful suits. And he always wore charcoal gray because he said it went so well with his hair."

She smiled, completely forgetting where she was and why. "He had the most beautiful hair ever put on a person. It was gray and very thick, so it clouded about his head. He used to say that his hair was like smoke. In fact, once he made a joke that *he* was the original Smokey, not some overweight bear."

Slowly, Ace put down his binoculars, then looked at her. "What did you say?"

She was startled by his wide-eyed look. "Nothing. I was just talking about my father. He died in Florida."

"No, not that part. You said something about his clothes. No, something about his hair."

"Great listener you are," she snapped, getting him back a bit for his earlier bad temper. "I said that he had beautiful gray hair."

"What about the bear?"

Fiona looked at him in consternation. "There are bears here? In addition to alligators and a million creepy crawlies and—"

Ace leaned toward her and put his hands on her shoulders, his fingers digging into her flesh. "What about the bear? What did you say about that fire bear?"

She drew back from him. "I said that my father said that he was the original Smokey the Bear. It was just a joke."

When Ace spoke, his voice was very quiet. "Did your father have a scar across the back of his left arm?" He held out his own arm, then drew a line with his finger all the way from the elbow to between his two smallest fingers.

"Yes," Fiona said, blinking. "At least he had a scar across the back of his hand. I never saw my father undressed, so I can't tell you about his arm, but it was there on his hand. He was injured while working in South America where he was charting an area of the Andes. Wait a minute," she said. "Did you know my father?"

For a few seconds Ace just blinked at her; then he stood up and raised his arms skyward as though in prayer; then he looked back down at Fiona. "We found it. That's the link. Your father is the link."

Fiona was aghast. "Then you *did* know my father?"

"Smokey? Are you kidding? Everyone knew Smokey."

At that Fiona began to smile.

"Every person in this state and I imagine quite a few of the residents of several other states knew Smokey. If you've ever been down on your luck, if you've ever been involved in some shady, underhanded deal, then you've met Smokey. I met him when I inherited the park and found out that my uncle had gone to loan sharks to borrow money to keep the place afloat. I don't know why he didn't go to my father and ask for help, but instead he contacted Smokey, who put him in contact with—"

"Hey!" Ace said. "Where are you going? We need to talk. Now that we've found the link, we can figure out how we're connected to Hudson."

He caught Fiona by the arm just as she reached the cabin, and when he spun her around to look into her eyes, he drew in his breath at the rage he saw there. "What's happened?" he asked.

"Happened?" she said in a deceptively quiet voice as she turned back toward him. "What has happened?" She took a step toward him. "You have just accused my father—my eminently respectable father—of being a... a... I don't know what you were calling him, but I'll not hear it, do you understand me?"

With that she turned on her heel and went into the cabin, where she began to throw her personal items into her backpack.

"What are you doing?" Ace asked from behind her.

"I'm leaving, that's what. I'm going to do what I would have done in the first place if you hadn't decided that *you* were in charge of my life. Thirty-two years I have managed without you, and now you think that I can't even decide my own future without your telling me what to do."

Grabbing her upper arms, Ace spun her around to look at him. "I don't understand what you're talking about. Don't you realize that this is it? This is what we've been searching for for days. Now that we've found it, we need to explore it and—"

"Get out of my way," she said as she used her backpack to shove him aside.

But Ace stayed where he was and didn't let her pass him. "I think you should sit down and let's discuss this."

"No," she said quietly, her jaw rigid. "I don't want to listen to another word you say. You got me into this mess, and—"

"Me?" he said, aghast. "Me? I didn't wake up with a dead body on top of me."

"No, you just took me away from the scene of the crime and made the police think I was guilty."

"Of all the ungrateful things I have ever heard of in my life, that wins the prize. Somebody murdered Roy Hudson in a very nasty way, and I didn't think it was you, and I knew it wasn't me, so that meant there was a killer at large. I saved your scrawny neck!"

"Are you finished?" she said. "Now may I go?"

"Go where? You didn't know where you were until minutes ago, so how can you leave? Plan to follow one of your father's maps?"

That's when Fiona slapped him. She hit him with a right arm that had been strengthened by years of carrying a portfolio that weighed the same as a sturdy toddler. And Ace, caught off guard, took the full blow on his left jaw; his head jerked hard to one side.

While he was recovering from shock at her unexpected action, Fiona pushed past him and stalked out of the rickety old house.

But she only reached the bottom of the porch steps before a bullet whizzed past her head.

Ten

Anger kept Fiona from realizing what had just torn past her ear. For all she knew it had been an especially virulent type of Florida mosquito.

But Ace knew that sound. He was standing on the top step of the porch, and he flew, not jumped, but put out his arms, pushed with his feet, and flew through the air to land on top of Fiona, knocking her to the ground hard.

She couldn't get her breath, couldn't understand what had hit her.

"Stay down," Ace hissed into her ear, his hands over her head, his body still on top of hers. "When I say the word, I want you to start running with me. We'll get to the car and get out of here. Understand?"

Fiona was still too stunned to answer him.

"Understand?"

When she didn't answer the second time, he put his arm under her waist as though he meant to carry her. "Up!" he said, then pulled her upright and did his best to run with her, but she was a hindrance as she tripped at every step. "Come on, come on," he said. "What if Smokey saw what a wimp you've become?" he taunted when she nearly fell for the third time.

His words had the desired effect as Fiona remembered all that had happened in the last few minutes. Rage put muscle back into her legs, and she straightened out and began to run.

Away from him.

"Damn you!" Ace said as he turned and ran after her, catching her just as she disappeared into the surrounding jungle. Once again, he tried to tackle her, but this time Fiona was ready for him. She hadn't played years of team sports without having learned a thing or two. She evaded his tackle and kept running as best she could through the tangle of vines and plants.

The next time Ace tried to bring her down, he caught her heel and hung on as though his life depended on it.

Turning over onto her back, her backpack under her, Fiona kicked out and caught him a hard smack on the collarbone. "Let go of me," she screeched. "I'll have you arrested."

Ace was busy holding onto one foot while trying to catch the other that was kicking him. "I'm trying to save your life," he said, trying to keep his voice down. "Don't you realize that that was a bullet that went past your head?"

That word stopped Fiona's struggles. But as she looked about her at the mass of vegetation, she thought, Who could get through this? "You're lying. You're lying about everything," she said, meaning about her father, too.

But as she raised her foot to kick out at him again, there was another crack and this time she could feel the heat of a bullet as it went very close to her head.

"He wants you," Ace said, "not me."

His words were so chilling that she knew he was telling the truth, and her mind seemed to go blank. Nothing in her life had prepared her for such a situation as this.

But Ace didn't hesitate. "Let's go," he said as he rose to a crouch and held out his hand to her.

Fiona took his hand and followed him, this time without stumbling. When he leaped over a fallen log, she leaped with him. When he ran across what looked like a piece of rotten fence over a stagnant pond, she was right behind him, never letting go of his hand. Only once did he let go of her hand and that was when he reached up to grab a horizontal tree branch and swung himself over a nasty-looking bit of mushy sand. She didn't want to ask if it was quicksand.

"Don't think," he said. "Just grab it and swing toward me. I'll catch you."

She did take time to give him a look of, Get real; then she grabbed the branch and swung hard—and landed half a yard *behind* him. "Can stubby little Lisa do that?" she said over her shoulder.

Ace almost smiled; then he grabbed her hand and started running again.

They had run through the wilderness for at least forty minutes when he suddenly plunged into the underbrush and grabbed a huge leaf. Under it was a car door.

"We made a circle!" Fiona cried, half in wonder, half in annoyance. She knew that the car couldn't be too far from the cabin, which meant that they weren't far from the cabin.

While she was considering this, Ace had uncovered the other side of the car and was inside it and he'd started the engine. The car was already moving when Fiona threw open the door and jumped inside. "Were you just going to leave me there?" she said as she slammed the door.

"Throw that thing in the back," he said, referring to her backpack, "and get down on the floor."

When she bent over in the seat, he yelled at her that he wanted her curled up on the floor and that she was to hold on. She did the best she could to curl her long body into the small space. Fear made her obedient.

She was no more in the small space than Ace hit a bump that would otherwise have sent her through the ceiling. As it was, she hit her head on the underside of the dashboard. "Ow!" she said, rubbing the place and looking up at him as he jerked the wheel first one way then the other, swerving around potholes.

"Is he following us?" she shouted up at him, for the noise of the car and the gravel and crunching plants under the wheels was deafening.

"Yes," Ace said, and his tone let her know that he needed to concentrate on driving, not on answering questions.

Three times she heard what sounded like a gun going off, but maybe it was the call of a unique and special bird, she told herself as she hugged her legs to her, making herself as small as possible. What had he meant when he'd said, "He wants *you?*"

If tires could screech on gravel, then Ace would have laid rubber several times. Instead, he seemed to turn in one ninety-degree circle after another until Fiona was as dizzy as she'd ever been on a carnival ride.

Just when it seemed that the harrowing ride was never going to end, Ace pressed the gas pedal to the floor and sent the car flying. It bottomed out when it hit something hard and solid, but it kept going, and Fiona felt the smoothness of asphalt.

"We lost him," Ace said quietly, and after

137

the noise of the last minutes, the car suddenly seemed almost silent. He held out his hand to help her uncurl from her painful position.

Gingerly, she pulled herself up onto the seat, but not before she looked out the window, almost expecting to see hordes of men with guns, all aimed at her.

"You want to tell me what's going on?" she said, trying to sound brave and strong, but there was a quiver in her voice.

"You have something to drink in that pack of yours? I find that I'm a mite thirsty," he said.

Bending over the front seat and retrieving her pack gave her time to regain some of her composure.

"I always carry bottled water when I go to the office," she said, but then she almost lost it, as her hectic office now seemed like a haven of peace and security.

"You did well back there," Ace said as he took the water bottle from her. "Look, I'm sorry about what I said about your father. It's been a bad morning, and I took it out on you."

At that Fiona looked out the car window and took a deep breath. They were on a highway, which highway she didn't know, and where they were going she didn't know, but she knew that "bad morning" in their situation was very bad. Very.

"All right, tell me," she said as she took the water from him and drank from the bottle. "What's happened now?"

"I called my brother. Eric was killed."

She didn't understand. "But isn't that good? He's the only one who says that you and I killed Roy. If Eric is dead, that means there are no eyewitnesses."

Ace kept his eyes on the road. "He was killed while he was in the hospital under a full police guard. And they have two eyewitnesses who say they saw you and me in the hospital."

"But we were here in the swamps. We weren't anywhere near the hospital."

"And who saw you? Or me? Think the state trooper is going to identify us? Me with skin much darker and you with just your eyes showing? The distinguishing characteristic of the two of us is your height. Any dark-haired six-footer is going to be taken for you."

"Thanks a lot. You make me sound like a freak."

"No, just easily recognized and easily impersonated." Reaching into his shirt pocket, he withdrew a round plastic object and handed it to her.

"What's this?" she said, then drew in her breath because she knew what it was. "It's a bug, isn't it?"

"Yes. It can be bought in any of those spy stores that are in the malls all over America."

She held the thing but didn't want to. "Where did you find it?"

"After I talked to my brother and found out about Eric, I got suspicious. I couldn't get over the feeling that someone was outside last night, so this morning I started looking around.

I found this in the kitchen stuck under the table."

"But it looks new. It couldn't have been there for very long, and how did the killer know that's where we'd be?" she asked; then her eyes widened. "It wasn't put there before we arrived. It was put there..."

"Last night while we were both sleeping the sleep of the dead. I think a shotgun could have gone off and I wouldn't have awakened."

"So much for my sex appeal," she said under her breath, then was rewarded by a huge grin from Ace.

"That's my girl," he said.

"So where are we going now?"

"It's a long shot, but Smokey had a house about twenty miles from here and—"

At the mention of the name, Fiona turned her head away to look out the window. She wasn't saying anything, but her body was rigid and her hands were gripping the seat so hard that her knuckles were white.

"I want you to listen to me," Ace said softly. "I said that Smokey *knew* people. He did. He knew everyone: senators to drug dealers. He had a way about him that enabled him to work with anyone. I don't know anything about map making, but I know that he was a sort of liaison person between—"

"The underworld and good, respectable people like you," she spat at him.

"I never said that. As far as I know, Smokey never took a drug, never sold one. He just... I don't know exactly what he did. He just used to say that he had an..." Abruptly he stopped and glanced at her; then his voice lowered. "He said that he had an angel to support."

Fiona threw up her hands. "Great. Now *I* am the cause of my father having to deal with criminals. No doubt it's one of the jailbirds on parole who killed Roy, killed Eric. I wonder what he thinks my father did to him?"

"Do *you* think your father was capable of what you seem to think that I told you that he did?" he said loudly; then when Fiona looked at him in question, he smiled. "Okay, so maybe I don't make any sense. Truth is, I don't know anything about your father. I met him only once. I had the problem with the loans that my uncle had taken out on the park. Truthfully, I was afraid that those men had killed my uncle. I asked someone what I should do, and I was told to ask Smokey, so I did. He gave me excellent advice, I slipped him a hundred, and that was that."

Fiona cocked her head to one side. "So what did he tell you to do?"

Ace hesitated before answering, and she was sure she saw a bit of a blush on his neck. "He, uh, told me to go to a bank and get a loan and pay off the sharks."

Fiona blinked at him. "But that's what anyone would tell you to do. Why didn't you think of that yourself?"

"Youth. Grief over my uncle's death. Too many gangster movies. When I look back on it, I don't know why I didn't think of that."

"So why didn't your uncle go to a bank in the first place and not the sharks?"

For a split second, Ace looked at her out of the corner of his eye, and she knew that he was hiding something. She had just touched on something that he didn't want her to know about his life.

"My uncle had major personal debts from a divorce. No bank was going to lend him more. The sharks didn't care about his lack of assets. As they say, He had knees. But I had no debts, and as far as the bank knew, Kendrick Park was unencumbered, since the sharks didn't have any paperwork on the money they had given my uncle."

"So they gave you the loan," she said, then looked away. His answer had been simple and easily believable, but he wasn't telling her all of it. She could sense that he was holding something back, hiding something.

"So how are you feeling?" he said in a false voice, obviously attempting to lighten the mood.

"Dirty," she said instantly. "My hair is dirty, my nails are ragged, even my toenails feel as though they haven't been trimmed in years. And I have hair on my legs and my under—"

"How about some music?" Ace said as he switched on the radio so he wouldn't be able to hear the rest of her feminine complaints. But he didn't get music.

"...notorious John Burkenhalter, aka 'Smokey'—" Ace turned off the radio.

Fiona closed her eyes and tilted her head back. "I've destroyed my father's name. Before

142

this happened everyone thought my father was wonderful. *I* thought he was wonderful."

"Why don't we—"

"What?!" she half shouted, and she could hear the hysteria in her voice. "What can we do? Check in to a hotel? Have a nice dinner and a rest? Or better yet, why don't we just get on a plane and get out of this mess?"

Leaning forward, she snapped the radio back on.

Immediately the announcer's voice came on. "It was announced today that Fiona Burkenhalter has been discharged from her job at Davidson Toys. The owner of Davidson Toys, James Garrett, said that he knew something was wrong when Burkenhalter refused to leave New York to go to Florida during the winter. 'I had to threaten her to make her go,' Garrett is quoted as saying in a press conference this afternoon. He went on to say that Burkenhalter had been relieved of all her duties at Davidson Toys. As is known by every little girl in the country by now, Burkenhalter was the creator of Kimberly."

It was Ace who switched off the radio; then he pulled the car off the highway and onto a side road. During the time it took to do this, Fiona didn't move so much as a muscle. She just sat there, staring out the window, not moving. When he looked at her, as he did every few seconds, she appeared to be relaxed. Her hands were lying limp by her sides, and her face was smooth, undistorted by the anger he would have expected to see.

He would have thought she was unaffected by what she'd just heard except that there were tears running down her face. Slow, silent tears just flowing out of her eyes and running, unchecked, down her cheeks. She made no attempt to wipe them away. In fact, she didn't seem to be aware that they were there.

When he stopped the car and turned the engine off, he leaned over her. "Are you all right?"

"Sure. Fine. Why shouldn't I be? It was just a job. I'll get another one, and they should fire someone accused of murder, shouldn't they? Especially when you work for a toy company. Children are involved with toys, you know. And they look up to the people who create for them. If I were Garrett, I'd fire me. I wouldn't hesitate. I'd fire me right away. I'd take Kimberly away from me too. Children look up to us. We have a responsibility to the children. That's important in a toy company. We—"

"*Sssssh,* be quiet," Ace said as he smoothed the hair back from her forehead. "Everything's going to be fine. I'll take care of it all, trust me."

"Gerald can take care of Kimberly. He's wanted to for a long time. The children will be all right. Garrett will figure out something to tell them."

Ace got out of the car, walked around to the passenger side, and pulled Fiona out; then he helped her into the backseat. "I want you to lie down," he said gently. "I want you to rest while I make a phone call."

"You know what's funny? Kimberly is going to work with a cartographer. I used my father's maps. Isn't that a good joke? Do you think I'll be arrested for using the maps of a criminal? But then *I* am a criminal too. Like father like daughter. Isn't this just the greatest joke you've ever heard?"

Ace got a blanket out of the trunk and spread it over her; then he rummaged in her backpack until he found the borrowed cell phone. "Be quiet now," he said. "Just close your eyes and be quiet."

"Might as well," she said. "Nowhere to go. Nothing to do. No one needs me anymore."

Ace stepped away from the car and punched the buttons of a number he knew well.

"How bad is it?" he said as soon as the familiar voice of his cousin Michael Taggert answered.

"Oh, God, Ace, am I glad to hear from you! It's real bad, but Frank has lawyers working and they all think you two should turn yourselves in. The lawyers will be with you every step of the way."

"Right," Ace said. "And will the lawyers be there when she's fingerprinted and they take her mug shot?"

Michael was silent for a moment. "What about you? You'll be taken into custody too."

"I can take it, but she's beginning to crack up." Holding the phone to his ear, Ace looked in the backseat of the car, where Fiona was curled, the blanket held to her tightly. She looked like a frightened three-year-old, he thought. He turned his attention back to the phone. "We stayed at Uncle Gil's place, and—"

"Everyone knows that!" Michael snapped. "Aren't you listening to the news?"

"No. Every time we turn it on, something new and horrible is reported and she nearly comes apart. She's had a tough life. A lonely life, but she doesn't know that. The only relative she's ever had has been her father, and he was—"

"An underworld character."

"He was not!" Ace snapped.

"I'm just quoting what the media is saying. You two have a powerful enemy out there. Someone knows a great deal about you two."

"And he's taken years to set this up against us."

Michael hesitated. "Actually, it's not you, it's her. I think she's the target, not you." When Ace didn't say anything, Michael continued. "And you agree, don't you?"

"That information's from the lawyers, isn't it? They can get me off because of my family name, right?" There was anger and even bitterness in his voice.

"Yeah, they can get you off. Your father can prove—"

"And what am I to do, *leave* her? Abandon her? Say, 'Nice knowin' you, babe, but I'm outta here'?"

"Calm down; I'm not the enemy. I just need to know what you want to do."

"I want to know who's behind this. Why is there an advantage to her being killed?"

"Killed? I thought she was being accused as the killer."

"This morning someone was shooting at her. Not at me, at her."

"You think it was the police?" Michael asked. "Or maybe someone looking to be a hero by bringing in the two most-wanted..." He broke off as though he'd thought better of finishing that sentence. "What do you think?"

"I have no idea, but I'm sure he was after her alone, not me. What I want to know is why. Any luck with the detectives?"

"None. The trail is ice. They hadn't even found out who her father was, but the police received a tip. Seems there are always tips from the same male voice."

"Yeah. He planted a bug under the table in the cabin, and I'm sure there was someone outside during the night. The pattern in the birdsong was different."

"Ace, you're out of your element. This thing is big and it's well planned. You've got to fight it with—"

"I know: money, guns, and lawyers."

Mike's voice was quiet and serious. "Lots of money, lots of lawyers. No guns."

Ace paused, took a breath to calm himself. Fiona looked as though she were sleeping. "Mike, who is Kimberly?"

"Kimberly? Lord, Ace, where do you live? On this planet? No, I know, you live in the sky with those damned birds of yours. If you ever took the feathers out of your eyes, you'd know that Kimberly is a doll, a—"

"A doll?" he said stupidly.

"Yeah, a little, what do you call them? A fashion doll. My girls are mad for them, not to mention adult collectors."

"You mean it's a doll like that other one? Bar—"

"Don't say that name. I mean it! The war between those two is very real. If you're a Kimberly girl, you don't buy Bar—" Michael broke off before he finished saying the name, and he sounded as though he were looking around to see if anyone was listening. "The other one," he said, and his voice was so low Ace could barely hear him. "Your Miss Burkenhalter created Kimberly. That doll is a whole world. She's got an occupation, and twice a year she's reissued with new clothes, new friends, and a new task." Mike's voice dropped even lower. "And twice a year I have to spend new cash on the bloody things. I tell you, it's one of the most brilliant schemes ever thought of to rook parents out of money. Every Christmas and birthday, Sam has to—"

"All right, I get the picture."

"Okay," Michael said in a normal voice. "Where do we meet you?"

Ace took a deep breath. "You mean to take us to the police?"

"Right. You can't remain fugitives forever. This has to end."

Ace took a while to answer. "We can't go in like this. Her hair is dirty and... and..."

"Okay," Mike said slowly, "I understand. Tell me where you are, and I'll send a car. You

148

can stay tonight at Frank's place. And I'll have Sam get things for... What's her name?"

"Don't send a car. I'll drive to Frank's. Just have his private elevator waiting and the room ready. Fill it with flowers and fruit and chocolates. And when we arrive, send up a lavish spread of food and champagne. And her name is Fiona, as you well know since it's being broadcast all over the world."

"Yeah, I know her name. I just wanted to hear you say it. You know, the photos of her remind me of someone."

"Ava Gardner, the fifties movie star. Fiona can make herself up to be a dead ringer for her. She's even got a faint cleft in her chin."

"Does she?"

"Don't use that tone with me. I want you to have Sam get her some clothes. She's been wearing men's clothes, and she's tired of them. Get something in silk. And shoes. Size seven. And get her some jewelry. Something tasteful. And real."

"She'll have to relinquish it when you two go to the police," Mike said softly.

"Yeah, but photographers will be there, and..." Ace's voice trailed off, as if the coming scene was too horrible for him to imagine.

"Oh, by the way, Ace, Lisa flew in last night. She said you'd called her once, but she hadn't heard from you in days, so she was coming apart with worry. She flew in on the same plane as Fiona's fiancé."

"Boyfriend," Ace snapped.

"Oh. I see."

"No, you don't see anything. I'll call Lisa soon. It's just that all this takes precedence."

"All this being Fiona, right?"

"All this being that *we*—the two of us—are charged with murder."

"Ace, am I remembering correctly that you used to own a tape of some old movie starring Farley Granger and Ava—"

"Shut up, Mike," Ace said, then closed the telephone and cut him off.

With a heavy heart, he walked back to the car. Fiona wasn't sleeping as he thought, but just lying there, her eyes full of fear. When she saw him, she looked up. "I can't take this anymore," she said. "I want out."

"All right," he said. "I'll get you out."

But when he started to get back into the driver's seat, she said, in a panic, "Don't leave me," so he half carried her as he put her into the passenger seat, and all the way to the hotel, she explained to Ace *why* she was giving up, why she thought they should stop running. Why they *had* to turn themselves in.

Eleven

Fiona couldn't seem to think clearly. There seemed to be something that she should remember, but she didn't know what it was.

She was vaguely aware when Ace opened the car door and helped her out. She was sort of aware when he led her into an elevator and the doors closed.

But when the elevator doors opened, she couldn't really focus on the fact that they were in a marble-floored foyer and Ace was opening the door to a living room. Light flooded in on them, and she had the sense of bright, happy colors.

As she stood there blinking, Ace moved away from her, then returned with a plate full of food. Holding it under her nose as he would to a wary animal, he moved the plate back and forth. And Fiona followed him. There was nothing like the smell of warm, delicious food to perk one up.

When she was near the table, he picked up a fork and held a bite to her mouth. Out of habit, she opened her mouth.

"Good, huh?" he said, then gave her another bite. It was chicken stuffed with crab and meltingly delicious.

"Sit," he said softly. "Eat, have something to drink."

Maybe it was that she was at last in her element, not in a shack that had bugs crawling in through the cracks, but she began to wake up, began to come out of her stupor caused by too much too fast. "Will you stop treating me like I'm crazy and hand me one of those?" she said, frowning.

Ace grabbed the rolls she was pointing to and kissed her on the forehead.

"And stop kissing me," she said, her mouth full.

"Right. Next time I'll have to slap you to make you return to our world."

She ignored his sarcasm. "Is there a bathroom in this place?" she asked, looking around. "A *real* bathroom?"

"Follow me," he said, then led her through a sumptuous bedroom and into a bathroom of green-and-peach-colored marble. The sinks were shaped like shells and had gold faucets. On the counter was the unmistakable layout of toiletries of a fine hotel.

Turning, Fiona looked at Ace, frowning. "Where are we and who's paying for this place?"

"Don't worry about it. It belongs to someone I know, and it's free."

"But—"

"If you'd rather go back to—"

"Sorry I asked. Could you give me a little privacy?"

"Sure," he said, "but don't let the food get cold."

Five minutes later Fiona was trying to decide whether she wanted to shower first or soak in the huge tub. One glance in the mirror at her hair, matted with dirt and sweat, and she turned on the shower taps. The steam coming from the water made her close her eyes in happiness. It was amazing how one could miss the simplest things in life the most, she thought.

"Aren't you hungry?" Ace called through the door, his mouth full.

"I'll eat later," she said as she tore the dirty clothes from her body; then when they dropped to the floor, she kicked them across the room in disgust. She never wanted the horrid things to touch her bare skin again.

She got into the shower and lathered her hair three times, then put some heavenly smelling conditioner on it and left it while she used shower gel to clean the rest of her body. And when she'd rinsed her hair, she got out, wrapped herself in a thick, warm towel, and filled the bathtub, dumping about half a cup of some expensive-looking bath salts into the water and watching the bubbles rise.

When she slid into the hot, hot water, she knew she'd never felt anything so wonderful in her life. She wanted to slide down under the water and close her eyes and float.

"Are you decent?" Ace called to her.

"No," she called back, but she heard the door open anyway. He had a plate heaped with food in one hand and a glass of champagne in the other. He also had his eyes closed, but since he was walking straight, she was sure he was pretending.

"Go away," she said in feigned disgust, but truthfully, she was glad he was there. Too much had happened in the last days for her to want to be alone. If she were alone, she might start to think.

Ace sat down on the marble edge of the tub. "Nice bubbles," he said. "Dense."

"Very funny. Are you going to share that?" She lifted one soapy hand to take the fork, but he moved it around her hand and fed her a bite of scallops marinated in lime juice.

"So how do you feel now?"

"Better. Superficially." She looked at him over the mountain of bubbles. "So what's on the agenda? Handcuffs at dawn?" She was beginning to know him well enough that she could see that there was something serious on his mind.

As for Fiona, she had a feeling that there was nothing more bad that could happen to her, for the worst had: she had lost Kimberly. Right now she couldn't seem to truly grasp what that meant. In a way, it was as though her life were over.

And maybe it was, because she had this feeling of, What the hell? that made her consider asking Ace to join her in the tub.

"Do you think we could discuss this later?" she said, frowning at him, trying to control herself. "Perhaps when I'm less..." She motioned toward the tub.

For a long moment Ace looked at her, and suddenly it seemed that the room grew a great deal warmer. Until now, they had been on the run and every moment had been charged with fear and anticipation. But now Fiona kept thinking that maybe this was her last night of freedom. Maybe tomorrow she'd be turning herself in to the police, and maybe tomorrow night she'd be in prison, and the next day—

She looked up at Ace and opened her mouth to tell him to leave the room, but he put down the plate of food and walked to the sink.

154

"We don't have time to waste," he said. "We have plans to make, and they have to be made now."

"But couldn't they wait until—"

She stopped because he'd looked about the counter and picked up men's shaving gear and begun to lather his face.

"Don't you think you could wait until after I'm out of the tub?" she said, trying to sound deprecating. But her tone seemed to be lost on him, and Fiona drew in her breath when—heaven help her—he removed his shirt.

For a few moments Fiona just lay there. Had bird-watching given him *that* body? She was looking at the back of him as broad shoulders topped a muscular back that tapered down to a small waist. Jeremy spent a lot of time at the gym, but he didn't look like this man, not at all like Ace with his honey-colored skin and muscles that moved as he shaved.

She became aware of him when she realized that he was looking at her in the mirror. Quickly, she turned away and tried to think of something other than the man's seminude body.

Ace started shaving again. "We have to plan how we're going to turn ourselves in," he said. "My cousin Frank has hired lawyers for us, two each, I think, so they'll be with us all the way. At least as far as they can go with the police, that is." He dipped his razor into a basin of water, then looked at her in the mirror. "What's wrong?"

"Nothing," she said. "Is there another razor

there? Could I have it?" She had eaten all the food on the plate that Ace had left beside the tub, and when he handed her another razor, she lifted a leg out of the bubbles, soaped it, then began to shave her leg. "I hate shaving," she said. "It leaves such a nasty, sharp stubble. Waxing is the only way to go." When she glanced up, she had the satisfaction of seeing Ace staring at her in the mirror with an open-mouthed expression. Good! she thought, two could play at this game.

"What were you saying?" she asked sweetly.

"I was making plans for our surrender," he said, then returned to shaving, but she could see that he was watching her. And when he let out a muffled, "Ouch!" she smiled. "My recommendation is that we wait until the morning, but if you want to turn yourself in tonight, we can arrange it."

"No," she said hesitantly, "I can wait." When Ace said nothing else, she put down her left leg and started on the right one. "Will it be really awful?"

"I don't know from experience, but I doubt that being fingerprinted and having your picture taken, then being put into a jail cell will be very pleasant."

For a moment Fiona tried to picture that actually happening to her, but she couldn't. She had never committed a criminal act in her life. She had never so much as cheated on her taxes. She didn't even jaywalk! Yet tomorrow she was facing...

"But it won't be for long, will it? I mean, lawyers can be very clever and they can get us off, right?"

"Truthfully, I don't think so. My relatives have had private detectives on this for days, and they've found nothing. You and I figured out that our connection to each other was through your father. No one knows Smokey's connection to Roy, or why you and I are Roy's heirs. You going to be in there long? I'd like to take a bath."

"Sure," Fiona said thoughtfully, then watched absently as he left the bathroom.

Still thinking hard, she got out of the tub and put on a thick terry cloth robe, then went into the bedroom. On a table was a large white bag on which someone had written, "Fiona." Opening it, she found it full of cosmetics and moisturizers. She could have wept at the sight of them.

As she was slathering Chanel cream on her face, she opened the closet and found it full of clothes, women's clothes, that fit her. And in the drawers were underwear and a simple white cotton nightgown. As Fiona held up the deceptively plain nightgown, her New York eye calculated that the garment had cost someone at least eight hundred dollars. She tossed the heavy terry robe onto a chair, put on the nightgown, then pulled a silky peach-colored robe from the closet.

Someone had gone to a great deal of trouble and expense to furnish this hotel suite, she thought. "Chalk up more mystery to Mr. I'm-just-a-simple-guy Montgomery," she said aloud.

Once she was dressed, with her face and body feeling less like sandpaper, she went into the sitting room, where Ace, still wearing only his trousers, was sitting on a chair reading a newspaper.

When he saw her, he didn't seem aware of her dishabille. He just put down the paper and said, "I think you should read those so you can see what we're accused of"; then he walked past her toward the bathroom.

When he was gone, she walked toward the stack of newspapers and picked one up.

"The Teddy Bear Killers," one newspaper said. " 'He was just like a big teddy bear,' the fellow employee of the brutally slain Roy Hudson told the press yesterday. 'He was sweet and always had a joke for everyone. How someone could have killed such a teddy bear of a man, I don't know,' the woman said."

Fiona sat down, and as she read on, her hands began to tremble, for she read horrible things about herself. According to the papers, she had been raised without love, abandoned to boarding schools. One magazine had an interview with a psychiatrist who told how Fiona's upbringing had obviously made her cold and loveless. "Such a person wouldn't be able to feel what others felt. My guess is that she's a sociopath."

"A sociopath," Fiona whispered.

Her former assistant, Gerald, had given an

interview in which he said that he thought that Kimberly had been a surrogate for the children Fiona never had.

It was when she was on the fifth paper that she realized that Ace was hardly mentioned. The press seemed to believe that she was the instigator, while he was just someone led about by her. There was even a hint that he was being held captive by her.

When Ace came out of the shower, wearing a terry robe and toweling his hair dry, she looked up at him.

"Horrible, isn't it?" he said. "I guess we did the wrong thing in running. The press has cut us up pretty bad."

"Me," she whispered. "And my father. You seem to have been disregarded."

At that Ace turned away, and again she knew he was hiding something. Did he have some underworld connection that could keep his name out of the papers?

He turned back to her. "Look, I swear that I'll do all that I can to straighten out this mess and—"

"How?" she half shouted. "How can any of this be straightened out when no one is looking for the *truth*? All of these papers have condemned me. They're all trying to figure out *why* I did it, not *if* I murdered some man. Or men."

"But you did work for the toy company that was going to franchise the toys from Roy's TV show. And you were in his will to make millions."

"I didn't know that," she said loudly.

Ace put up his hands in mock surrender. "You don't have to persuade me. I was there, remember?"

"Not really. You didn't see anything, did you? You didn't see someone else kill Roy, did you?"

"No," he said. "Unfortunately, I didn't. I was sleeping up on deck and heard a noise and came downstairs about the time you discovered his body on yours."

For a moment, Fiona looked away. She didn't like to remember that horrible night.

"How about if we make a pact not to talk about this tonight? The decision is made, and we have one last night to enjoy ourselves. We can't leave this room, but we can have anything you want brought to us. You can try on all your new clothes and—"

"And what? Take them to jail with me? Will the police keep them while I serve a life sentence for a murder I didn't commit?"

"Two," he said. "We'll probably be charged with two murders." He picked up the TV remote control. "You want to watch a movie? Or we can have my cousin bring us any video we want."

"No!" she shouted. "I don't want to watch any movie. I want to—"

"I think you should calm down," Ace said patiently; then he went to the table and poured her another glass of champagne. "Here, drink this. Eat some chocolate. And there's cheese-cake topped with fresh raspberries. You have

160

to calm down. There's no other way than to give it up," he said softly. "You've seen it out there. Someone tried to kill you. He, or she, was shooting at *you*, not at me, at you. At least in jail you might be safe from murder."

She downed the champagne in one drink, and Ace refilled her glass. And when she had the third glassful in her, she began to relax. At least her feeling of panic was subsiding.

"Come on," he said, as he held out a plate full of luscious desserts. "Let's go lie down and relax. We're going to need rest for tomorrow."

"Are you trying to seduce me?" she asked; then, to her horror, she giggled.

"Do you want me to?" he asked seriously.

"I just bet you're the life of the party, Ace Montgomery. Tell me, why are you called Ace if your real name is Paul?" she said as she followed him into the bedroom.

"I was first in my class—Ace," he said without smiling as he put the plate on the single, huge bed that took up a good portion of the room. "I should have asked for two beds," he said.

"Why? We've slept together before and in a much smaller bed than this one."

"Maybe you slept," Ace muttered, then picked up the remote control. He stretched out on the bed, but he was so far away from Fiona that they might as well have been in separate rooms.

She was eating cheesecake, and all the champagne seemed to quiet something inside her. And seemed to clarify her mind.

161

"The public seems to have judged me and found me guilty, so even if I do stand trial for a crime I didn't commit, I'll still be found guilty," she said quietly. "Maybe I *should* try to fight this thing."

Ace changed channels on the TV. "And maybe you could be shot. Did you forget the person who's pursuing you?"

She took a deep breath. "I don't want to sound melodramatic, but I'd rather die than spend the rest of my life in jail."

Ace made no answer to that, and if he hadn't been so still, she would have thought he wasn't listening.

"Don't you see? Unless I clear my name, I'll never have a life. Even if I beat the charges through a trial, I'll still be tainted and I'll never get another job in the toy industry."

She waited for him to respond, but he kept his eyes straight ahead. But she could see that his shirt was moving quickly over his heart. He's working to stay calm, she thought. He's trying to keep himself still so I can say what's on my mind.

"But if I *clear* my name, that's a different story," she said softly, leaning toward him.

"And how do you do that?" Ace asked just as softly. The volume on the TV was so low that she could barely hear it. "The police and the lawyers plus half a dozen detectives haven't been able to find out anything that could come close to clearing us."

"That's because you and I have to find out what we know." She took another breath.

"Separate us and we'll never find out the truth."

Ace turned to face her, and his eyes were intense. "What if we find out really horrible things about your father?"

"What if we find out really horrible things about your *uncle?*" she shot back at him. "I think he's involved in this too." She narrowed her eyes at him. "Or what if I find out some of the secrets you're so carefully hiding from me?"

"You mean like your secret that Kimberly is a doll?"

Fiona threw up her hands and lay back on the bed. "Is that supposed to be a revelation? It's shocking that you didn't know who she was. Do you know about anything at all except birds? I guess if I'd ever made Kimberly an ornithologist, you'd know all about her. Or maybe I should just put wings on Kimberly herself."

"Not a bad idea. You could make a bird doll to replace the alligator you destroyed. A sort of crocodoll."

Fiona's growing anger immediately left her, and she laughed. "You can't imagine how much it would cost to manufacture a top quality fashion doll, then launch her. You'd have to be as rich as Bill Gates to do something like that."

He took time to reply to that, as though he was thinking about her statement. "You mean like Disney drawing a few cartoons, then franchising replicas of the characters?"

"Disney, *Star Wars...*" She looked at him. "And *Raphael.*"

"And we're back to the beginning. It's what got us into all this in the first place."

"But what's going to get us out?" Fiona asked quietly. "That's the real question, isn't it?"

"The lawyers will. They'll investigate, and there are detectives trying to solve this thing. And my cousin—"

Fiona could no longer stay still. She got off the bed and walked to the foot, to stand between him and the TV. "Why do you trust those people so much? It's your life involved too. For all that the papers seem to have disregarded you in this—after all, you're not famous, *you* didn't create a doll like Kimberly—but you are involved in this."

"What choice is there?" Ace said, moving his head to try to look around her, as though he was much more interested in the TV than in what she was saying. "We can't continue as we are. You can't stand living in cabins that don't have hot-and-cold running water, and you break down at every little revelation. You're too soft to stand it on the outside."

So many words went through Fiona's head that she couldn't get them all out. "Soft?" she said, and her quiet tone was louder than a shout. *"I* am *soft?* I raised myself, you... you... Everything I am I did myself, without any help from anybody."

She put her hands on her hips and began to pace back and forth at the end of the bed. "Do you know how I got started with Kimberly? I created her, that's how. When I got out of college, I had no connections, nothing; I might as well have been an orphan. And I was *not* going to use my friends as ladder rungs. 'That poor little Burkenhalter girl,' is what I was called. But I wasn't going to let *anything* stop me."

Turning, she glared at him as he was stretched out on the bed, his ankles crossed, one arm behind his head, the remote in his other hand, and gazing up at her, a bland expression on his face. Soft! she thought.

She resumed her pacing. "After a couple of years of dead-end jobs, I got a job as a personal assistant to an executive at Davidson Toys. I thought I was going to help create, but she just wanted me to fetch her coffee and pick up her dry cleaning. I was little more than a maid, and paid about as much as one."

Turning, she raised her arm and pointed at him. "But I didn't let that get me down. I kept my mouth shut and my ears open, and one day I heard—" Fiona had to take a deep breath before she could say the man's name.

Her voice lowered and she calmed down. "I heard James Tonbridge Garrett say that he'd give the earth for a B clone." Fiona glared at Ace. "I do hope you know who *that* is."

Ace nodded, his face still showing no emotion.

"I didn't sleep for three days and nights," she said, over her anger now. Turning, she looked toward the curtained window. "I thought about nothing but making... not just a new toy but a whole new concept in the

165

doll world. I created a doll with a story, a story that changed twice a year as she learned and grew as a person."

She looked back at Ace. "I hired an artist to draw my ideas, then pushed my way into Garrett's office one Monday morning and presented the whole concept to him."

Ace didn't say anything for a while, just lay there looking at her. "I see. You're great in the business world. As long as the surroundings are clean and you have a flush toilet, you're fine."

"Damn you!" she said, her hands made into fists at her sides. "You don't see anything at all. Nothing. New York is a jungle too, just like the one here that contains crocodiles."

"Alligators. Not too many crocs."

"Whatever. My point is that..."

"Yes? Exactly what is your point? You want to go back to New York and play with your doll? You can't do that. What's happened isn't your fault, but it's happened and you can't change it. So what is it that you're saying?"

Fiona sat down on the foot of the bed. "I don't want to go to jail."

"Neither do I, but right now that's our only choice. Someone or maybe a whole gang of people are out to get us. We have no idea why they want us, but we have to leave that up to the lawyers and detectives and the police to find out. They—"

"They know nothing." She gestured toward the newspapers and magazines stacked on the chair. "Haven't you heard a word I've said? No one is trying to find out the *truth*. They're just trying to find *us*. We're the killers at large, the—"

"The Teddy Bear Killers."

"Right. We've been judged and found guilty of killing a teddy bear of a man." She stood up again. "But, you know, Roy Hudson wasn't a teddy bear to *me*. I thought he was a slimy old man who kept putting his hands all over me."

Ace rolled over a bit, opened the bedside table drawer, and withdrew a pencil and notepad. "That's good. We'll get the detectives to check that out."

"Fat lot of good that's going to do. The woman who was quoted in the paper has now made a name for herself. She isn't going to go back on her word and be made a laughingstock."

"Right," Ace said, then put the pencil and paper back in the drawer and closed it.

Fiona took two steps around the bed and opened the drawer again; then she tossed the pencil and pad onto Ace's chest. "There are other things we could check out."

He held the pencil, ready to write. "Such as?"

"I don't know. If the connection between you and me is my father, then maybe the connection between us and Roy is my father."

"But again they may be separate. The reason Roy chose you could have nothing to do with the reason he chose me."

"True," she said, turning away again. "But it would make more sense that my father is the link between all of us. When did my father and Roy meet? Did my father help Roy in some way?"

"Or did Roy hurt your father in some way?" Ace said quietly. "Maybe Roy hurt your father *and* my uncle and he felt he owed them."

At that Fiona turned toward Ace and blinked at him; then she sat down on the bed beside him. "You've been thinking about this, haven't you?"

"Quite a lot actually."

"If we turn ourselves in, we'll never find out anything, will we?"

"I doubt it," he said softly.

Fiona looked into his eyes, and for all his seemingly relaxed position, his eyes were burning. "You don't want us to turn ourselves in, do you?"

"You went berserk when you found out your father wasn't what you thought, and you nearly lost your mind when you were fired from your job," he stated flatly.

Fiona looked away from him. "True," she said.

"And you hated the cabin. People on the run can't stay in five-star hotels, not if they're digging for information."

"True, I hated that cabin."

"And someone seems to be trying to kill you."

She looked back at him. "And he's succeeded, hasn't he? What am I now except dead? My work, my life, everything has been taken from me. One night I went to bed and when I woke up, there was a dead man on top of me, and since then..." She trailed off.

"Since then you've been in the company of a man you heartily dislike and you've had to do without even basic comforts."

"I don't—"

"Don't what?" he asked. "Don't mind doing without a shower? Doing without a deli? Doing without—"

"I don't dislike you," she snapped. "You're... That is, you've become... I mean, that you..."

As Fiona looked down at him, she saw a tiny glint in his eyes; then, suddenly, her head came up and her eyes widened. "You bastard!" she said under her breath. "You've planned this, haven't you? You *never* meant for us to turn ourselves in, did you? You've manipulated me so that I've been trying to make *you* want to continue."

"I want you to make decisions of your own free will," he said, trying to keep a straight face, but there was a bit of a smile playing around the corners of his mouth.

"I more than dislike you," she said, standing up, hands on hips and glaring down at him. "I hate you, hate and despise you, and I hope you're found guilty and that they bring back the guillotine and that you—"

Ace started laughing. "Come on, you don't mean that. Why, just two seconds ago you were saying that you didn't dislike me."

"I was lying." She started to turn away, but he caught the edge of her robe.

"I don't think you hate me," he said softly.

"I do!" She was pulling at her robe, trying

169

to get it out of his grasp. "You are the coldest, most unfeeling man I've ever met. And boring. All you do is watch TV about birds. Listen to birds. Look at birds. Write about birds. *Think* about birds." She must have hit home, because she had the satisfaction of seeing that at last she'd wiped that smug look off his face.

Smiling sweetly, she continued. "You seem to think that every woman wants you. Well, maybe your blue-haired old ladies want you to beg them for money, but I don't want anything from you. You share nothing! You keep everything secret and hide inside yourself. I pity any woman fool enough to agree to spend her life with you. She'll freeze to death being in the same bed with *you.*"

"Is that so?" Ace said, and the next moment he gave such a hard yank on her robe that she fell down on top of him. Instantly, his arms went around her and pulled her close.

Maybe it was all they'd been through, all the danger and excitement, or maybe it was their lengthy no-touch proximity, but when they did touch, it was flammable.

Ace's hands seemed to be over her everywhere at the same time. Fiona wrapped her legs about his and held on as her mouth opened under his and she felt his tongue in her mouth.

Passion did not describe what she felt. Had she been thinking about him all these days? Wanting him? Or was she just desperate for any human contact?

They rolled about on the bed, hands and mouths moving. Ace's mouth moved to her neck; her legs moved up to his hips. The top of his robe came open, and she could feel his chest against her skin, just the thin layer of cotton of her gown separating them.

In their rolling, they moved on top of the TV remote, and a body part hit the volume control. In an instant the television sound blared to a deafening level.

"Ace, my darling," came from the TV. "If you hear me, I want you to know that I'm doing everything to help you."

Ace, on the bottom, his arms around Fiona, his legs now around Fiona, took his mouth off Fiona to look at the screen to see his fiancée, Lisa Rene Honeycutt, staring back at him. He froze.

As the voice was unfamiliar to Fiona, she didn't react instantly, but she was aware that something had turned Ace off. Turned him off completely. "What?" she mumbled.

But in the next moment she, too, froze when she heard Jeremy's voice. "Fiona, dearest, please give yourself up to the police."

Slowly, she turned her head to look at the TV. The screen was so large Jeremy's face was almost life-size, and the picture was so clear that he might have been standing at the foot of the bed.

"Fiona, please, I beg you, turn yourself in," Jeremy was saying into the camera. "If you hear this, if you've ever cared anything for me, please call the police and let them bring you in. I know you couldn't have killed anyone, and I'm staking my career on that belief. I'm working night and day to find out the truth of this matter, but you aren't helping me by being a fugitive. Please call—"

"And there we have it," the announcer said as his image replaced Jeremy's. "The betrotheds of both of the alleged Teddy Bear Killers have flown here to Florida to help in this statewide manhunt. And we must say that they have both been a great help to the news media and to the police. Miss Honeycutt has undergone such extensive grilling that she's now under a doctor's care. And someone here said that Jeremy Winthrop hasn't slept in days.

"That's true love for you," the announcer said, smirking. "Not even cold-blooded murder can stay the course of true love."

Turning in his swivel chair, he looked back at the camera. "So now let's get an update on the whereabouts of the so-called Teddy Bear Killers. It's believed that they have left the state of Florida and are now in Louisiana. The police there have—"

Ace removed the remote control from under his hip and turned off the TV.

"Don't fall apart on me again!" Ace snapped when he saw Fiona's face.

She rolled away from him. "You *are* a bastard," she said quietly but with great feeling.

"Look, I have personal commitments," he said, nodding toward the bed where they had almost made love. "I can't do this kind of thing. I have—"

Turning, she glared at the back of him as he

172

was sitting on the opposite side of the bed. "And what is that supposed to mean? That I don't?"

"I just mean that I'm a man and I'm susceptible to long legs being shaved in front of me and—"

Fiona was sure that never in her life before had she ever been so angry. "In front of you?" she said, and her voice was little more than a hiss. "In front of you? *You* were in the bathroom *with me,*" she said. "I was taking a bath and you came in, took your shirt off, and... and... what was that all about? Were you trying to turn me on? Is that what you were doing? You think—"

"I don't think anything," he said, standing and glaring at her across the bed. "So maybe I was in the bathroom with you, but I was afraid you might try to drown yourself. If you recall you were pretty much suicidal today."

"And how would you know what I was? And what business is it of yours anyway?"

"You exit and I'll still be accused of something I didn't do. Remember that Hudson named me his heir too."

At that Fiona sat down hard on the chair by the bed. "I see," she said softly. "I see."

"I didn't mean it like that," he began. "I meant—"

"It's all right," she said, interrupting him. "It's good to know where I stand. After all, I broke your alligator and—"

"You want to cut out the feel-sorry-for-Fiona crap?" he snapped. "From where I'm standing, we have a job to do together and that's the only way it can be done—together. We don't have to like each other." He held up his hand before she could speak. "Or worse, if we do like each other, I think we should keep our hands to ourselves."

"Oh, so I guess I was the one who pulled innocent *you* onto the bed. You should write that down on your pad and tell it to your attorney. 'Fiona tried to seduce me.' "

Ace came around the bed and grabbed her by the shoulders. "Damn it! You didn't try to seduce me. You don't have to *try* anything! You're a beautiful woman; you're interesting; you're intelligent; you're... you're..." He let go of her, and Fiona fell back onto the chair.

Taking a breath, Ace took a moment to calm himself. "Okay, so maybe I am cold. You can call me what you will, but what you and I are going through now isn't real. We're isolated; we have only each other; so of course we're attracted to each other. In a physical sense, that is. But in a greater sense, we couldn't be more mismatched."

He was looking at her as though he meant for her to understand his thinking without his saying another word.

"Go on," she said. "I want to hear what you have to say."

"You and I come from two different worlds. You're a city girl, and I'm country through and through. I'm..." As he looked at her, there was a tiny smile at the corners of his lips. "I'm this century's biggest male chauvinist."

"Pig," she finished for him. "MCP. Male chauvinist pig."

"Right there. That's the attitude that sets us apart. Do you know why I'm marrying Lisa Rene?"

"No, but please tell me; I'm fascinated." Her voice was heavy with sarcasm.

He gave her a tight-lipped look. "Because she wants the life I want. And because she's the most opposite of me that I could find. She is as outgoing as I am reclusive. She's as friendly as I am—"

"Taciturn?"

"Right. And I like the life I'll have with her. She has no ambitions past wanting to be a wife and mother. I like the idea of having a wife and kids to go home to."

"You *are* a throwback! No career woman for you, right? No woman who spends her day at corporate headquarters and leaves the kids with a nanny, right?"

"Exactly."

"Sounds like you've planned yourself a *very* boring life."

"And I guess you and Jeremy have your life perfected."

"I am not engaged to him, but—"

"But you'd say yes if he asked."

"Of course," she snapped. "He likes a woman to be more than a pair of long legs."

Ace sat down on the edge of the bed, looking at her for a moment, and when he spoke, he was calm. "We have just established that, outside of a basic physical attraction that would happen between any two normal people, we don't like anything that the other stands for. You can't abide men like me, and I still think women should stay in the kitchen. Are we agreed on this one point?"

"You know, through all of these last days I've wanted to know more about you, but when I do get to know you, I find that there's very little there to like."

"Exactly." He took a breath. "So now that we're agreed on some basic issues, I suggest that we do our job as quickly as possible and separate. You will return to your life, and I will—"

"Return to your cave. Or is it your eyrie above the real world?"

"Wherever it is, it works for me. So, are we agreed? No more of this." He motioned toward the bed. "I want to be able to face Lisa when I get out of this mess."

"Suits me," she said, "but what about tonight? There's only one bed."

"I'll have a bed sent up and put in the living room. Now, I think we should get some sleep, and in the morning I want you to make a clearheaded decision about what you want to do. Maybe you should think of all this as a business deal with nothing personal in it."

"Great with me," she said. "So maybe we should start by getting some sleep. You want to leave *my* bedroom?"

"Of course," he said, then got up and walked out of the bedroom, closing the door behind him.

And once he was in the living room, he leaned against the door and closed his eyes for a moment. She'd swallowed it, he thought. He couldn't believe it, but she'd swallowed it.

Twelve

Ace walked away from the door and went to a cabinet, opened a door, and looked at the selection of liquor there. He poured himself a triple shot of bourbon, then took the glass to the window to look out.

She had believed him, he thought. And her anger had put the steel back into her spine.

Ace had let her see the newspapers, but what he hadn't let her see were the reports that Michael had sent to him while she was in the shower. It was one thing to see the situation from the point of view of smirking newscasters but another to see it from the lawyers' point.

So far nothing had been found as a reason for Roy Hudson to leave his worldly goods to Fiona and Ace. The detectives could find nothing. His brothers and cousins had men working around the clock. Records were being checked, people were being questioned, but nothing, absolutely nothing, could be found.

And Ace knew that if he and Fiona turned

themselves in, they didn't stand a chance of going free. Because of Eric's statements and the fact that they'd been in the same hotels at the same time, on three separate occasions, it was assumed that they had planned Roy's death. And they both stood to inherit what could be millions.

The only chance that either of them had of going free was to find out what was hidden inside Fiona's memories, for Ace had a firm belief that it was something about her father that was behind everything.

But how did he ask her to risk so much? How did he keep her from collapsing as she had today when she heard that that bastard Garrett had tried, judged, and condemned her without so much as hearing the facts?

The only answer Ace could come up with was anger. If he could keep Fiona angry, she wouldn't feel defeated. Hadn't he seen that when she was angry, she had the willpower of half a dozen men? It was anger that had made her able to run across razor-sharp plants to escape the gunman. Fear made her freeze up. Bad news frightened her and made her withdraw into herself. But anger made her *move*. Anger gave her courage.

So anger it was, he thought, then took a deep drink of his whiskey.

Too bad the anger had to be at *him*, because, truth was, she was beginning to grow on him.

At that he looked down at his glass and smiled. Well, maybe she was getting to him more than he wanted to admit. She did have an ability to make him laugh, and that was unusual in most females. In fact, she could make jokes under some pretty rotten circumstances.

And she was courageous too, he thought. Maybe she was a little slow at realizing certain things, like the fact that someone was shooting at her, but she had faced the bullets with bravery. Sort of.

He smiled. And then there was her innocence. The thought of that made him chuckle aloud, then he looked toward the closed door and listened. He wouldn't want her to hear him laughing.

For all that Fiona liked to think that she was a big city hardnose, she was about as innocent as they came. For one thing, it was as though she had no idea how beautiful she was. To her, making herself up to look like an old movie star was a joke. But when he'd first seen her, with those dark eyes, dark hair, that red mouth above a cleft chin, he...

He broke off his thought and looked out the window.

"You wanted her," he whispered aloud, then took another drink. But then "wanted" didn't quite cover it, did it? What man wouldn't want a six-foot-tall sultry goddess?

But there was more involved than just lust, he thought, and remembered how much she'd hated that cabin of his uncle's. Ace hadn't been there in years, and he'd been shocked at how badly the place had deteriorated. If they'd tried to live inside the mound of a dung beetle, they would have had a cleaner time of it than in that shack.

But Fiona had pitched in and cleaned, and after her initial shock, she'd made jokes. In the end, she'd made it a pleasant evening for both of them. How many women could have done that? he thought. Lisa would have been complaining about her nail polish being chipped.

At that thought Ace finished his whiskey. He had been intending to marry Lisa Rene in just a couple of weeks. If he didn't go to jail for murder, that is.

Turning away from the window, he looked at the couch. It was plenty big enough to sleep on, and he'd better get his sleep because tomorrow they had to start searching. Searching for what, he didn't know. Nor did he know how they were to start looking.

All he was sure of was that if he was going to succeed, he was going to have to keep Fiona furious at him. As he settled down on the couch, he closed his eyes, and the image of Fiona in the tub, raising one of her long, long legs came to him. Furious, he thought. Yes, indeed. Furious.

Thirteen

⟡⟡⟡

"Good morning," Fiona said brightly when Ace opened the bedroom door. She was up and dressed and sitting at the little desk across from the bed, and when Ace returned from the bathroom, she smiled at him.

"All right," he said warily. "I'll bite. What's happened?"

"Nothing," she said, still smiling.

Ace gave her a narrowed-eyed look. "What are you up to?" He walked to the desk and saw that she had written on every piece of paper from the drawer. Besides using all the stationery, she'd scribbled all over the room-service menu and on the inside of the binder that held the directory of hotel services.

"I've decided you're right," she said.

At that Ace groaned. "When a woman says that, I know I'm in for it."

Fiona's face changed as her eyes brightened with anger. "I've been up most of the night, and I've been telling myself that you couldn't possibly be as horrible as you say you are, but here you are proving me wrong."

"I like to please," he said, then sat down on the foot of the bed. "Make any decisions yet?"

"I don't like the way you did it, but you're

right: we can't turn ourselves in or we'll never get out. Is that your opinion too?"

"Pretty much. So what have you been writing?"

"Trying to figure out what we know and what we need to find out."

"And?"

Before she could speak, there was a knock at the door in the living room. In a movement faster than Fiona could breathe, Ace leaped up, grabbed her arm, and shoved her out onto the tiny balcony. "Say nothing no matter what happens," he said, then shut the door on her.

Fiona stood outside on the balcony, seesawing between rage and terror as she heard voices inside the room. Would she hear shooting at any minute? Should she be inspecting the drainpipes for possible escape routes?

"It's all right," Ace said, sliding the door open. "It's my cousin."

Fiona kept her head turned so only Ace could see the look she gave him. She was going to have a talk with him. He could *not* be allowed to thrust her in and out of rooms whenever he felt like it.

"How do you do?" Fiona said, stretching out her hand to shake the man's hand as he rose from the living room sofa. A heavy-looking briefcase was on the floor beside his feet. "So good to meet a relative of... Paul's." The man was very good looking, shorter than Ace and heavier built. Fiona thought he looked like a longshoreman next to Ace. Even their hands were—

She stopped that thought. "What have you found?" she asked, sitting down across from him.

The man was looking from one to the other as Ace sat down by Fiona. "I'm Michael Taggert, by the way," he said. As he spoke, he put a thick stack of papers on the coffee table. "I've had a thorough search done on Roy Hudson, at least as thorough as can be done in so short a time." Michael looked at Fiona. "Hudson and your father, John, went on a fishing trip together some years ago."

"To Alaska," Fiona said under her breath. "Yes, he wrote me about it. A dreadful trip as it rained the whole time and they got to do no fishing."

"Right," Michael said. "Our guess is that during the time the men spent together, your father told him about you. Maybe Hudson felt sorry for Smo... er, ah, John's daughter."

"Go ahead, call him Smokey. It seems that everyone else did."

Michael reached into his briefcase. "Just to make sure that we're talking about the same man, is this your father?"

Even before she touched the photo he held out to her, Fiona's hand was trembling. It was a picture she'd never seen before, but then she'd seen few photos of her father. She owned only four, and they were back in her apartment in New York. This was a picture of her father standing in front of a tent with Roy Hudson, and they were holding up empty fishing poles and laughing.

As she looked at the picture, Fiona realized that what she'd not wanted to believe was true: there was another side to her father than the one she knew. She'd never met this man in the picture. This laughing man with a week's growth of beard was not the elegant gentleman who took her and her friends to French restaurants.

"Yes, that's my father," Fiona said quietly, then handed the picture back to Michael. "But all that proves is that he knew Roy Hudson. I can't imagine that my father painted such a sad picture of his little orphaned daughter that Hudson would feel he needed to leave me all his worldly goods."

"Especially not one as old as you," Ace said thoughtfully.

"We can't all be eighteen-year-old cheer-leaders," Fiona snapped at him.

When Michael blinked at her odd statement, Ace said, "Lisa."

"Oh, yeah, sure," Michael said, then looked away for a moment. "Basically, I came to say that we can find nothing except this trip to link your father with Hudson. And we can't find anything at all to link you and Ace, or Ace to Hudson, or even Ace to Smokey."

Michael took a breath. "Therefore, I came to say that it's the opinion of all of us that you two must turn yourselves in."

"Someone must have known my father," Fiona said, acting as though she hadn't heard Michael's last sentence. "Someone must have an idea what my father did for that awful man."

"She means Hudson," Ace said, looking at his cousin. "Is everyone still saying that Hudson was a dear, sweet man?"

"The teddy bear," Michael said. "He'd led a boring life, and until he came up with the idea of the show *Raphael,* no one ever noticed him. But once he wrote that show and put that little local TV station on the map, everyone loved him."

"I didn't!" Fiona snapped, then saw the way the two men looked at each other. She stood. "Oh, no you don't. Don't you two start thinking that I disliked him so much that I killed him." She looked at Michael. "I dislike your cousin much, much more than I ever disliked poor old Roy Hudson yet I haven't killed *him.*"

When Michael looked at his cousin, Ace was leaning back on the sofa and smiling.

"Women often dislike Ace," Michael said solemnly. "Tell me, was it his obsession with birds or just his lack of dazzle that did it for you?"

At that Fiona sat down by Ace on the couch and leaned toward Michael. "Both," she said. "He twists my head around to make me do what he wants me to do."

"Sounds like him. My wife says—"

"Before you two start sharing recipes and quilting squares," Ace said, "I think Fiona and I need to talk. We have to decide where to go from here."

"There isn't anywhere to go," Michael said. "There're no clues about anything. That's what I'm trying to tell you."

"You mean that our only alternative is to give ourselves up to the police?" Fiona said quietly.

"I'm sorry, but it looks that way. We've done everything that the Montgomery mon—" Michael broke off at a sharp look from Ace. "Anyway, we've done what we can. Look, here are the reports, and you can read them if you want. Maybe there'll be something in them that rings a bell." He said this last to Fiona. "Oh, and I nearly forgot. I got videotapes of some of the *Raphael* episodes that were shown locally in Texas. I haven't seen them, but I heard that the show was awful."

"Bad? Then what's all the hoopla about?" Ace asked.

"Beats me. But Frank saw the tapes and he said they were disgusting, nothing but a bunch of wastrels. A sort of Three Stooges become pirates, is what he said."

"That would be ironic if the show is shown nationally and it's a flop," Ace said.

"Then the estate he left us wouldn't matter because there wouldn't be any money," Fiona added.

"Exactly," Ace said, looking at her.

Michael cleared his throat to bring their attention back to him. "Why don't you two spend the morning here and this afternoon—"

"We'll let you know," Ace said, cutting him off; then he stood. "You hear anything else,

186

let us know." He was dismissing his cousin.

"Sure," Michael said, looking in his briefcase to see if he'd missed anything. "I'll call you in a couple of hours."

"Right," Ace said, then walked Michael to the door, and when he returned, Fiona was already reading the bio of Roy Hudson.

ໝ

"Nothing!" Ace said as he threw about fifty pages onto the coffee table, then kicked them when they went spilling.

Fiona knew it was her turn to be the calm, sane one. "We're not going to figure out anything if you keep destroying the evidence." She reached down to pick up the papers, but then leaned back against the couch. How could such a beautiful room feel like a prison?

The thought of prison made her look back at the papers. They had been reading for hours but they had found out nothing, for there was nothing to find out. Roy Hudson's life had been without excitement—unless you thought that having three wives was exciting. Each of his former wives had cited his attraction to other women as the cause of the separation.

"But this is the teddy bear everyone loved," Fiona said bitterly. "I bet they didn't love him before he was a national dead man."

Ace smiled. "As opposed to a national celebrity?"

"Exactly. You find out anything at all?"

187

"Nothing." His papers dealt with Smokey, and there was very little information in them. He'd wanted to read them before Fiona in case they needed to be censored. But Smokey was a man who kept to himself and what dealings he'd had with people weren't put on paper.

At one o'clock, Fiona yawned and said she was going to take a shower.

"Another one?"

"I think some of the mold in that cabin took root in my hair."

"When you get back, let's talk about what you wrote during the night. Maybe you had some ideas."

"Yeah, sure," she said as she headed for the bathroom.

"I'll put that video in and get started on that," Ace called after her.

"Sure," she mumbled as she closed the bathroom door. Truth was, she wanted privacy so she could give way to the tears she was holding back. She'd spent most of the night trying to find some connection between her and Ace. She'd tried to remember anything her father might have said about his own life, but she'd always been filled with so much that she wanted to tell him, and John Burkenhalter had been an excellent listener.

She got into the shower and let the tears flow. She was a doer, and this inactivity was maddening to her. If they could just find a clue, some connection in all this, then they could *do* something.

It was quite some time before she got out

of the shower and went into the bedroom to dress. She put on a scrumptious Italian silk blouse, man-tailored but feminine at the same time. As she fastened the silver belt buckle over gabardine trousers, she thought, I won't get to wear silk in prison.

As soon as she opened the door to the living room, Ace muted the TV. "Frank is right," he said in disgust. "This is the most horrible show I've ever seen. I can't even figure out why it's called *Raphael.* "

She kept her face averted so he couldn't see her eyes. She'd tried to cover the redness with makeup, but her tears were still obvious. "How's it bad?" she asked.

"Mike included copies of reviews printed in Texas and a couple from New York, where the show has already been shown. They can say it better than I can. Listen to this. '*Raphael* is a cross between *Home Alone* and *Treasure Island,* and it is deceptively complicated. Six of the most degenerate men imaginable are looking for treasure—and they will do anything to anyone to get it. Is this what we want to teach our children?' "

Ace looked up at Fiona, but she said nothing. "Here's another one," he said. " 'Even though *Raphael* is said to be for children, the show has sexual overtones—especially homosexual. There's thievery, betrayal, and not a likable or honorable person in the show. Ma Mills is obviously a madam, and Ludlow, with his lisp and twirling pearl-handled knife, is despicable. Craddock has—' "

189

"A nervous tic," Fiona said, her head coming up, her eyes widening.

" 'A nervous tic,' " Ace said in unison. " 'And Hazen has...' " Trailing off, he looked at Fiona in question. "I thought you said you'd never seen the show."

"Give me that paper," she said, then half snatched it from him. " 'Hazen, with his—' " She looked up at Ace. " 'Hazen, with his scar across his hand that reaches up his arm as though he had fought some monster and nearly lost—' "

At that Fiona sat down on the couch, and the paper fell from her hands.

Ace could see that she was in shock, but he didn't know why. "Have you seen this show before? Is that the problem? Maybe Hudson knew—"

"This is my father's story," Fiona whispered. "And it's not called *Raphael*, it's *Raffles. The bastard stole the story from my father.*"

For a moment Ace just sat there blinking at her; then he smiled; then he smiled some more; then his face nearly cracked as he grinned so wide. The next moment he leaped up from his chair, grabbed Fiona about the waist, and lifted her into his arms. "We found it!" he said, then began to dance about with her. "We found it."

Fiona was still in a daze at hearing her favorite childhood story, her own very private story, being read aloud.

Ace had no mixed feelings as he led Fiona across the room; then he punched some buttons on a sound system and the room came alive with music—ZZ Top.

And it was the music, the wild acid rock that Fiona played when she was alone and wanted to celebrate, that made her come out of her daze.

She raised her arms above her head and began to gyrate in a way that she only did when she was alone—and Ace was right with her. Hip to hip, shoulder to shoulder, the music blasting away.

"On the trip to Alaska," Ace shouted as he leaned over Fiona, making her bend backward.

"It rained," she shouted back. "My father loved to tell stories."

Ace parted his knees and went down, moving his hips all the way; Fiona was with him. "Hudson felt guilty," Ace shouted, "so he left everything to Smokey's daughter."

"Me!" Fiona shouted back, then came up, her arms again lifted. *Ahhhhh haaaaa!*" she yelled, country style.

Ace grabbed her in his arms and whirled her about. "We did it. We did it. We did it," he said over and over as he went round and round. "We did it."

Fiona twisted away from him and danced harder and as lustily as she'd ever danced in her life, tossing back her head and letting the wild music seep into her. "Jeremy hates this music," she yelled.

"So does Lisa," Ace shouted back.

"I'd never have thought *you* would like it!" she yelled. "Not Mr. Birdman."

"There's lots you don't know about me," he said in a suggestive way; then in the next moment their arms were around each other and they were kissing. Fiona's leg came up Ace's leg, he grabbed it and pulled it onto his hip, then began to move his hips into hers, closer and closer and—

The song ended, the CD ended, and suddenly they were in silence. And the quiet was deafening.

Fiona pulled away first. "I, ah," she said, her body still wrapped about his.

"Right," Ace said, then dropped her thigh.

Fiona stepped back from him. Her chest was heaving both from the strenuous dance and from the emotion of kissing him, of feeling him close to her. "Jeremy," she said firmly, as though the word were a battle call. "We have to think of them, of Jeremy and Lisa," she said. "They're risking everything for us, working night and day and—"

"Sure," Ace said. "Now, if you'll excuse me." With that he left to go into the bedroom.

And Fiona sat down on the couch, trying to calm herself. Hands off, she told herself. This situation is not real. In a way it was as though they were stranded on a deserted island and they had no choice of companion but each other. In a normal situation she would never, ever be attracted to a man like Ace. A man who could be depended on in any emergency, who kept a cool head no matter what, who protected her, who—

She picked up the remote control and

started the tape. Better to put her mind on getting them out of this unreal situation than to think about what wasn't to be.

Fourteen

❧◎◎◎❧

"So what have you found out?" Ace asked thirty minutes later. He was wearing a thick sweat suit with the heavy terry cloth robe over it, and he had another towel about his neck.

"You all right?"

"Sure," he snapped. "I asked if you'd found out anything."

"You don't have to take my head off. What's with you anyway? Minutes ago you were all over me, and now you can't even be cordial? And why are you bundled up like you're on an Arctic trek?"

He didn't answer her question, but picked up the telephone on the side table. "What do you want for lunch? My cousin will bring up anything you want."

She was still puzzling over his attire when realization suddenly hit her. "You took a cold shower, didn't you? A very, very cold shower."

Ace frowned, the phone receiver in his hand. "Tuna salad sandwiches? Or you want a hot lunch?"

Fiona smiled sweetly. "I'll have what you're having. But *you* better ask for a pot of coffee to be sent up. Hot coffee."

At that Ace unfastened his robe, gave her a quelling look, and said into the receiver that he wanted a dozen oysters on the half shell.

Laughing, Fiona turned back to the TV. Ace was a man who could give as good as he got, she thought, then remembered that Jeremy hated to be teased.

"Enough of that," she mumbled.

Ace sat down beside her. "Did you know that you talk to yourself?"

"And you snore, so we're even."

"And would you mind putting the cap back on the toothpaste? And don't use my razor."

"I will when you stop leaving your wet towels on the floor for *me* to pick up," she snapped. "And you ate all the strawberries off the pancakes this morning. Strawberries are my favorite."

"Mine too," Ace said. "Lisa likes bananas."

"So does Jeremy," Fiona said in surprise; then she realized that she and Ace were staring into each other's eyes. "Bananas and strawberries are fabulous together," she said, her mouth set in a firm line.

"The best," Ace said, then looked back at the TV. "Now tell me what you've found out."

"Nothing that I didn't already know."

"Come on, you must have seen something more."

"More?" As Fiona spoke, she seemed to

read what was in Ace's mind. "Oh, yeah, I see. I guess I killed Roy in revenge for stealing my father's story."

"Exactly. So tell me everything about this story that you know."

"All right." She picked up the remote, rewound the tape, then played it back. "See that man there?"

"Darsey."

"Very good. I assume he's the one the critics are connecting to homosexuality, right?"

Ace nodded. "He lusts after the other men."

"No, *she* lusts after the other men. Darsey is a woman. My father revealed it well into the story."

"Okay, so give me an overview of the story."

"There's a treasure, a couple of gold lions, that a man named Raffles—*not* Raphael—was taking back to the U.S. back in eighteen-something-or-other, but the ship went down and everything was lost."

"Except for the lions."

"They were lost too, but they were so big that a diver found them; then he and some other men pulled them out of the sea and hid them. The men made a map telling where the lions were; then they all died in rather mysterious and gruesome ways." Fiona gave a wicked grin. "All of which my father described to me in gory detail."

"When did your father tell this story to you?"

"He didn't actually tell it to me. He wrote it over the course of six months while I was laid up with a broken leg when I was a kid. He sent me a letter every day, with the story unfolding more in each letter."

"Okay," Ace said, "go on. What happened after the men were murdered?"

"The last man died in a freak accident. He—"

"Ah," Ace said, "saved by the bell." He got up to answer the door for room service.

Fiona craned her neck around to see who was wielding the cart, but the person kept out of sight. Ace talked to the person for some minutes, then returned pushing the room service table. "Go on," he said as he motioned for her to take a seat.

"The man died, but the map survived. The story goes that it was in his effects and no one knew what it was for many years. His landlady thought it was pretty, so she had it framed and it hung on her wall for many years. When she died, the map was sold along with everything else to pay her debts."

"You want chicken or fish?"

"Some of both, and don't take all that salad," Fiona said, reaching for a roll. "It wasn't until... Let's see, I'm thirty-two and I was eleven that summer that I broke my leg, so—"

"Twenty-one, if you're trying to subtract," he said. "I wanted that roll. Why don't you take the one that has raisins in it?"

"Too sweet," she said as she broke the roll in half and gave him a share. "Butter," she said, and he handed it to her. "Okay, according to the story—and my father worked hard to make it seem real—about twenty-three years ago someone saw the map, realized it was genuine, then got with five other people and began searching for the lions. Only they didn't know that lions were the treasure. At first they had no idea what the map led to."

"Wait a minute. Where did your father hear this story?"

With her mouth full—the food was very, very good, everything fresh, as though it had just been taken from the sea or plucked from the vine—she almost snapped that he had *not* stolen it, if that's what Ace was implying. Instead, calmly, she began to backtrack as she told Ace about that Christmas holiday when she'd broken her leg and as a result, she'd been so alone. She couldn't go home with any of her friends, since she was in a cast from crotch to toes. And she'd been nearly hysterical when her father said he wouldn't be able to make his usual Christmas visit.

"I was the most miserable child on earth," she told Ace. "But my father said he'd keep me company while I healed by telling me all about his job." Fiona smiled in memory. "That first letter made me cry harder because what could he write me about drawing maps? 'Dearest Fee, Today I measured six acres and tomorrow I measure four.' That's what I expected."

"But instead you got *Raffles.*"

"Exactly. I knew my father had a great sense of humor. Every year on my birthday he sent me a fantasy map, something about far-away places with exotic names like Caramel Lake and Ice Cream Mountain."

"Very exotic," Ace said, refilling her iced tea glass.

"They were wonderful to a child," she said, sounding defensive.

"I just meant..." Pausing for a moment, he smiled. "Never mind. Go on. How did he create *Raffles?*"

"He did it day by day, I guess. But he wrote as though he were actually on the trip, actually with the five other people, and that everything was really happening and..."

Trailing off, she looked up at him. Ace wasn't saying a word. His head was bent over his food, and he was saying nothing.

"Oh, no you don't," Fiona said.

"Don't what?" Ace blinked at her in puzzlement.

"Don't give me that look, Montgomery. I've seen it before, and I know you're up to something."

"What if the story isn't made up? What if it was really happening just as your father said?"

At that Fiona gave a look of disgust. "You have no idea what you're saying. When I was a kid, I thought the characters my father wrote about were the funniest people on earth. But what did I know? I was a kid and what I loved was seeing adults humiliated."

"Not to mention murdered," Ace said. "And robbed and betrayed and—"

"Exactly. As an adult I can see how really horrible the people were." She leaned toward him. "And don't forget—if it really happened then my father was one of those people looking for the treasure. But I still don't believe that's possible."

Ace got up from the table and went to the newspaper clippings that his cousin had included with the video. " 'Hazen, with his scar across his hand that reaches up his arm as though he had fought some monster and nearly lost,' " he read from the paper.

"Oh, no," Fiona said. "You're not going to do this to me. The story was made up; it was stolen by Roy Hudson, and that's why he was murdered."

"In that scenario, only *you* have a reason to kill him, since the stories were your father's alone, and you wanted to prevent Hudson from making money on them."

"If I was to inherit, it would have been in my best interest to have them make lots of money."

"So you waited until *Raphael* went national; then you offed Roy and now you stand to inherit."

"But why would I have killed him so publicly?" she half shouted, the logic of his words making her angry.

"I didn't say you were smart, just greedy."

When Fiona lifted a spoon to throw at him, he gave her a knowing smirk and said, "I knew you couldn't take it. Want me to call the police and turn us in?"

Fiona started to make a comeback to him, but suddenly she was deflated. "You do realize, don't you, that, actually, we aren't any further along than we were before? Roy Hudson stole stories my father made up or maybe my father actually lived them."

"If these are true stories, then I don't think the participants would want them shown on national TV. Someone is bound to recognize the people involved."

"Great. I just hope the bad guys are recognized before we get the gas chamber," she said.

"Didn't you say that your apartment was robbed and someone took letters your father wrote you?"

"Aren't you clever to remember that?" she said, one side of her mouth turned down.

"The *Raffles* letters?" he asked.

"The *Raffles* letters," she answered.

Before Ace could make another comment, the telephone rang and he picked it up. "Yes. Sure, why not?" he said, then hung up and looked at Fiona. "That was my cousin Frank and he said he's sending up something that he thinks we should see." As Ace said the last words, the doorbell rang. He answered the door, and in moments he was back with a thin parcel in his hands.

"I don't want to know how many people know where we are," she said, peering over his shoulder as he began to unwrap the package.

"No one who isn't named Montgomery or Taggert," he said, as though that explained everything. "Passports?" he said, holding up the two blue booklets.

"And a set of keys," Fiona said, taking the package from him, "and a letter. Dear Miss Burkenhalter," she began to read. "Your father once did a great favor for me, a favor so great that I wouldn't be alive today if it weren't for him. I know what you are looking for. I know who you are looking for. You will find what you want at the Blue Orchid."

Fiona looked up at Ace. "That's all. There's no signature, no identification at all. Do you think the Blue Orchid is a nightclub? Are we to meet someone there?"

Ace closed the passports he was studying and looked at her.

"Oh, no," Fiona said, backing up. "I don't like that look. Last time you looked at me like that, we ended up in a swamp."

Ace gave her a bit of a smile. "The Blue Orchid is a beautiful gated community about fifty miles north of here."

"Yeah?" she said, narrowing her eyes at him. "What's the catch? Alligators in the pool? Or, knowing you, it's vultures on the roofs."

"Nothing wrong with the place at all. It's quite nice. Of course I haven't actually seen it, but I've heard that it's..."

When he trailed off, she was sure there was something wrong. She snatched the passports from him and looked at them. At first she saw nothing wrong with either of them. They were for two people named Gerri and Reid

Hazlett. "Who are these people?" she asked. "Are we to meet them at this Blue Orchid?"

"Look at the photo of the woman," Ace said softly.

When Fiona first looked at the photo, she didn't get the connection. It was a picture of Ava Gardner as she was in her fifties, not looking as most people remembered her when she was the star of movies. "Who is this Gerri Hazlett?" Fiona asked, but as she said the words she knew.

Still holding the passport, she sat down hard on the sofa. "We're to go in disguise, aren't we? And our disguise is that we're *old*, isn't it?"

" 'Fraid so," Ace said. "We get new names and new ages. The Blue Orchid is a retirement community. There's lots of them down here. No one's allowed to live there who's under fifty."

Fiona looked as if she wanted to weep. "Why is it that on TV when a woman's in disguise, she gets to dress in tiny skirts and wear great dangly earrings? *I* go in disguise and I get knitting needles and a rocking chair."

"It's not that bad. You'll be about my mother's age, and she has no idea how to knit."

"Very funny. And what kind of name is 'Gerri'?"

"I'm more curious as to what your father did for whoever it was who sent us these. These passports are big-time illegal."

Fiona's head came up. "When does *Raphael* premiere on national TV?"

"In about a week, I think, why?"

"Because a whole lot of people are going to recognize themselves on TV."

At that Ace sat down beside her. "And when they do, they're going to know that there's only one innocent person on earth who knows the whole story. Only one person who can turn them in without being part of the dirty story."

Fiona looked at him. "A person who is innocent no longer. That one person is now wanted for murder. And if she's convicted, who's going to listen to her from prison?"

"Bingo," Ace said; then he leaned forward and picked up the set of keys from the coffee table. "Well, Mrs. Hazlett, you ready to join the old folks in shuffleboard and canasta?"

Fiona whimpered. "I hope Roy Hudson is where he deserves to be," she said with feeling.

"All this because it rained on a fishing trip," Ace said as he stood, then held out his hand to help her up. "Come on, Ma, let's get crankin'."

"Get me my rheumatiz' med'cine, Pa, and we better stock up on prune juice."

"We'll get some gray dye for your hair and—"

"We make my hair gray when you shave your head bald."

"Ah. Well, in that case, I think we can say you dye your gray black."

"And I'll pass around the name of your wigmaker."

"You do know, don't you, that sometimes women of your generation actually cook."

"If you'll eat it, I'll cook it."

"I just became a retired cook. What about you? What did you used to do? No one will believe you were a housewife."

"Actress?"

Ace looked at her.

"Okay, how about fashion designer for a small clothing company operating out of the Midwest?"

Ace laughed. "Not bad. And what about..."

The sun set and they were still talking. They ordered dinner and talked through that, laughing over the new lives they were creating for themselves. And their laughter was much needed to relieve the tension of the previous days, their mad flights, bullets whizzing about them.

It was only at night when they finally parted, him to the living room to sleep, her to the bedroom, that Fiona thought again about how little she knew about him. Tonight they had created two whole people, having a good time making up a story about how they'd met and married only recently. "That'll explain why we know so little about each other," Ace had said.

"Of course we'd know more about each other if you didn't leave the room every time I ask you something about yourself."

"I thought women were sick of men who did nothing but talk about themselves."

"Women are sick of men who don't share, and that means whether they talk all of the time or none of it," she shot back at him.

But her gibe didn't make Ace reveal anything about himself.

So now, when she went to bed, she had a feeling of loneliness that was deeper than the situation. What was wrong with her? she thought. She should be thinking about how to get herself out of this problem, not lying there wondering what Ace was doing. Did he have a blanket? The air-conditioning was turned up quite high, and he'd need a blanket. What about a pillow?

She put the pillow over her head and chanted, "Jeremy. Jeremy. Jeremy," until she finally went to sleep.

Fifteen

"If I eat one more bran muffin, I'll be sick," Fiona said. "What do you think these people do, judge the things by weight? If you drop it and it goes through the floor, that's the best recipe?"

"Only if the floor is brick," Ace said, deadpan as he looked across the breakfast bar at her.

It was early on Sunday morning, and they had been in the house in the retirement community for three whole days. And neither of them had ever been so exhausted in their lives.

From the moment they walked through the front door, they were inundated with invitations. At first they'd been gleeful. "We'll find out everything now," Fiona had said the first night, and Ace had smiled in agreement. Both of them had imagined a community of elderly people whose memories needed prodding, but they were both confident that they were up to the task. They agreed that the problem was going to be making their neighbors believe that she and Ace were old enough to live in the fifty-plus community.

But the first woman who'd seen Fiona had said, "Wow, you look great. Who's your surgeon?"

Fiona had stood there gaping at the woman, unable to say a word, for she had the body of a twenty-year-old. She was wearing tiny red shorts and a T-shirt barely large enough to cover an infant, much less her large, firm breasts. Her blonde hair was pulled back into a thick ponytail, and Fiona couldn't see a line on her perfect skin. She was jogging in place as she talked. "Let me know if you want to work out," she said, looking Fiona up and down and obviously thinking she was too soft. "Maybe I can give you some pointers."

"Uh, sure," Fiona mumbled. "Maybe next week."

Behind her, Ace snorted. It looked as though all their talk of disguises had been for no purpose. Thanks to plastic surgery and fierce workouts, some of the people in the Blue Orchid looked *younger* than they did.

They had only one week before the national airing of the *Raphael* show, and during that week they had to find out all they could about what had happened back in 1978, when Fiona was eleven.

But now they'd been here for three days, and they'd found out nothing that helped them solve the mystery.

"Do you think they *all* went to Woodstock?" Fiona asked as Ace turned the omelettes. The house that was theirs was bright and cheerful, and in a mere three days Fiona had almost come to think of the place as "home." It had been one of the model houses for the community and had been professionally decorated, completely furnished down to dishes and a fully equipped office. It was a bit too much black-and-white for Fiona's taste, but it was a wonderfully comfortable house, and she could almost imagine living there permanently.

She was making coffee. It was the kind Ace liked, with three different types of beans, a teaspoon of each ground together. "Where's your... ?" she said absently, then looked to where Ace had directed his glance. He'd known that she was looking for his coffee mug, a big one with a big handle, not the pretty, dainty cups that came with the house.

"According to them, they were all there," Ace said with a sigh as he slid her omelette onto a plate. It was just the way she liked it, with more green pepper than onion and not as much black pepper as he liked.

"Do you think they're liars?" she asked as she took the bagels out of the toaster: sesame seed for her, poppy for him, little butter for her, half a stick for him.

"Truthfully, I don't think they remember. I think they were all stoned." As he put the two plates on the table, he gave her a one-sided grin.

"What have you done?" she asked, her eyes twinkling. "Come on, tell me."

"Nothing," he answered, teasing, but as he backed away from her, she could see that he had something behind his back.

"What is it?" she asked, moving toward him.

"Nothing," he said, smiling, backing up more. "Nothing at all. Only..."

"Only what?"

"What did you try to get at the store but couldn't?"

"Nothing," she said, puzzled. "They have everything." Just outside the gates of the community was a small grocery that had every exotic foodstuff you could imagine. You could get all the ingredients for Thai cuisine as well as Indian, but they didn't carry Velveeta.

Suddenly, Fiona's eyes widened. "You didn't. You couldn't have," she said. "They said it wasn't made anymore."

"True, but maybe I have some connections," Ace said then stepped back until he was against the kitchen counter.

"Let me see." She moved toward him as Ace lifted a short, fat jar above her head. "It is!" she squealed, then reached for the jar, but he twisted about and tossed the jar to his other hand.

"If you break that, I'll kill you," she said, pivoting, reaching again. The first night they were there a neighbor had served them the hated bran muffins but with an exquisite apple-plum marmalade. Fiona had liked it so much that she had nearly eaten the entire jar. The neighbor had told her that the little store carried it, but when Fiona had asked at the store, she was told that the manufacturer no longer made that particular flavor.

But here Ace had a jar that he was waving above her head. But not out of reach of Fiona's long arms. She stretched, grabbed his wrist, and pulled. When one hand couldn't bring his arm down, she latched on to his wrist with the other hand too. Then, to steady herself, she wrapped one leg about his and put all her effort into getting the jar from him.

Ace was laughing as Fiona was struggling against him.

"Oh, my, I can tell that you two really are newlyweds," came a voice from the sliding glass doors that led from the kitchen to the pool.

As though they were naughty children caught in the act, both Ace and Fiona stopped their wrestle and turned to look at the woman. She was named Rose Childers, and she and her husband lived four doors away. On the first night they'd asked Ace and Fiona to "wife swap." They called themselves "swingers." "We're the last of a dying breed," Rose had said.

Ace had mumbled, "Let's hope so," and Fiona had kicked him under the table.

But now here Rose was standing in their kitchen, no knock, just opening the door and letting herself in. "Don't mind me," she'd say when she walked into someone's house. "I used to live in a commune, and we never had locked doors. If we walked into something, you know, private, we usually just joined in." After this oft-repeated statement, she'd laugh so hard she'd roll herself into a ball—a ball that usually found itself next to Ace.

"Don't mind me," Rose said. "I just came to ask if Lennie and I could use your pool today. Ours is on the blink again, and the pool people can't come fix it until tomorrow."

Straightening up, reluctantly moving away from each other, Ace set the jar of marmalade down on the counter, and Fiona walked to the table. She wanted to tell this awful woman to go away, but she and Ace were in too tenuous a situation to offend anyone. In spite of their fake names, they both knew that there were people in the community who knew who they were. But then there were a couple of people that Ace said he recognized from somewhere. Fiona had a feeling that she and Ace weren't the only couple who never walked outside the gates of the compound.

So now they were faced with a day of Rose and Lennie using their pool. Maybe if the two old hippies didn't always swim in the nude, it wouldn't be so bad. But the thought of a day spent fending off the advances of two naked leeches was turning Fiona's stomach.

"Sure, Rose. We'd be glad to have you here," Ace said cheerfully, and Fiona looked at him to see if he'd lost his mind. She very well knew that Ace couldn't stand the woman. "Truth is, the little lady and I are going out today."

"Out?" Rose said sharply. "I thought you two couldn't—I mean, what's out there that you can't get in here?"

"Mothers," Fiona said quickly. "Uh, I mean, my mother."

Ace took Fiona's upper arms, her back to his front, and started leading her out of the kitchen. "My wife's mother is ill."

"I thought you were an orphan."

"Oh, no," Fiona said airily. They were almost to the front door now. "I said that if I didn't visit my mother soon, I was going to be declared an orphan. You know how that is, don't you?" Rose said that long ago she'd given birth to three children, but she had no idea where they were now.

Ace picked up the car keys from the narrow table in the foyer, opened the door behind him, stepped out, pulling Fiona with him. Once outside, they started to run like schoolchildren about to get caught playing hooky. And once they were in the Jeep, they started laughing. When they reached the entrance gates, they laughed harder.

"We're going to get caught," Fiona said. "We can't leave. We can't—Oh, the hell with it! That place is as much a prison as prison is. 'And do you remember the year 1978? My father said that was his favorite year. Maybe you knew my father? Smokey?' " Fiona mimicked herself. "Maybe we should give a square dance and make an announcement that we're on the run from the police and—"

"Hootenanny," Ace said. "Not a square dance, a hootenanny."

"Oh, right. And do we serve marijuana brownies?"

"I think the guy in the pink house makes LSD in his basement."

"And the police are after *us*," she said sarcastically, then looked out the window at the open highway they were on. "By the way, speaking of police and roadblocks and illegal acts, where are we going?"

"Where do you want to go?" he asked softly.

"Truth?"

"The whole truth," he said, smiling at her.

Fiona turned away so she couldn't see that smile. Maybe they hadn't found out anything about who had killed Roy Hudson, but in the last three days she and Ace had found out a lot about each other. By necessity, they had had to stop bickering between themselves and work together to find clues to what had happened and what was going on now.

For three days, they had accepted nearly every invitation extended to them, and they had encouraged the people to talk about the "old days." Unfortunately, this seemed to open floodgates, and in a mere three days, she and Ace had unintentionally started a sixties revival—and everyone knew that what people remembered as happening in the sixties had actually happened in the seventies.

So Fiona and Ace, as Gerri and Reid Hazlett, had been bombarded with hippie nostalgia. There had been home movies, music (if she heard "can't get no satisfaction" one more time she was going to set fire to their headbands), food (which seemed to consist mainly of bran muffins), and reminiscences. Lots of stories were told with dreamy eyes about a time that the participants seemed to remember as ideal.

But, as far as Ace and Fiona could ascertain, not one of their neighbors had been in Florida in 1978. But then there were lapses in memory. "I was stoned that year and don't remember too much," was a common reply to their queries.

And at night, finally alone in the cozy little house, she and Ace had discussed what they'd heard and been told. They compared notes about people and discussed what they did and did not believe.

"I thought she was lying too," Fiona would say, agreeing with Ace.

It only took one day before they started finding out how alike their perceptions of people were. "Me too!" they often said, again in agreement.

So now, when Ace asked her where she wanted to go, all she could think of to say was, *With you. Anywhere you go, that's where I want to go too.*

But she didn't say that.

"Let me guess," he said, looking at her out of the corner of his eye. "Have your hair done? Nails? Waxing?"

"Ha!" she said. "Obviously you don't know anything about me. Not the real me." There was a bit of a whine in her voice, and she could have kicked herself for it.

"Big city gal like you?" he asked. "Wasn't it you who just a few days ago was mincing about in sand-filled shoes and complaining about Florida?"

She looked out the car window. "That seems like another person and another life," she said softly, and the thought of the last days came back to her. What was going on at her office? No, not *her* office any longer. Now *the* office... and Kimberly belonged to someone else.

"So?" Ace said, interrupting her thoughts. "If you don't want to get hair removed, or cut, or curled, or colored, what *do* you want to do?"

"I want to work!" she spat out. "I'd like to do something other than listen to hippie stories. Or think about what happened when I was a kid. I'd like to... I don't know, design one of your crocodolls, maybe."

"Really?" Ace said, turning to look at her in surprise. "I would have thought you'd be finished with that."

"About as much as you're finished with looking at birds. And where *are* we going?"

"You better check the map on the backseat."

Turning, Fiona leaned around the front seat to look in the back. There was no map anywhere, but there was a pair of high-powered binoculars sitting on top of a notebook, and beside them was a package wrapped in pink-and-white birthday paper, a pink ribbon about it.

"No map," she said as she turned around, then waited for him to say something, but he didn't.

"I guess the notebook and the binoculars are for your bird-watching," she said after a while.

"*Mmmm,*" he answered.

For a moment she sat still, staring straight ahead. She was not going to ask him who the gift was for. But maybe if she said something ordinary, like, "So whose birthday is it?" that would be all right. Pink paper usually meant a female. So who had Ace bought a birthday gift for? One of the women in the Blue Orchid? Surely he wasn't hot for a woman who had to be at least twenty years older than he was. Was he? Or was it business? But if he'd found out something, then why hadn't he told her?

Without thought for what she was doing, she doubled up her fist and smacked him on the shoulder.

Ace burst out laughing. "You lasted longer than I thought you would. It's for you."

Part of her was annoyed that he knew she'd be eaten with curiosity, and another part of her was annoyed that he seemed to know her so well. Whatever, she was definitely annoyed with him.

But not enough not to grab the package

and open it quickly. Inside was a sketch pad and a set of drawing pencils and a fat, soft, stretchy eraser. It was such a very personal gift, something that she wanted so much, something that was for her alone, that she could just look at it in wonder. Every man she'd ever known gave women either perfume or jewelry. Right now she'd rather have this sketch pad than the Hope Diamond.

"Come on, Burke, you aren't going to get maudlin on me now, are you?" he said, one eyebrow raised as he glanced at her.

He'd never called her that before. Truth was, he'd never called her any name except "Miss Burkenhalter."

"So give me an idea about how I can make money for Kendrick Park."

"What?" She had to work to haul herself back to the present.

"You owe me, remember? Remember the 'gator you broke?"

"Oh, yeah. I saved your life. I forgot that."

He signaled, then turned left off the highway. "So save my park. When we get out of this mess, I'm going to need a way to make it pay. And you said that you could create a doll for my park."

At the way he said, "When," she had to turn away and look out the window. "When" they get out. "When" they can stop hiding. "When" they can again join the world.

"Well..." she said hesitantly, looking back at the sketch pad, running her hand over it.

"I see. You're a one-book author."

"And so was Margaret Mitchell," she shot back at him, making him laugh.

"So what would you do to market Kendrick Park? If it were yours, that is?"

"I'd..." She hesitated as she thought about his question. "I'd try to come up with something that kids would want and drive their parents crazy for but they could only get here, at the park. Kids are the true consumers of the world. Hook them when they're young and they'll get their parents to buy it for them, and when they're parents, they'll buy it for their own kids out of nostalgia."

Ace gave a great sigh. "So maybe I could do some mechanical birds."

She didn't seem to hear him. "You know, I've had some ideas over the years. I've often thought that if I had it to do again, I could create a doll that would knock Kimberly off the market."

Ace pulled off the paved thoroughfare onto a gravel road. "Don't tell me," he said, "she turns into a blue heron at night?"

"No," Fiona said slowly, thinking about the idea of a doll that would be connected to a bird sanctuary. "She owns the park, so she has to be a vet during the day and attend glamorous fund-raisers at night. She drives a Jeep and deals with poachers. Kimberly doesn't have any villains in her life. And Kimberly..."

"Kimberly what?" Ace said as he drove the Jeep into what looked like virgin swamp. But he must have known where he was going, because they didn't sink into water.

But at this point Fiona was only barely aware of where he was driving. When she spoke, her voice was hardly a whisper. "This doll is secretly in love with a man who can breathe underwater." Her eyes were alight. "And when they get into jams, if her boyfriend is out of water too long, he dies." She paused, then sighed. "No, no, been done. I'll have to think of something else."

She looked up when Ace opened the car door for her, then reached out his hand to help her out.

Once outside the car, she glanced about her. "We're back at your park, aren't we?"

"I thought we could have a day out, a day away from *Raphael* and Roy Hudson, and anyone who can make a peace symbol. Okay with you?"

"You can watch birds, and I can sketch."

"You don't like that," he said flatly, and she could hear the disappointment in his voice.

"It's a great idea; it's just that..."

"Out with it, what's wrong?"

"Money. It would be enjoyable to fantasize about such a doll, but it would be just that, a fantasy." She took a breath. "I told you: Starting such a doll would take millions. I would refuse to work on some cheap doll with over-sized eyes. Only the best vinyl, the best clothes, the best..." She paused. "So why aren't you making fun of me?"

"Because it's not a bad idea. This place eats money. It would be nice to find a way to earn some back." He paused. "Does Kimberly have her own TV show?"

Fiona couldn't hide her contempt. "No, those things have those nasty action figures. They are *not* dolls. No one has ever..." At the words of "no one has ever," she hesitated, then looked up, her eyes wide.

With an I-told-you-so smile, Ace took her hand and led her down a narrow path to a tiny dry hill, then made a motion for her to sit down.

"Not even Disney?" he said as he put his binoculars to his eyes.

"Puhlease. Those people pop them out for the movie, then two weeks later you can't find them. I'm talking about something that lasts for twenty years."

Fiona glanced down at her sketchbook, but she hadn't opened it yet.

"So what's her name?"

"What?"

"What's the doll's name? Swamp Girl?"

"Oh, something to do with the sun," Fiona said, then smiled. "Octavia 'Tavie' Holden. 'Holden' for William Holden the actor who later turned conservationist. Tavie has two boyfriends, one who lives in civilization and one who is a guide in the Everglades."

"Kind of like you," Ace said softly. "One man on dry land and another from the swamps."

But Fiona wasn't listening to him. "The guide is named Axel and the other man is named Justin." She opened her sketchbook and began to draw.

For hours, until about one o'clock, they were silent, Fiona furiously drawing, Ace scanning the horizon and making notes in his book. And it wasn't until he waved a pastrami sandwich under her nose that Fiona came out of her trance and looked up.

"You planned this, didn't you?" she said, her mouth full, her sketchbook on the ground beside her.

"Self-defense. I couldn't take the smell of marijuana. You know that those plants you were admiring at the Joneses were grass, don't you?"

"Grass as in—"

"Two to five, or whatever the charge is now," he said.

"I guess you and I will soon get to find out all there is to know about sentences." She hadn't meant to add a sobering thought to the day, but she had.

"Show me what you've drawn," he said, then sat down beside her.

Fiona could smell him. He didn't wear aftershave, but she knew his smell. After all, she shared a house with him, shared a car, had shared a hotel room and a bed. He leaned across her, and she could feel the warmth of his hair near her face. He'd been in the sun again without a hat, without any sunscreen. She'd told him not to do that.

When she said nothing, he turned to look at her, and Fiona's breath drew in sharply. Their lips were inches apart, and she could smell his breath, feel the heat of his body.

"Ice?" he said abruptly, then rolled away from her.

"Yeah, sure," she said as briskly as possible, to cover the pounding of her heart.

"You were going to tell me what you've come up with," he said as he handed her a cube of ice from the cooler, but he stayed at arm's length.

Fiona took the ice and wondered that the little cube didn't instantly turn to steam in her hand. All morning she'd been sitting near him in perfect contentment, but now she was suddenly aware of him and of their isolation. But they were always isolated, weren't they? They lived together in a perfect little house, and they were—

" 'Adventure Park, add more schooling. Not for commerce, for teaching,' " he read aloud, and she looked up to see that he had her sketch pad in his hand. "What's this about?"

"Just some ideas I had. How can children learn what happens when they throw their drink cans out the window if they don't see the results? You could use the park to teach them."

As she talked, the shaking of her body began to recede and she focused on the ideas she'd had for making Kendrick Park a paying concern. "You could offer free tours to anyone showing up with ten children or more. Hire poor but smart and zealous college students to act as tour guides. Do some Disney stuff with fake birds of prey coming at them. Impress the kids for life."

"And who pays for all this?"

"The doll, of course."

"What about the boys? And don't you dare tell me that you're going to 'educate' them into liking dolls."

Fiona gave him a blank look. "I have no idea. What do little boys play with?"

"Something with more action than a doll," he said, deadpan.

"Right. Violent things. Well, then sell them some plastic alligators that you can open up and there's a man's arm inside the belly. With a watch on it."

To Fiona's shock, Ace suddenly became furious. His dark brows drew together in a scowl. "I don't think you should joke about things you know nothing about."

At that he turned away, and she feared that he was going back to the car. Had she somehow managed to ruin their precious day out?

Immediately, she went after him. "I'm sorry," she said quickly, but she didn't really know what she was apologizing for. Truth was, she could hardly remember what she'd said. Going to him, she put her hand on his arm. "I didn't mean to insult your state. In fact, I'm growing to like the place. It's—"

"That's how Uncle Gil was found," Ace said softly.

Fiona couldn't understand what he was saying. "Found? I don't—" She drew in her breath. "You mean... ?"

"One day he went out birding and didn't return. We found... his gold watch a couple of weeks later."

Fiona didn't want to ask more, didn't want to hear more. Sometimes there were images that entered a person's mind and never left.

"Look, maybe we should go back," he said. "The mosquitoes will—"

He broke off when he saw her face.

Fiona didn't know what put the idea in her head. Maybe it was thinking of the watch. The *gold* watch. And behind Ace's head was a knotty old tree and the way the sun hit it made something in the side of it sparkle.

With her hand over her mouth, her eyes as wide as twin moons, she took a step backward.

"What?" Ace whispered.

"Gold," she managed to get out.

"What's gold? Where?"

"The lions. If..." Her throat closed.

They had been together in such intimate circumstances for so long that Ace read her mind. "If the story is real, then where are the lions? Good point."

Slowly, Fiona raised her arm and pointed to the old tree behind Ace. He looked behind him, but from the angle he was looking, he could see nothing unusual. But when he looked back at Fiona, she still had her mouth covered and she was still pointing.

Ace put the binoculars down, climbed over eight feet of spike palms, and ran his hand along the side of the tree. On the third pass he found the protrusion. The tree had nearly grown over it, but using his pocket knife, he extracted what looked to be a long, thick nail, with an inch-diameter head. The number four was on the head. And the nail was made of gold.

When Ace climbed down to Fiona, his outstretched hand had the nail in the palm.

But she didn't take the nail. Instead, she stepped away from him, her face showing shock.

"What is it? *Tell* me," he demanded.

"I..." She cleared her throat, then lowered her voice. "I... My father..."

"So help me—" Ace warned, taking a step toward her.

"I have the map to the treasure. My father sent it to me. I know where the gold lions are hidden."

Ace stood still for a moment, looking at her, then at the golden nail in his hand. If the nail was part of the map and he'd found the nail here, then...

"The lions are on my property, aren't they?" he said softly. "And my uncle probably found them, so he was killed."

Sixteen

ᕦᐧᐧᕤ

"Okay, so forgive my terminal stupidity, but please tell me just one more time. You did *what* with the treasure map?"

Fiona glared at him. Her hands were crossed over her chest, and her mouth was a tight line. It wasn't easy to be self-righteous while standing in a swamp. "I didn't *know* it was a real map. Look, could we get out of this place?"

He acted as though he hadn't heard her. "If you could remember what the map looked like, maybe I could go from here to the lions. If they're still there, that is."

"My father sent me a total of twenty-two maps. The first one arrived when I was one year old, and it was a map to Lollipop Mountain, and he sent twenty-one maps after that. How was I to know that one of them was real?"

"All right," Ace said, turning away from her and trying to conceal his frustration. He'd asked her about the maps days ago, but she'd said they couldn't be real, but now he had a gold nail in his hand and she was saying that her father had used such nails in one of his treasure maps.

When he turned back, he was calmer. "Okay, explain it to me again."

Fiona gritted her teeth. He was acting as though she had *willfully* withheld information from him. "When I was nine he sent me the Map of the Nails. At least that's what my friend Ashley called it; it was her favorite map."

"Nine." With his hands behind his back, Ace began to pace. There wasn't much land to walk on. Around them was swamp, and Fiona was sure she could see the outline of something slithering just below the surface of the water.

"But you received the *Raffles* story when you were eleven. And weren't those the letters that were stolen? Was the map for when you were eleven also stolen?"

"Yes," she said, her anger seeping out of her

225

as fear began to replace it. Ace had always said that this had been in the planning for a very long time. Now she was beginning to realize just how long someone had been planning this. But why? she wondered. If the thief missed the map the first time, why not just make a second burglary? Or did he want something more than just a couple of gold lions?

"So your father sent you the map two years *before* he sent the story?"

Ace's voice was so insistent that she almost thought he was reading her mind and hearing her horrible thoughts. "Yes."

"And all these years the maps, including the one from when you were eleven that was later stolen, have been hanging in the hallway of your New York apartment. Right?"

"Exactly."

"But now they are... ?" He waited for her to answer.

"The last time I saw the originals they were sitting on the floor of my office in a Saks Fifth Avenue shopping bag, waiting for me to take them home."

"Great," Ace said as he sat down on a stump. "Think we can call your boss and he'll send them overnight down to us?"

"I *knew* you weren't listening to me," she said, then put her fists to her sides. Why did he always work so hard to make her angry? Why couldn't he have listened from the first and—

"I'm listening. Explain, please. I have all day." With that he crossed his arms over his chest and looked up at her with a smile.

Fiona took a deep breath. "All right, I will try once again to explain. Twice a year Kimberly is given an assignment. It's hinted that the assignment comes from the president of the U.S., but Legal said we couldn't say that outright. Anyway, she's worked in a circus, been a tour guide in a restored early American village, an Elizabethan actress, an interior designer, a—"

"And you get to sell clothes and accessories for every new character she plays."

"Someone in this world has to make money exchange hands," she said more sharply than she intended.

"Was she ever a philanthropist?"

"As a matter of fact, she was," Fiona snapped; then suddenly she laughed, and her anger and her fear left her. When she'd first realized that she had a real treasure map in her possession, her fear had made her unable to speak. Then Ace had been his usual pain-in-the-neck self, blaming her for not thinking of the map sooner, not understanding a word she said, but now his joke seemed to release the pent-up emotion inside her.

Turning, she smiled at him. "Actually, that was one of our more successful launchings. A very rich old man hired Kimberly to give away his millions so his greedy relatives wouldn't benefit by his death. We improved the lives of lots of people with the money we gave away that year."

"And this year?"

"This year Kimberly had to learn about

227

maps so she could become a cartographer. Seems there are some places in the Montana mountains that no one has explored, and the president—"

"Right," Ace said, cutting her off. "So what did you do with the maps your father made for you?"

"Lined her trunk. You see, accessories are available with each persona. When she went undercover in England in an old house as a Victorian parlor maid—"

"*Very* old house," Ace murmured.

"It was a tourist place. Kimberly has only time-traveled once. Anyway, that year Victorian clothes and household gadgets were available, as well as a book about Victorian life."

"So a cartographer would have a trunk."

"A trunk filled with instruments and textbooks."

"And the lining of this trunk is a map."

"The art director and I made a collage of my father's maps; then he had them printed into wrapping paper. We used the paper to line the trunks that came with Cartographer Kimberly."

"So all we have to do is buy a trunk and open it up to see the map, is that right?"

Fiona turned away to look at the trees for a moment before looking back at him. There was a white bird sitting on a branch, and she was tempted to ask Ace what kind of bird it was. Anything to delay telling him the truth. Taking a deep breath, she turned back to look at him. "Not quite. There are twenty-one maps that cover a piece of paper about ten feet by fifteen feet. My father's maps were large and detailed, so even when we reduced them, they were still big."

For a moment Ace just looked at her, trying to figure out what she was saying. "How big is the lining of each trunk?"

"Oh, about..." She held up her fingers as though measuring distance. "I'd say about four inches square."

Ace swallowed. "In other words we're going to have to buy hundreds of these trunks to be able to piece the whole thing together so we can find the one map that we need."

"I think it may be more like thousands, because you could buy half a dozen trunks and they could all be cut from the same square foot of the master sheet. In fact, that's likely if you buy them all in one area. And, too, the trunks come with Cartographer Kimberly."

"You have to buy the *doll* to get the trunk?"

"The objective is the doll, not the trunk," she snapped, refusing to hear any disparagement of Kimberly.

"Maybe I could hire someone to break into Davidson Toys and steal—"

"You have no idea what the security is in a toy manufacturer, do you? Do you have any idea what my people are offered to reveal who Kimberly is to be next? They..." She trailed off as she realized that she was no longer involved with Kimberly.

Ace's head came up. "Girls," he said, then stood. "Little girls buy them, don't they?"

"By the millions."

"If we could get lots of little girls to buy lots of doll trunks, then steam off the linings and fax them to us—"

"And offer a reward for any new puzzle piece that we don't have—"

"As a reward, how about dibs on Olivia the Bird Girl?"

"Octavia the naturalist," Fiona answered instantly. "But if we go public to reach lots of little girls, say on the Internet, how do we keep the police from picking up on this?"

"Easy. We don't use real children, we use relatives."

Fiona gave him a blank look. "Relatives? You'd have to have hundreds, and they'd have to live all over the U.S., and who's going to pay for all those dolls?"

"Relatives," Ace said; then he grabbed her hand and started pulling her toward the car.

And "relatives" was the only word she could get out of him until they were on the drive back to the Blue Orchid. He said, "It was a killdeer."

"What was?"

"The bird you were looking at."

"Oh? I wasn't aware that I was looking at any of your boring old birds." When she looked at him, he was smiling in such a way that she smacked him on the arm.

"Oh!" he said in mock pain, rubbing his arm. "You really are the most violent woman. I bet Jeremy is black-and-blue."

That was a sobering thought, and Fiona realized that she hadn't thought of Jeremy in days. Instead, her life had become this man. Although much about this man remained a mystery, in a way she knew more about Ace Montgomery than she ever had known about Jeremy. For all that she and Jeremy had been to bed together hundreds of times, she had never *lived* with him. She knew more about what Ace ate, what he liked to wear, what he thought about, than she had ever known about Jeremy.

"I think I'll call him when we get back," she murmured.

"Right after we get the map," Ace said quickly. "Then you'll have something to tell him."

"Good idea," she said too quickly. "After we get the map."

⤙◈⤚

"Three?!" Ace said into the phone. "Why you conniving little demon. Who taught you to do business?"

Turning, he put his hand over the phone and said to Fiona, "Every doll, dress, shoe, hat, whatever, that comes out for one year she wants in triplicate. And she has a list of friends who want the first doll."

"You are bargaining with something we don't have and will probably never get," Fiona said nervously. "And what kind of family do you have if nine-year-olds can negotiate contracts?"

"*Mmmm,*" was all Ace would answer to her question before he turned back to the phone.

"How do I know you can deliver the goods? I have a fax machine sitting right here, and nothing has come through it yet." He listened for a moment.

"Yeah, well, maybe we can talk more when I see some maps.

Mmhmm," he said into the phone. "No way. Miss Burkenhalter does that and she does it alone, got me? Now get out there and *buy!* I want faxes within an hour."

Fiona was sitting beside him on the couch, her eyes wide. She couldn't believe he was talking to a child. When he put the phone down, she said, "What did she want?"

"To be on the board of directors of the new doll company. She wants a say in the planning of the new doll. Is there anything to eat?"

"Come on and I'll make you a sandwich." Once in the kitchen Ace sat on the opposite side of the island while Fiona got bread, mustard, roast beef, tomatoes, and lettuce out of the refrigerator. "How can you talk about giving away a doll that doesn't exist and probably never will?" she asked. "Even if we did get out of this mess, where would we get the money?"

"We'd have to think of something," Ace said, looking across the granite countertop to the sandwich she was making. "Mayo too, if you don't mind, and—"

He broke off when the phone on the kitchen desk rang. They instantly looked at each other in a quick moment of fear. Only Ace's cousin

Michael Taggert knew the number, but they had talked to him just minutes ago.

Ace snatched up the phone, then waited in silence for a moment. "Yeah, yeah, she's here," he said gruffly.

Puzzled, Fiona took the phone from him.

"Fiona, darling," came Jeremy's voice, and she was struck with how long it seemed since she'd heard his voice. Had he always called her darling?

"Yes," she said, feeling guilt wash over her. The last time she'd "seen" him he'd been on TV when he was begging her to turn herself in.

"How are you, darling?"

"Fine," she said, swallowing. "And you... darling?" Ace was sitting on the barstool looking out the window toward the swimming pool, his face unreadable.

"How can I be anything but miserable without you?"

Pulling the phone away from her ear, Fiona looked at it in consternation. Since when was Jeremy so lovey-dovey? "What's going on?" she asked softly.

"Nothing at the moment. The hunt for you is still on, but did you hear about the double murder last night? It's taken you and Montgomery out of the spotlight."

"No, Ace and I don't—I mean *I* don't watch the news very often as it upsets us, I mean, me. The news upsets me. Listen, Jeremy, Ace and I are on to something. I think we may be closer to finding out who killed Roy Hudson

233

and, more important, *why* he was killed, and after that—"

"Oh, dearest, I understand completely. You take all the time you need."

"But I thought you wanted us, me, to turn myself in."

"Yes, of course I do. As a lawyer that's the only thing I can recommend, but, as you know, I'm a man too. You do remember that, don't you, darling?"

"Jeremy, you're frightening me. What's going on?"

At those words, Ace turned around to look at her, one eyebrow lifted in speculation.

Fiona gave a puzzled shrug. "Jeremy, why did you call me? How did you get this number and have you given it to the police?"

"Of course I haven't, darling," he said, ignoring the first half of the question. "And if they find out that I have it, I'll have to say that I had no idea that it would reach you. That's why I'm calling from a pay phone."

"Why *did* you call?" Fiona asked. There was something strange about his voice and his attitude. The Jeremy she knew would be bawling her out for running from the law. The Jeremy she knew never stopped being a lawyer for a moment, and he was very aware of his civic duty. But here he was talking to a criminal fugitive and telling her, more or less, to have a nice day.

"Just to touch base, to see how you were and if you needed anything."

It was on the tip of her tongue to say, "A

234

map," but she wasn't going to hint at the truth to him. For all she knew he was sitting in a police station right this moment. "I'm fine. *We* are fine," she said pointedly.

Jeremy gave a fake little laugh. "Ah, yes, you and Ace. I have heard so much about him. He seems like a fine young man."

"The best," Fiona said, tight-lipped.

Again there was that little laugh. "These are difficult times for both of us. Well, darling, I'll speak to you later. Good luck." With that he hung up.

For a moment Fiona just stood there holding the phone. What had just happened? Had she been given the brush-off? Because Jeremy the lawyer didn't want to be associated with a near-criminal? Not likely. If he could try her case and win, his career would be made. Fiona's problems were Jeremy's dream.

"What was that about?" Ace asked as he took the phone from Fiona and set it down.

"He..." She hesitated. "He just called to tell me he loved me."

"Ah, right. And to beg you to give yourself up, no doubt."

"Actually, he didn't ask. Was there any salad left from last night?"

Ace got up and followed her to the refrigerator. "He *didn't* ask you to give yourself up? Isn't that a little unusual in a lawyer? Don't they have to take an oath?"

"That's doctors. Lawyers do what they can get away with, remember?" She pushed past him to put pickles and relish and ice cream and fudge syrup on the countertop.

"But he upset you, didn't he?"

"Of course not. After what I've been through lately, nothing can upset me. Shouldn't the fax be ringing by now?"

Reaching across the countertop, Ace put his hands over her wrists. "I don't think you want to eat that."

Looking down, she saw that she'd smeared mint ice cream onto her bread, then put sweet pickle relish on top of that.

"Unless you're pregnant, that is," he said, smiling at her.

When she looked up from her ridiculous sandwich, there were tears in her eyes. "I want to go home," she said softly. "I want to have a home. I want to go to work in the morning. I want—"

"Hush, baby," he said as he drew her into his arms. "Be quiet. I'm going to fix everything, promise."

She slid into his arms and against the body that had become so familiar to her sight. His hands were stroking her hair, and it felt wonderful to be near him; then he was kissing her neck and she was kissing his neck and...

"Oh, baby, I've waited a long time for this. Do you have any idea what you do to me, watching you, being near you, talking, listening, I—"

She put her mouth on his so his words were blocked. "Make love to me. Please. Please."

"Yes," he said, then swept her into his arms

and headed for the stairs up to the bedroom.

Fiona curled against him. She'd always been too tall to be treated as a Scarlett O'Hara, being carried up the stairs to a night of passion, but Ace was tall enough and strong enough that he could do it.

His neck felt so good, and her lips on his skin were searching, seeking. It was as though she'd been aching, hungering, to touch just this spot.

When he was at the top of the stairs, he turned right to the bedroom, and Fiona's heart began to pound harder. Days and days of foreplay, she thought. That's what they had lived through, days of wanting each other.

At the doorway she felt Ace's body grow rigid, and he halted.

"It's all right," she said against his neck. "It will be all right." She didn't want to think about what she was saying, didn't want to think about Lisa or Jeremy, and especially not about their temporary circumstances.

Abruptly, Ace turned around, still holding her, set her down, grabbed her hand, then started down the stairs with her.

"What in the world are you doing?" she asked, halfway down the stairs. He was pulling so hard and moving so fast she was about to fall. With a sharp twist, she wrenched her hand from his and bounded up the stairs two at a time.

And she reached the bedroom door before he could stop her.

It was the bedroom Ace was using, the

larger master bedroom. The curtains had been drawn, but the lamp on the left side of the bed was on. It was almost cozy looking, with the sleeping woman lying on the bed, looking so peaceful, the pretty spread tucked up to her collarbone.

If it hadn't been for the gold nail in her throat and the thin trickle of blood running down the side of her neck, no one would have guessed that anything was wrong.

As Fiona stared, her pulse raced.

Pushing past Fiona, Ace went into the bedroom and bent over the woman in the bed.

It was Rose Childers, the woman who had pursued both of them, trying to persuade them to do a bit of "wife swapping."

"Poor old woman," Fiona said, standing at the foot of the bed and trying very hard to control herself. As Ace said, they couldn't afford hysteria now. "Should we call an ambulance?"

Ace gave her a look of disbelief, then straightened and went to Fiona. Grabbing her shoulders, he ushered her to the chair in the corner. "Sit down and be quiet. I need your brain now. We have to figure out what to do. If she's missed, the police could be all over this place in the next few minutes."

When Fiona lifted a hand to push her hair back, she was trembling so that she decided to sit on her hands as she watched Ace carefully pull back the bedspread. The woman was naked, the way she said she was most natural. "Nature" and all forms of the word were what had come out of her mouth the most often. "Being natural is what nature intended," Rose used to say.

"I wish I hadn't disliked her so very much," Fiona whispered. "Whatever she was, she didn't deserve to have... to have this done to her." She couldn't bring herself to look upward to the nail in Rose's throat. And she couldn't allow herself to think about what the woman had felt when that had been done to her.

Her naked body was not a pretty sight, and now lifeless, it was embarrassing to look at her. When Ace put his hands on the body and gently turned it over, Fiona looked away. In her old life one didn't handle dead bodies.

"Wonder if she called herself Rose before or after *this?*" Ace said, making Fiona look up.

The woman's buttocks were covered with a huge tattoo of a bouquet of roses.

One second Fiona was sitting down, a weak, nervous wreck, and the next she was on the other side of the bed staring at the woman's behind. "Oh, my God," she said, her hand to her mouth.

"What is it? And so help me, if you clam up on me like you did this morning, I'll make you regret it."

Fiona swallowed the lump in her throat and took a breath. "In *Raffles,* the man who is actually a woman had..." She pointed at the tattoo.

Ace dropped Rose back against the bed with a thump and straightened. "Now we're getting somewhere."

"Where?" Fiona's voice was rising. "Closer

to death? Closer to having nails put into *our* throats?"

At that Ace bent over the woman and pulled the nail from her throat and started to examine it. "Number three," he said.

Fiona thought she was going to be sick. Her knees gave way, and she sat back down on a chair.

When the telephone rang, both of them jumped. Fiona put her hand to her mouth, her eyes wide as she looked at Ace.

"It's line two," he said, "the fax. Stay here and I'll go down and—"

She didn't bother to answer him but took one stride with her long legs and was right behind him as he went down the stairs. When he reached the fax machine, Fiona was as close to him as his underwear.

"You're so close I don't have room to move my arms," he said as he tried to pick up the papers, but there was no annoyance in his voice.

Reaching around him, her front plastered to his back, Fiona snatched the papers from the machine. Looking at them, she said, "Good girl," then handed them to Ace, and he carried them into the dining room, where they were already set up with tape and scissors.

Minutes later they had half of two maps and a third of four others. "Very good, don't you think?"

"Yeah sure," Ace mumbled, looking at the papers. "I was thinking," he began slowly. "Maybe you'd be safer in—"

She backed away from him. "You aren't

going to say, 'in jail,' are you? You stay on the outside and I get put behind bars? You follow a treasure map while I fight off hairy women? You—"

"You stay safe while I risk—" He broke off when he saw her face. "Okay, we're in this together, right?"

Looking into his dark eyes, she nodded. At that moment she wanted to say that she'd follow him to the ends of the earth.

"Hey, Burke," he said softly. "You aren't falling for me, are you? It's one thing to have a good time together, but love is something altogether different."

"I..." she began, then stiffened. "Who could fall for *you*? You're the last man on the earth who I'd—"

She stopped talking because the doorbell rang, and after a fearful glance upward toward the bedroom, she looked at Ace in fear.

"Stay here and keep quiet."

Again, Fiona didn't pay any attention to his order, but glued herself to the back of him as he walked to the door. After giving her a push backward, which had no effect in putting any distance between them, he opened the door. It was Suzie, the jogger, again in tiny shorts, her fabulous legs exposed to the point of indecency.

"Sorry to bother you, but could I borrow a cup of sugar?"

"Sure," Ace said, holding wide the door so she could enter, and it wasn't easy to move since Fiona was attached to his back. As he led the way to the kitchen, Fiona didn't leave him. Once in the kitchen he managed to peel her hands from his arms and put them on the end of the countertop. Then, giving Fiona a stern look, he went to get the sugar from the cannister on the countertop.

"Nice day, isn't it?" Suzie said, looking about the kitchen.

Fiona gave her a weak smile in answer. She was much too aware of what was in the room over their heads to be able to think clearly.

As Ace handed Suzie the sugar in a paper cup, he said, "So how's Rose this morning?"; then he had to grab Fiona's elbow to keep her from falling to the floor in shock.

"Fine, I guess," Suzie said, smiling so wide her perfect ponytail bounced. "You wouldn't have any coffee, would you?"

"No, but I can make some," Ace said pleasantly, then turned his back on the two women as he went to the coffeepot.

Suzie gave her megawatt smile to Fiona. "Is that a telephone ringing?"

When Fiona didn't answer, Ace said, "It's the fax. Sweetheart, you want to go see what someone has sent us?"

Fiona had no idea who "sweetheart" was, so she just stood there staring at Suzie. What if she found out about the dead body upstairs? But then she and Ace were already accused of having committed two murders, so what was one more going to matter? They couldn't be hanged more than once, could they?

"I think the fax might be part of the map,"

Suzie said softly, "and we wouldn't want to miss that, would we?"

It was Ace who suddenly remembered that the house was probably wired for listening devices and that they were giving someone an earful. In one swift movement, he grabbed the arms of both women and half shoved, half pulled them outside. Once they were outside by the pool, in a silent gesture, he looked at Suzie and pointed around the pool.

She shook her head no.

"You want to tell me what's going on?" Fiona said impatiently. "Or are you two planning to open a mime school?"

"Bugs," Ace said as though that explained everything.

"Lots of bugs in Florida," Fiona said; then realization dawned on her. "Oh. *That* kind of bug."

Ace gestured to Suzie to take a seat on one of the four green chairs around the glass-topped table, then sat across from her. He left Fiona to stand or sit, her choice. She sat.

"You want to start talking?"

"Is Rose... ?" Suzie asked.

"Yeah, she's dead," Ace said. "In our house, in our bed. I'd like to know who knows what."

"Do you mean whether or not everyone in the Blue Orchid knows who you really are?" She didn't wait for them to answer. "Of course they do. We'd have to be blind and deaf not to know. And, honey," she said, looking at Fiona. "No surgeon is good enough to make a woman look as young as you do."

Right then and there, Fiona decided that she liked the woman.

"Half of us in this place are looking for the lions," Suzie said.

At that Fiona drew in her breath. So much for great secrecy.

Suzie leaned across the table toward Ace. "And if you find them, there will be a dozen people right behind you with guns."

"Except for Wallis," Fiona said quietly. "He only used a knife."

At that both Suzie and Ace looked at her. "I don't think either of you realize how much she knows," Suzie said quietly. "There are some people who want her dead for that knowledge, and some who want her alive because of what she knows. Truth is," she said, looking directly at Fiona. "You'd be a lot safer in jail."

"I think so too," Ace said quickly; then, under the table, he took Fiona's hand in his and squeezed it, and he didn't let go when he felt her trembling.

"Who killed Roy Hudson?" Fiona heard herself ask. She was trying to pull herself away from this whole matter and look at it logically. Forget the woman dead upstairs. Forget that the fax was ringing again and it was probably more of a map to a treasure that people had been killing each other for for a couple hundred years.

"One of them," Suzie said with a shrug. "I wasn't there and I don't know much about it. And now I try to stay out of it; I don't like to know things that could get me killed."

244

"Neither do I!" Fiona said with passion, then felt Ace's hand tighten on hers.

"But you were Smokey's daughter, so you were told things. Who would have thought that entertaining a kid with a broken leg could—"

"How do you know about her leg?" Ace snapped.

"I was there," Suzie said, contradicting herself. "I mean I wasn't part of the expedition that was searching for the lions, but I—"

"You were one of the women who researched the story," Fiona said, eyes wide. "You were the girlfriend of... of..."

"Edward King," she said slowly, looking into Fiona's eyes. "In the story he's called Wallis. And that's with an *i-s* on the end, not *W-a-l-l-a-c-e,* as the papers call him in the reviews."

For a moment Fiona blinked. "Of course, as in Wallis Simpson." She looked at Ace. "You know, the man who gave up being king was Edward and the woman was..." She broke off because Suzie and Ace were exchanging looks.

"*Now* what have I missed?" Fiona said with great sarcasm, but she knew that, once again, she'd revealed that she knew more than she thought she did.

"Who was the other researcher? If you were 'one' of them, who was the other one?" Ace asked softly.

"Lavender," Suzie whispered.

"Oh, no, you don't," Fiona said as she stood up so suddenly she knocked the chair over. "There was no one in the story named

245

Lavender. Not now, not ever." With that she started back toward the house.

Standing quickly, Ace reached out for her, but Fiona sidestepped him, moved past his grasp, and went into the house. Once he and Suzie were alone, Ace turned to her. "What was that all about? I haven't heard anything about anyone named Lavender."

Suzie took a deep breath. "From her reaction, I guess that Smokey told his daughter that one of the researchers was a prostitute, but he doesn't seem to have mentioned her name."

Ace was still puzzled.

"There wasn't much about her in the story, but what was there was pretty awful. You know, drugs, men, a lifetime of involvement in some very nasty dealings."

Ace just looked at Suzie, still not understanding.

"She hadn't always been such a loser. I was told that a few years before she'd been a tall, dark beauty. I was told that she even had a kid and the father named the kid after its mother."

When Suzie didn't say any more, Ace stood there looking at her. It took him a moment to remember that he'd seen the initials FLB on Fiona's backpack. Fiona Lavender Burkenhalter.

"Her mother was..."

"Yes," Suzie said just before Ace turned on his heel and went into the house to find Fiona.

Seventeen

❧⊚❧

It took Ace a few moments to find Fiona. She was in her bedroom, the borrowed cell phone to her ear. "You'll do it for me?" she was saying. "WordPerfect, yes, that's right. And, Jean... I... Okay, so I won't say anything, but you must know how much this means to me." With that she put down the phone; then, without a look at Ace, she went to the closet and began pulling out clothes—jeans and T-shirts, thick cotton socks—then started stuffing them into her backpack.

"Would it be too much to ask that you tell me what you're planning?" he asked. "Or maybe I should ask where you're going."

"Hunting," she said quickly. "This isn't going to stop until those—" She meant to say, "those damned lions are found," but the warning look on his face stopped her. "I'm going to look for what's lost," she finished.

"With or without me?" he asked. He was leaning against the doorjamb, his arms folded across his chest.

"Your choice," she said.

"I see. You're going to go to *my* park, tramping through the swamp by yourself."

"Maybe I can hire a guide. I'll cut him in for the profit. No, better yet, I'll make him a present of the... the lost goods once we find them."

"Ever hear of 'trespassing'?" Moving away from the door, he started to take her arm, but she pulled away from him. "Since when did *I* become the enemy?"

"Since I became a prostitute's daughter," she snapped, then looked at him in horror. She hadn't meant to say that; she hadn't meant to even think that.

At that, Ace put his hands on her shoulders and pulled her to face him. She tried to jerk away from him, but he held her firmly.

"We don't have time for this right now. Do you understand me? It doesn't matter who your father was, or your mother. Right now all that matters is that we find out who is killing these people and clear our names."

"Your name maybe," she said, jerking away from him, "but my name will never be cleared. It will be all over the papers about my... my ancestry." She stopped shoving clothes into the backpack and took a deep breath. "You could never understand," she said softly.

"I couldn't understand that you have lived your whole life believing you knew who and what you were and in a few days you've found out that everything in your life is a lie?"

"Yes," she said, deflated; then she sat down hard on the bed.

Ace sat beside her and put his arm around her, drawing her head down to his shoulder. "I know what it's like not to belong. I grew up in a family that thinks they're alone if there aren't a dozen people around them. All I wanted was to live with my uncle in a shack with no plumbing and look at birds. There would be days at a time when he and I never said a word to each other, and when we did talk, it was..."

"Birdcalls?" Fiona heard herself say, then looked at Ace in surprise. How could she make a joke at a time like this?

Ace laughed. "That's better," he said; then, as naturally as a bird flies, he bent his head to kiss her.

"Is she all right?" Suzie said from the doorway.

Fiona laughed when Ace said a bad word. "Padlocks," he added under his breath before turning to look at Suzie. "Fine!" he snapped. "She's just fine."

"Oh. Right," Suzie said as she started backing out the door. "I was just wondering what you planned to do with, uh, with Rose."

"Take her with us," Ace said loudly, then put his finger to his lips and pointed around the room. Had both women forgotten about the listening devices planted in the house?

"Yes," Fiona said, standing. "She'll go with us. You know Rose, the most natural person on earth. It would be natural to take her with us, since we're 'going back to nature' so to speak. Right, darling?" she said to Ace. "You *are* going to take me on that daylong picnic, aren't you?"

"Right," Ace said a little bit less loud. "A

picnic tomorrow. I think it's a bit late to go today, though, don't you, dear?"

"And I'm so glad that you've invited me to go with you," Suzie said. "I'd be happy to go with you."

Both Fiona and Ace vigorously shook their heads no, but Suzie tightened her lips and nodded yes, that she was going whether they liked it or not.

"In fact," Suzie said, "I think I'd better spend the night here with you, so I'll be ready to leave bright and early in the morning."

"But first, how about a swim?" Ace said. "It might do us all good to get outside for a while."

With that the three of them ran for the doorway and tried to get through it all at the same time. After some shoving, Ace stepped back and let the women go first; then he followed them down the stairs. Once they were outside, he turned on them.

"I think I can handle this better by myself," he began. The women were sitting while he stood, his hands behind his back. "I'm the only one who knows the park, so I should go alone."

"How will you know which map is the right one?" Fiona asked, a small smile curving her lips. "Suzie, would you like some iced tea?"

"Love it."

"Sit!" Ace ordered when Fiona started to get up.

She sat. In fact, both women sat still, their hands clasped on the tabletop, looking up at him as though awaiting his orders.

After a moment of looking down at them with his most stern face, Ace sat down hard on a chair. "All right, go on. Make the tea, then get out here fast," he said to Fiona.

"And leave you two here alone to plot my future," she said sweetly. "Not on your life."

With a sigh from Ace, the three of them silently trooped into the kitchen and made a huge pitcher of iced tea, added salsa and chips, then carried the tray out to the table by the pool.

"Okay, so which of you goes first?" Ace asked. When neither woman answered, Ace narrowed his eyes at them. He would, perhaps, have been more threatening if he hadn't had a mouthful of corn chips. The crunching seemed to take away his edge.

"If you two don't tell me what you know, I'll take you into the swamp and leave you there. With the snakes."

"He's bluffing," Fiona said. She had the strangest feeling that nothing horrible could ever happen to her again. It was as though the worst had happened and now nothing could top what she'd seen and felt. Her father wasn't what she'd thought. Only once in her life had she asked her father about her mother, and he'd told her a beautiful story she now realized was worthy of a Pulitzer.

In between having her personal life shattered, Fiona was finding dead bodies with regular frequency. Right now there was a dead woman just inside the house, yet here she sat munching chips and drinking tea. And all she could think was that she should have dumped some vodka into the tea.

"All I know is what we—" Breaking off, Suzie looked at Fiona. "What Lavender and I found." With that she reached out to clutch Fiona's hand but the younger woman moved away and Suzie stiffened. "Actually, I don't really remember too much about anything. It was a long time ago."

"You think Lavender might remember something?" Ace said softly.

It was one thing to learn that your mother wasn't the fairy princess that your father told you she was but quite another to think that she was alive. Fiona wasn't ready for that.

"I don't think the story of where the lions came from will be of any use to us but, if it helps, we should get the information tonight," Fiona said loudly and quickly.

Both Ace and Suzie looked at her sharply. It took Ace only seconds to start scowling, as it seemed that, once again, she had concealed information from him.

"Don't start on me," Fiona snapped. "You never asked if *Raffles* was the *only* story my father ever wrote me. It was just the best one. There were others."

"Let me guess," Ace said, his voice thick with sarcasm. "There was a story that came with the Nail Map."

"Aren't you clever?" Fiona said, smiling at him.

"I thought the papers said you two weren't married," Suzie said. "You sound as though you're married."

"Actually, we're both engaged," Ace said. "But not to each other."

"No, she likes some lawyer who calls her 'darling.' "

"You were eavesdropping," Fiona snapped. "You were listening in on my private conversation."

"I hate to interrupt you two, but could we stick to the subject?" Suzie said, looking from one to the other. "Did Smokey send you the story of the lions?"

"Yes. And the map. But I didn't realize they were real until..." She took a breath. "Until today. And the truth is that I still don't see the significance of the story."

"Maybe if we knew the story, we could judge for ourselves," Ace said. "Oh, but then both of you know it, don't you? I'm the only one who's left out in this."

At his whining, petulant tone, both women laughed.

"I called my friend—" Fiona began.

"One of The Five?" Ace asked, interrupting.

"Exactly. After my father's letters from when I was eleven were stolen, I spent a few evenings typing the rest of his letters into my computer. I had an idea of someday publishing his stories in a book for children, and—"

"Children!" Suzie exploded. "You'd want to have children read something like *that?*"

"I read them as a child and I came out normal," Fiona said, defending her father.

"If this is going to turn into a catfight, let

me know. For some reason, I have an extreme aversion to cats."

Fiona thought that was a very funny statement, but Suzie, who didn't know him, didn't understand and didn't laugh.

"So you have the stories on floppy?" Ace asked.

"All of them. And The Five—well, I guess it's The Four at the moment—are going to get into my apartment in New York tonight and get the disk. Jean will print it out and fax me the pages as soon as possible."

"That's wonderful," Suzie said, smiling.

Ace reached across the table and took Fiona's hand in his. "If your friends live all over the U.S., then that means they've stayed in New York since... since all this began. They're staying until they know you're safe."

With her head down, Fiona nodded. She didn't want to look into his eyes or she might start crying, but she didn't let go of his hand.

"I think maybe friends like them are worth more than the reputation of a woman you never knew," Ace said quietly.

"Right," Suzie said cheerfully. "And that they're willing to risk their own necks to break into your apartment, which must be under police quarantine, and risk getting involved in two brutal murders—three if you count Rose—as well, is a real show of friendship."

At the end of that little assessment, both Ace and Fiona were looking at her with their mouths open.

When she'd recovered enough to speak, Fiona stood. "I have to call Jean and tell her not to go. It's too dangerous."

Ace pulled her down to the chair; then he went to get the cell phone. But when Fiona called her friend, she only got her answering machine. "Too late," she said, looking at Ace. "They must have already gone. What is wrong with me that I didn't think of this? If Jean gets caught, I'll never forgive myself. I'll—" Pulling her into his arms, Ace held her tightly. After a moment, Suzie stood up and went into the house.

"Don't think about this," he whispered, "because tonight I'm going to make love to you. I have wanted you from the first moment I saw you, and I have waited long enough. For one whole night we're going to put all this aside and we're just going to enjoy each other. There's cold champagne in the fridge and the water in the tub will be very hot. Are you listening to me?"

She could only nod against his shoulder. Oh, yes, she was listening, listening with every cell in her body. "Tonight," she whispered. "Tonight."

Eighteen

❧❦❧

Bad didn't begin to describe the mood of Ace and Fiona the next morning as they got into the Jeep and headed for Kendrick Park. Fiona wanted to sit in the back with the bags they'd put in the car the night before, but Suzie insisted she sit back there, so the front seats were occupied by two people who weren't speaking to each other.

After last night when he'd made his declaration of intention to make love to her, Fiona had been nothing but a quivering mass. It was embarrassing to be her age and certainly no virgin and yet suddenly find herself thinking about sex as though it were her first time. When she thought about it, she didn't know when she'd started lusting after him. But then if she were honest with herself, it was probably at the airport when he came at her with the double row of teeth attached to his arm. There'd been something truly primitive in that situation, something very Tarzan and Jane, that appealed to her.

Of course since then, there had been the days spent in each other's company. So, all in all, last night his hot words had done to her what no amount of touching had ever done. She could have ripped his clothes off and leaped on top of him right there beside the pool. Then in the pool. And in the kitchen. And in...

But there had been Suzie. For days and days there had just been the two of them, but now suddenly there was another person: Suzie in her tiny shorts with her bouncing blonde ponytail, with her high firm breasts that didn't jiggle when she moved. Whether or not parts of her were real, the fact that she was actually there was certainly real enough.

"What's your husband doing?" Ace had asked Suzie last night by the pool. "Won't he be worried about you?"

"He's having an affair with his secretary, and this is their day together," Suzie said without blinking. "Besides, you're not going to get rid of me. I deserve a cut of this."

Before Fiona could explode, Ace put his hand on her arm. "If we did find these lions, we'd give them to a museum. No one is going to make a profit from this. All we want to do is clear our names."

Suzie gave him a little smile. "You cut me out and I'll tell the police you're here and that another body is in your house."

It was Fiona's turn to calm Ace down. "In that case, we'd love to have you," she said as sweetly as she could. "So maybe tonight you'd like to help us get rid of Rose's body." She hoped that this prospect would send Suzie running to the front door.

"Sure," Suzie said with a smile. "How about acid in the bathtub? Or should we dismember the corpse and stuff it in a trunk?"

Ace gave Fiona a raised-eyebrow look as though to say, I told you so. "Speaking of trunks," he said, "I think I'll check the fax machine."

"Me too," Fiona said quickly as she looked at Suzie. "He can't do anything if I'm not there to help him." With that she ran into the house after Ace, and once they were in the dining room, where he was sorting map pages, she opened her mouth to speak, but he put his finger to his lips in warning.

What do we do to get rid of her? Fiona wrote on the back of one of the fax sheets that did not contain the correct map.

Make her number four? Ace wrote back.

"Very funny," she said aloud as she took the pages from his hand and began to piece them together.

But then her hand touched his and instantly, electricity flashed between them.

"So how're the maps coming?" Suzie said from the doorway. "Got everything pieced together yet?"

"Just about," Ace said through clenched teeth, then stood between Suzie and the sheet of maps spread on the table so she couldn't see anything. But Suzie didn't seem to want to see them and soon wandered into the living room, where she could see but not necessarily hear everything.

We have to do something about Rose, Ace wrote. *We can't leave her here when we leave in the morning. Any ideas?*

This is out of my experience. What would you do if she were a bird?

Put her back into the nest so her mother could find her.

After Ace wrote that, he and Fiona looked at each other; then they smiled. "We'll take her home," Fiona whispered. "Let Lennie deal with her."

What followed after that, Fiona didn't like to remember. She and Ace spent a couple of hours piecing together the maps that Ace's little girl relatives kept sending through the fax machine. "Don't they have regular bedtimes?" Fiona snapped at eleven-thirty when she was yawning. The events of the day had pretty much worn her out, and she wanted nothing more than to...

She looked across the table at Ace. She wanted nothing more than to climb into bed with this delicious man and...

As he often did, he seemed to be reading her thoughts as he reached across the table and took her hand; then his fingers began inching up her arm.

But then Suzie sneezed and the spell was broken.

At twelve-thirty P.M., Ace decided that it was dark enough and quiet enough to take Rose down the street and leave her in her own house. He tried to persuade Suzie that she should remain behind; in fact, he tried to get Fiona to stay behind too, but neither woman would listen to him. And Fiona was ready to murder Suzie when the blonde woman reached out and grabbed the front of Ace's trousers.

"Keys," she said, turning to Fiona. "He

259

has the car keys with him. He was going to leave us."

When Fiona looked at Ace, she saw his face redden. He was a little boy caught in an act of naughtiness.

It was Suzie who grabbed the stack of papers just coming in from the fax and tore them in half. "Half for you and half for me," she said, then gave a torn stack to Fiona.

Fiona didn't say a word, but she and Ace knew that the real map had come through the machine a couple of hours ago and that now a copy of it was nestled against Ace's heart.

Ace gave Suzie a scowl of anger, as though she'd just foiled him in some dastardly deed; then as he turned away, he winked at Fiona before heading up the stairs. When he returned twenty minutes later, he had a fat roll of beach towels over his shoulder, tied in four places with silk neckties.

At the foot of the stairs, he nodded to Fiona to open the door; then he checked that no one was about.

Once she saw the big roll and knew what was inside of it, Fiona's fear returned.

"Don't give out on me now," Ace said, close to her. "Did you bring the gloves?"

She nodded. He'd told her to get the yellow rubber gloves that were stored under the sink so they wouldn't leave fingerprints when they had to break into Rose's house.

They had to walk down the sidewalks of the Blue Orchid because to try to walk across the minuscule back lawns would mean having to navigate around swimming pools in the dark, and they couldn't risk that. But they saw no one; there wasn't a light on in any house, neither outside nor inside, which in itself was eerie.

"Wouldn't someone have left a porch light on?" Fiona whispered, clinging to Ace's arm, even though he was straining under his heavy burden.

"Do you think they're all watching us?" Suzie whispered, clinging to his other arm.

"You're on their side, so you tell me," he hissed down at her.

"Me?" Suzie said, looking around her as though she expected an army to jump out at her. "I'm on Smokey's side. He wanted to find the treasure so he could make his daughter proud of him."

Leaning around the back of Ace, Fiona said, "My father said that? That's what he wanted? Did he tell you about me?"

"Honey, you were all he ever talked about. Not to the others, of course, but to me and Lav, when we were all in bed—uh, I mean, when we were together having a glass of wine or something, he'd tell me about you."

"You and my father—"

"Could you two please stop talking?" Ace snapped. "We're here." With that he bent and put his heavy burden on the ground. "Stay here," he said to the two women just before he disappeared into the darkness at the side of the house.

Fiona and Suzie looked at each other over

the corpse on the ground, then took off running after Ace. Fiona slammed into him first; then Suzie hit her hard in the back.

Ace gave a muffled, "Damnation!" then turned back to the women and steadied them. Silently, he motioned for them to remain where they were, but one look at their faces in the moonlight and he gave a great sigh. With resignation, he put his finger to his lips, then waved his arm for them to follow him.

At the back door he crouched over the lock, then put on the gloves Fiona handed him and began to fiddle with it.

It was Suzie, bringing up the rear, who reached over the heads of the two of them, turned the knob, and opened the unlocked door.

The house was empty. There wasn't a stick of furniture anywhere, not a picture on the wall. In the bright moonlight it was easy to see that the place had even been cleaned so that it looked as though no one had ever lived in the house.

"So now what do we do, Mr. Hot Shot?" Suzie said, hands on hips and glaring at Ace as though he had caused all their problems.

"How would I know? My doctorate is in ornithology, not murder."

"What I want to know is how they moved everything so quickly and so quietly," Fiona said. "When I moved my apartment, it took three days for them to pack everything, and I can tell you that I don't own a houseful of furniture. Maybe—Oh!!!" she gasped.

"What is it?" Ace said anxiously.

"My rent was due yesterday. I'll be evicted if it isn't paid."

Ace gave a sigh of disgust. "Let's get out of here."

"I agree," Suzie said. "This place is giving me the creeps."

The two women stayed outside, looking about them, jumping every time the breeze rustled the tree leaves, while Ace carried the towel-wrapped body into the house, then shut the door behind him.

Silently and very quickly, they walked back to their house.

Ace double bolted the front door then leaned against it. "I suggest that we all get a good night's sleep. Tomorrow we need to leave early for our picnic," he said, saying the last for the benefit of the listeners—whoever they were.

Everyone agreed with that idea even though there wasn't much of the night left and all of them had never felt less like sleeping in their lives.

But then there was the question of who was to sleep where. Ace didn't trust Suzie not to do something underhanded during the night, so he didn't want her in a room alone all night. Therefore, it made sense that Fiona and Suzie would sleep in Fiona's room, while Ace had his own room. But he took one look at his bed, the covers still pulled back from where Rose had been, and he knew he didn't want to sleep in that room.

Had it been under different circumstances,

Fiona would have made a few gibes at his nervousness, but she didn't want to be alone with Suzie. Right now Fiona was wondering just how big a part Suzie really did play all those years ago when the men had failed to find the lions.

In the end, all three of them climbed into one bed, Suzie in the middle. And Suzie was the only one who did any sleeping.

"You don't have to go tomorrow," Ace whispered across Suzie's sleeping form. "You could stay here and wait."

"And end up like Rose?" Fiona whispered back.

"I could take you to"—he took a deep breath—"to Jeremy."

"And you could go to Lisa," she said; then both of them were silent. It seemed like another life when they had known those people. When Fiona thought about it, she couldn't even seem to remember Kimberly very well anymore. What seemed real to her was Ace and his birds and his park and what she'd come to know over the last several days.

"I'm not proud of what I've done to her," Ace said. "She's a nice person and she loves me."

And I don't? Fiona wanted to say, but she wasn't going to let herself think that, much less say it. They were under great stress, and who knew how they'd feel about each other when their lives were back to normal?

"When you get back to New York, do you think you'll ever want to return to Florida or do you think you'll hate the place too much?" he asked softly.

Fiona was saved from answering by Suzie. "Could you two stop talking for a couple of hours so one of us could get some sleep?"

Fiona didn't say anything more, but she didn't sleep. Sometimes it took something horrible happening to make a person look at her life. If someone had asked her three months ago, she would have said that she was the happiest person on earth, utterly content with what she had. But now she looked back at that life and knew she could never go back to it. There was something missing in a life that revolved around money. And try as she might to tell herself that there was a higher purpose in a doll that was reissued twice a year, now it seemed that Ace was right and she had dedicated herself to making money for an already rich company.

And in the end, she hadn't been important. She'd thought that her life was Kimberly, but now the company obviously hadn't gone under because Fiona Burkenhalter wasn't there to decide what to do with Kimberly. In fact, if Fiona were truthful with herself, she was sure that there were several people who could take Kimberly further than she would have been able to.

"High tide," she whispered into the darkness.

"What?" Ace said from the other side of Suzie.

"I feel like one of those heroines in a Gothic

romance. You know, she goes out for a walk, and even though she's grown up by the sea, she 'forgets' that the tide is about to come in, so she gets caught in high tide."

"Oh," Ace said flatly. "Does she get out?"

"Of course. And in the end she finds out that getting caught in high tide was the best thing that ever happened to her."

"Somehow I don't think that being accused of murder is going to be the highlight of your life."

Fiona took a deep breath. "Maybe not, but, like all those heroines, I think that I've learned something." And maybe it was that admission that released something in her so she could fall asleep, because the next thing she knew, Ace was waking her with kisses. It took her a moment to realize that they were in bed together, alone, and that he was at last going to make love to her.

Deliciously, she put her head back and kept her eyes closed as his kisses trailed down her neck, as his hand ran up her bare arm, then went down again until he found her breast. She brought her leg up between his and felt that he was ready for her.

Never in her life had she wanted anything as much as she wanted this man. She opened her mouth under his and felt his tongue slide into her mouth. With all the strength of her legs, she pushed him back and climbed on top of him.

"Oh, baby," he murmured, his hands running all over the back of her and down her body.

"It came!" Suzie said loudly from the door.

Ace and Fiona didn't so much as pause in kissing as he rolled her onto her back.

Suzie, seemingly oblivious of what was going on, sat down on the bed beside them. "The story came," she said, then took a sip from her coffee mug. "Fiona, I guess your friends were able to break into your apartment after all. Wow, that was really brave of them to risk so much. They must really think a lot of you. Do they?"

Fiona wasn't hearing too much at the moment, but some part of her was beginning to draw back from Ace's kisses.

"Do they?" Suzie asked louder.

When neither of the people on the bed answered her, Suzie leaned over them. "Do your friends think the world of you?" she asked loudly.

At that Ace lay back on the bed and opened his mouth to tell Suzie what he thought of her. But Fiona didn't want to hear it. Yes, she wanted to make love with Ace, wanted to very much, but there was something holding her back from giving herself to him fully. She didn't know what it was, but there was something between them that hadn't been resolved. Maybe it was that she didn't think they had a future, what with his being in love with Lisa and the fact that they had been together only under horrible circumstances, but, yet, there was something else too.

So she rolled off the bed and stood. "Yes, my friends think a great deal of me."

It was obvious that Suzie had wanted to break Ace and Fiona apart. But why? Fiona wondered. In fact, when she looked back on it, Suzie's many timely interruptions couldn't have been by chance. Every time that she and Ace touched each other, there was Suzie asking some inane question or doing things like insisting that she sleep between the two of them.

Whatever Suzie was doing, it was certainly intentional, and it was *very* personal.

"There's hot coffee downstairs," Suzie said cheerfully as though she were unaware of what she had deliberately interrupted; then she got off the bed and turned her back on them.

Fiona almost giggled as Ace stood up, made his hands into claws, and went for the back of Suzie's neck. But Suzie turned in the doorway. "Ace, dear, your clothes are in the other bedroom, aren't they?" she said and seemed determined to wait until he followed her. She was not going to leave the two of them in the room alone together.

To Fiona, it was funny. Yes, she wanted to make love with Ace, but there was something old world and chivalrous about Suzie's attitude, as though she were protecting Fiona from something. She smiled when Ace left the room.

After Fiona had dressed, she went downstairs, and there she saw Ace in a towering rage pulling Suzie out the back door. Fiona followed them outside.

"Look what you've done!" he was saying in a low voice that had undercurrents of murder in it.

"I'm sorry," Suzie was saying. "It was an accident, I can assure you. I didn't mean to do it."

"So what happened?" Fiona asked, yawning. It wasn't full daylight outside yet, and she'd had very little sleep.

"This woman," Ace spoke with contempt, "just destroyed the papers your friends sent us."

"No!" Fiona breathed, then looked at the sodden mess that Ace was holding.

"She dropped the glass coffeepot on top of the papers, then tried to clean the mess up with the wet papers."

"I just forgot, okay?" Suzie said, sounding as though she was on the verge of tears. "I put the papers down on the counter, then dropped the pot on top of them. It was a reaction to start scrubbing with the papers."

"Do you have any idea what those papers could have cost those women?" Ace said angrily. "I don't know how they got into Fiona's apartment, but it had to be by illegal means. Then they stayed up all night doing whatever they had to to transcribe them so they could fax them to us. If they'd been caught, those women would be *prosecuted.*"

Fiona didn't like to think about what he was saying, and she didn't like the way Suzie was shaking. Fiona didn't know what it was, but there was something about Suzie that she liked. Maybe it was the way she played chaperone to her and Ace.

Whatever it was, Fiona put her arm around the shorter woman's shoulders and drew her head against her chest. "It was an accident, so let up, will you?"

"Accident?" Ace said, scowling. "You know what? I think she did it on purpose. In fact I think her whole act is just that, an act. I don't think she's who she says she is or that she's as innocent as she pretends to be." He was advancing on her.

"Me innocent?" Suzie said, sniffing, and clinging to Fiona. "You're the one who's a liar. Why did you allow Fiona's *friends* to risk their lives to get these papers? Why didn't your family just *buy* their way into her apartment? In fact, why don't you just *buy* your way out of this whole thing? What would it cost you? A few million? What's that to someone as rich as you?"

By the time she finished, Suzie was hiding behind Fiona, her hands on the younger woman's waist, and Ace was going for her throat.

"I'm going to kill you," Ace whispered.

Fiona drew herself up and kept her place between the two of them. "What is she talking about?" she asked softly.

"Nothing important," Ace said, still trying to get to Suzie.

Fiona put out her arm, barring his way. She was looking hard at Ace and with great intensity. "Is this why we don't look at newspapers and TV?" she asked softly. "You didn't want me to find out that you were... rich?" She said the last word so quietly he could barely hear her.

Stepping back, Ace looked at her. "It wasn't a secret," he began. "I..."

Fiona turned to Suzie, pulling her hands away from her body. "How rich?"

In answer, Suzie made a sound in her throat. "Kings have run countries on less money than he has."

Fiona sat down on a barstool. "So everything you've told me has been a lie," she said softly.

"Fee," Ace said, reaching out his hands to touch her.

But Fiona put her hand up to halt him. "From the very beginning, everything has been a lie. You told me that you had worked for years to earn the money to buy the plastic alligator, but that was a lie. You could have bought it out of the cash you had in your wallet."

"I've never spent a penny of my inheritance," Ace said, his face twisted with emotion. "I've tried to make it on my own."

"I think it was Henry Ford who said 'Nothing kills ambition like an inheritance,' right?" she said. Her voice was flat and her eyes were even flatter. "Do you own the hotel where we stayed?"

"No," Ace murmured.

"But I bet his family does," Suzie said. "At least one of his relatives is a billionaire."

"Oh, my," Fiona said. "Not merely millions, but billions."

"Fiona," he said, his hands outstretched in pleading. "It hasn't been like that. I never meant—"

"To lie to me? Why not? Who am I to you? Tell me, is your beloved Lisa from a wealthy family?"

Ace didn't answer her, but just stood there with his lips tight.

Fiona turned to Suzie.

"You really haven't been reading the papers, have you? Miss Lisa Rene Honeycutt's family is almost as wealthy as the Montgomerys. Not quite, but nearly. According to the papers, his family, throughout history, has married money."

"Well," Fiona said, turning back to Ace. "In this case only I was available, so I guess you take what you can get." It was a nasty comment, but she wanted to hurt him for lying to her.

She waited for Ace to answer, but he didn't. He just stood there glaring at her. Part of her wanted to scream at him to tell her that the thoughts inside her head weren't true. But another part wanted to hold on to her anger and hurt. When a man has lied to you as completely as this man had, you couldn't be dumb enough to fall in love with him.

Fiona turned her back on both of them. "Is everyone ready to go? The sooner we get started, the faster we can get this over with."

"I'm ready," Suzie said, moving away from the protection of Fiona. "Just a trip inside to the little girls' room and I'm all set."

When Ace and Fiona were alone in the backyard, he moved to stand close to her. "I think we ought to talk about this. I never meant—"

Turning, she smiled at him coldly. "What you have in your bank account is none of my concern," she said with as little emotion as she could manage. "You don't owe me anything, and I don't owe anything to you. What has happened to us hasn't been exactly a party. We were thrown together under extraordinary circumstances, remember? And you had no obligation to tell me anything about yourself other than what was absolutely necessary. That you finagled me into telling you everything there is to tell about myself while you kept the basic essence of yourself, literally, who and what you are, from me, means nothing." Her voice was rising, but she didn't care.

"No," she said, putting up her hand when he started to speak. "You don't have to defend your actions. What were you going to say to me? 'By the way, Burke, I'm rich, and I'm just living on a run-down bird farm for a lark? I wanted to see how the other half lives. It makes great dinner party entertainment. I—'"

"I think you've said enough," he said just as coldly. "I don't think you should talk about something you know nothing about."

"You're bloody right there. I know *nothing*, do I? You know about my mother, my father, about my being the poor lonely kid in boarding schools, and about how I've felt about my job, about everything there is to know about me. But I know nothing about you."

"You know everything that's important to

know about me," he said quietly. "I have always considered that there was more to me than what I had in the bank, but if you think that that's the most important thing there is to know about me, then I've misjudged you."

"Misjudged *me?*" she hissed at him, but he'd turned away and started out of the kitchen.

"Everybody ready?" Suzie asked cheerfully, then was greeted with scowls from both of them as they stalked toward the Jeep. "Something tells me that this isn't going to be a pleasant excursion," she said, but she was smiling as she said it, smiling as though she'd accomplished what she meant to.

Nineteen

On the drive to Kendrick Park, all Fiona could think about was Ace's betrayal of her. How could she have thought that she knew him? She had been thinking that she knew the real him because she knew what he liked to eat for breakfast. And because she knew about his love of birds. But all this time he had been excluding her from the real him.

And why not? she wondered. What was she to him? They had been thrown together by a freak accident, because her father and his uncle had been involved in something that happened long ago. And because Roy Hudson had stolen the story from her father. And because—

"You want to talk about this?" Ace asked softly, glancing away from the road to look at her.

"Nothing to talk about," she said with as much carelessness as she could put into her voice. "Will we get there soon? I was wondering, you know Kendrick Park and you saw the map, so how long do you think it will take us to find the lions? If they're still there, I mean. I certainly hope they are because—"

Ace glanced in the rearview mirror and saw that Suzie appeared to be sleeping. He doubted that she was, but at least she was pretending to give them some privacy. "The reason I didn't tell you that my family has money," he said softly, "is because I didn't want it to matter."

She stopped talking and looked at him, one eyebrow raised. "I see. You just wanted to make me feel bad about smashing your expensive alligator and taking food out of your employees' mouths."

"Yes," he said simply. "At first that was true. I was angry. I had earned the money on my own to pay for the thing; then to have it smashed like that and know that I was going to dip into money I hadn't earned..." He glanced out the side window for a second before looking back at the road. "I wanted to blame you for everything, but then..." He looked at her.

"Then what?" she said, her voice still full of anger. "You what? Fell in love with me? Is *that* why you tried to get me into bed with you? You don't think I'm going to fall for that, do you?"

"Is that how I come off to you?" he asked, turning quickly to glare at her. "Do you think I set this whole thing up just to go to *bed* with you?"

Fiona looked out the window and realized how ridiculous she sounded. Her girlfriends often called her a prude. Jean had once gone to a Caribbean island and spent a week in bed with a young man she never planned to see again. But here Fiona was, at thirty-two, on the very edge of the twenty-first century, and she was acting like the virgin in a Greek play.

But logic had nothing to do with it! she thought. His lies went beyond the ordinary lies that men told to women. Ace's lies were fundamental, and they had almost made her believe in them. Believe in *him*.

"Look," she said as calmly as she could manage, "I have no right to be angry about anything. Your life is yours, and whether you have money or not, whether you pay for your alligators yourself or your daddy does, is none of my business. Maybe in another forty-eight hours we'll have found the lions and maybe found out who really killed Roy, and maybe... I don't know, maybe everything will be solved and you can go back to your rich family, and I can go back to... to..." For the life of her, she couldn't think what she had to go back to. Kimberly was no longer hers, and she had a gut feeling that neither was Jeremy. And the truth was, she didn't think that she'd ever be able to look at Jeremy without seeing Ace Montgomery. In fact, she wasn't sure she was ever going to be able to look at any man without seeing *him*.

Ace had pulled off the highway onto the overgrown back road that entered Kendrick Park, and now they were heading toward the cabin.

He didn't respond to her statement, and she wondered what he was thinking. For her, with every plant they passed, every bird they saw darting about, she remembered the first time they had been to his uncle's old shack. Fiona remembered being frightened, but she also remembered the simple camaraderie they had shared in those days. She remembered how Ace had protected her from bullets with his own body; he was ready to be shot rather than allow her to be hurt.

Had he been acting? she wondered. Was anyone that good an actor?

But even back then she had known he was hiding something. She hadn't had a clue what it was, but she knew that he wasn't who he seemed. And now she knew what it was that he had been covering up: Money. He was wealthy and he hadn't wanted her to know about it. Why? Wasn't she his social class?

When they were close to the cabin, Ace said, "Fiona, I want to tell you that—"

He didn't finish his statement because standing on the porch of the falling down old shack was Jeremy. And beside him was a lovely young woman who Fiona recognized from TV as Miss Lisa Rene Honeycutt.

Twenty

<small>ᐉᑯᏰᏰ</small>

"This is *not* a garden party," Ace said through his teeth to his cute, perky little fiancée.

Fiona had to turn away to hide her smile because when she'd first seen the adorable-looking Lisa, she'd been afraid that Ace was going to fall all over her, and Fiona wasn't ready to see that yet. She didn't know when she was going to be ready for that, but it certainly wasn't now.

Now they were inside the old shack, and from the looks of the place the animals were grateful that an attempt had been made to clean it, because they'd redoubled their efforts to make it their home. But Fiona happily sat down on a couch that a few weeks before she wouldn't have touched. Smiling, she patted the space beside her for Jeremy to take, but he gave her a curled-lip glance that asked if she'd lost her mind.

Everyone in the cabin was focused on the argument going on between Ace and Lisa, watching them as though they were the stars of a movie.

"Lisa," Ace said through clenched teeth. "Do you have any idea how serious what you've done is? If the police followed you, Fiona and I could be taken to jail before we get a chance to clear our names."

Lisa stuck out her lower lip in the prettiest pout imaginable. "If you talk to me like that, I won't tell you our surprise."

When Ace's face turned dark and his hands made fists, Fiona decided to step in before there was a fourth murder. "If your surprise is something to wear and in silk, I'm all for it," Fiona said, trying to inject humor into the situation, because, so far, there had been no humor. Jeremy had greeted her with a hand tightly gripping her upper arm, as though she were a wayward two-year-old and he were bringing her back into line. Had he always treated her like a child? she wondered.

At Fiona's words, Lisa turned to her, and her blue eyes were fire, a fire that asked who Fiona thought she was.

But instead of angering her, Lisa's hate-filled look made Fiona give a warm smile of congratulations to Ace. What a lovely lady you've chosen, her smile said.

"*He* is my surprise," Lisa said coldly, pointing to the door.

In the doorway stood an old man. But on second glance, Fiona thought that maybe he wasn't as old as he seemed but just beaten about by weather and time. His gray hair was sparse, as was his body, and his neck hung down in whiskery folds into a shirt that was clean but nearly worn out.

"Forget about these?" the old man said, then held out his thin hand to show three little listening devices.

"Did you find them easily because you put them in the cabin?" Ace snapped.

Fiona was staring at the man. There was something familiar about him, and when he turned to address Ace, she let out a gasp. The man turned back to her and gave a wide grin. He was missing his left incisor.

"Know me, do you, Little Smokey?" he said, laughing.

"Gibby," Fiona whispered, for she'd seen the green dragon tattoo going up the back of his right calf.

"Smokey always said you were smart," the man said, then turned sharply to look at Suzie. "You ain't changed much," he said, looking her up and down. "What'd you do? Sell your soul for youth?"

Suzie smiled at him. "Screwed the brains out of a plastic surgeon and he was real grateful."

Gibby laughed with her.

"All right," Jeremy said in his lawyer voice. "I want to know what's going on. This man said that if we'd take him here, he'd clear up this whole mess, so now I want to know what's going on."

But no one answered him, because Ace, Fiona, and Gibby were pulling on backpacks.

"We have to get going. We have a long hike ahead of us," Ace said, then looked at Jeremy in his lightweight suit. "We'll be back as soon as we can get back. The car keys are on the table." It was obvious that he planned to leave Jeremy, Lisa, and Suzie behind.

But Jeremy had other ideas. "If you think you're going to walk out of here and—"

When Ace turned a face full of rage toward Jeremy, the shorter man halted. "I'm in just the mood to take the head off somebody and if it's you, so be it," Ace said softly; then when Jeremy said nothing more, Ace fastened his pack and started for the door.

But as soon as they were on the porch, Jeremy was with them. "You're not leaving without me," he said through clenched teeth.

"Why?" Ace said, looking him up and down. "Concerned for your ladylove? Or do you want a cut of what we find?"

Before Jeremy could answer, Fiona got between the men. "Don't take your anger out on *him*. He was trying to help. Gibby is—"

"One of the original men who went with your father; that I could guess," Ace said, then turned to see Lisa emerge from the cabin, a little black nylon pack in her hand. "Neiman Marcus" was written across the top flap.

"Her mascara," Fiona said before she could stop herself, then had to look away because she saw just the teeniest bit of a smile at the corners of Ace's lips.

"Ace, honey, you're not going to let her snip at me like that on this whole trip, are you?"

"Lisa," Ace said patiently, "you can't go with

us. There are snakes and mosquitoes out there as well as alligators. It's too dangerous for you."

"But not for me?" Fiona asked.

"But not for her?" Lisa said at the same time.

At that Ace threw up his hands, then started down the porch steps. "Where are the police when you need them? Why can't I be arrested and put in a nice safe jail cell?"

Behind him Gibby chuckled. "I think I'm gonna like this trip better'n the last one."

An hour later Fiona wished she'd begged to be allowed to remain at the cabin rather than traipse through a swamp, but she refused to make a complaint. As it was, Lisa was doing enough of that for all of them. And with every word out of Lisa's perfect little mouth, Fiona smiled a little more inside.

"You hate her, don't you?" Jeremy said, moving to walk beside Fiona, dodging plants and constantly looking about for snakes.

There was something in his tone that made Fiona look at him sharply. He was shorter than she remembered and had he always had that pinched look? Maybe it came from a lifetime spent in front of a computer screen.

"But you like her," Fiona said softly. He hadn't touched her other than to grab her arm since she'd first seen him over an hour ago. Right now it seemed impossible to believe that they had once been lovers.

"Do you have any idea who her family is?"

"No. But I take it you do."

"She would..." Turning his head away, he

looked at Fiona out of the corner of his eye. "She could help me in my career."

At that Fiona took a deep breath. "Well, that's honest. And, you're right. Even if you were my lawyer and got me off, what would I be but an out-of-work executive? Right?"

"I wouldn't put it quite so bluntly, but, Fee, you know that there was nothing set between us. We were just—"

"You don't have to tell me that we weren't in love. I know that now."

"Now? Does that mean that you and Montgomery... ?"

"Nothing has happened between us, if that's what you mean," Fiona snapped, then lowered her voice. "We've been rather busy these last days, what with trying to find out who killed three people."

"Three? My God, Fiona, how deep are you into this?"

"As deep as I was put into it!" she said, then had to calm herself. "Look, if you want my permission to pursue your cute little"—she sneered the last word as though it were a deformity— "blonde, you have my permission." A leaf hit at her face, and she swiped it away. "But do you think your little cheerleader is going to want *you* when she can have a man as rich as I've heard... as I've heard... Montgomery is?" She couldn't bear to say his first name. He was now holding Lisa's perfect little ankle and turning it about in his big hand, checking if her lovely little bones were injured in any way. As for Fiona, she'd stepped wrong on a tree branch half an hour ago and was still limping, but no man was coddling her. Beside her, Jeremy hadn't even noticed her limp.

"Their marriage was to be a merger of two family fortunes," Jeremy was saying, and sounding as though he were quoting someone. "In these past days I've come to know Lisa very well. We've worked side by side, day after day, and—"

"Searching for us," Fiona said, deadpan. "While you were looking for us, trying to prove our innocence, you and Lisa were playing footsie under the table. Or was it in bed?"

"That's an example of what's wrong between us," Jeremy said. "No matter how bad things are, you always make jokes."

Fiona waited for him to finish the sentence, waited for the other shoe to drop. Where was the punch line to that sentence? Wasn't it good that she was the type of person who could laugh in the face of adversity? One of the things that Ace liked most about her was her ability to laugh no matter what was happening to them.

Turning, she looked at the head of the line of people and saw Ace helping Lisa over a fallen log.

"I don't think he'll let her go." She looked back at Jeremy. "And I can't see that she'd ever choose you over *him.*"

Jeremy gave a snort. "Are you kidding? He's one cold bastard. The only thing he ever thinks about are birds and—Would you mind telling me what is funny about that?"

She was staring at Ace with Lisa, staring very, very hard.

"There is nothing wrong with Ace Montgomery," she said. "Nothing whatever in this world." With that, she strode forward and got between Gibby and Suzie.

"So tell me everything," Fiona said, suddenly wanting to hear something other than Jeremy's whining and his calculations about his career.

⊸⊙⊶

When Lisa said that she was hungry, Ace motioned everyone to take a break and sit down.

Fiona dutifully sat by Jeremy, but the minute she saw Ace walk off into the bushes, she was up and after him.

"A man would like a little privacy," Ace snapped as he abruptly turned his back on her and fiddled with the front of his trousers.

She ignored him. "How many have you found?"

"I think we should return to the others," he said. "Lisa will be frightened and..."

"Don't you give me that, Ace Montgomery!" she snapped, then lowered her voice. "You are a sneaky, conniving bastard, and I know you're up to something."

"Would you believe I came out here to see a bird?" he asked, one side of his mouth curled into a smile.

"Not even for a blue-eyed blonde sap-sucker," she retorted, and Ace grinned.

"I've missed you," he said softly.

It was all Fiona could do to keep from falling into his arms. At the moment all she could remember was their time alone. Why had they argued so much? But then she remembered Lisa and the good humor left her.

Narrowing her eyes at him, she held out her hand. "Show me."

After a look about him to check that they weren't being watched, and with a chuckle, he handed her two gold nails.

"How did you know?" he asked.

"I know you. You're not one of those Southern gentlemen who helps ladies over fallen logs. You're more of a Get-off-your-rear-and-let's-*do*-it sort of guy, so when I saw you helping Lisa, I figured you were up to something, like hiding the fact that you were pulling nails out of trees."

"Lisa thinks I'm a gentleman," Ace said with a bit of a smile.

"Lisa likes your money, and if you don't know that, you aren't the man I thought you were."

At that Ace grabbed her, pulled her into his arms, and began kissing her. "I've missed you," he said as he kissed her hair and her eyes. "Do you hate me? I never meant to lie to you, but—"

"I know," she whispered as her mouth hungrily ran over his neck. "I know. You're sick of women who want you for your money."

"I never had a chance with a woman who didn't know who my family was, and—"

He didn't say any more, because his hand was on her breast and moving lower. And Fiona's knees were giving way as they both began to sink to the ground. Around them were luxurious jungle plants, and overhead the birds called to each other, and Fiona had never wanted anything like she wanted this man. It didn't matter that there were other people not more than twenty feet away. For all the two of them were aware of other people, they could have been alone on an island.

But Lisa's frantic screams brought them back to reality.

"What now?" Fiona murmured. "She see a spider?"

But Ace had lifted his head to listen; then in the next second, they heard the unmistakable sound of a shot, followed instantly by another one.

Fiona started to plow through the brush to go back to camp, but Ace grabbed her arm and led her around, quietly through the plants, so they were entering the camp from a different angle. At one point he halted, put his finger to his lips, then gestured. Fiona stood perfectly still while a snake that had to be forty feet long slowly slithered past them. When it was gone, he motioned to her to continue walking.

"Poisonous, right?" she whispered.

"Deadly."

"Of course."

He broke through the plants, then stood for

a moment staring; then, frowning, he turned back to Fiona and shrugged his shoulders in puzzlement. She stepped forward and looked ahead. Jeremy, Suzie, and Gibby were staring down at something on the ground. Lisa was lounging against a tree root looking as though she were about to die.

"She saw the snake," Fiona said in disgust.

"And they shot each other in terror," Ace added jokingly; then they both smiled.

Straightening, Ace left the shrubs and walked toward the campers. "I want to know who has a firearm," he said. "And I want it turned over to me now."

Lisa, who moments before looked as though she were dying, leaped up and threw her arms about Ace's neck. "It was me. I found her. She was... Oh, Ace, honey, it was horrible. I don't know how I'm going to recover from this. My therapist—"

Looking up, Ace saw Suzie step back from the little circle, and her hands made a motion that meant, Come and see for yourself.

And when Suzie stepped back, Fiona could see into the group. There on the ground, wearing men's overalls and a plaid flannel shirt buttoned up to her neck, was Rose.

"Not again," Fiona sighed, hands on hips.

"What does she mean, 'Not again'?" Lisa half screamed. "Ace, that woman is *dead*. Doesn't she realize that? What is wrong with her?"

Ace peeled Lisa's arms from around his neck, then walked to the body. "I guess it's too late to try to see footprints that we could follow."

Fiona didn't want to think about what the reappearance of Rose's body meant. They were being watched, being followed. She glanced down at the clothes Rose had been shoved into. "All cotton," she said. "At least she's still 'natural.' "

At that the fear left Suzie and Ace too, and they began to laugh.

"You three are sick," Jeremy said. "You're really sick. I'm beginning to think that you *did* kill that nice old man, Roy Hudson."

At that Ace spun around and grabbed Jeremy's shirtfront. Jeremy had discarded his too-hot jacket long ago.

"That's right, lawyer, we are all sick. And the person or persons who keep killing everyone involved in this is even sicker. Now, I want you to give me your gun, and do it now."

"I live in New York; I have a permit," Jeremy said, trying to pull himself up to his full height, but the top of his head only touched Ace's chin.

"This is not New York, this is *my* land, and here I'm the king, got it? Give me the gun."

Reluctantly, with a face that threatened, but with no words, Jeremy handed Ace the small handgun he had carried inside his coat pocket.

Ace put the gun in his backpack, then started to put the pack on. "From now on, everyone stays together. There is someone following us, someone ahead of us. Anyone have any questions?"

"We aren't going to leave her here, are we?" Lisa asked in a whisper.

"Would you like to take her back to the cabin?" Ace asked, his eyes cold. "Would you like to move away from the protection of the group and go back there alone? Is that what you want to do?"

"I don't see why you have to be so rude about it," Lisa said, sticking out her lower lip. "Maybe you two are used to seeing murdered people, but Jeremy and I aren't."

At that Ace blinked a couple of times, then looked from Lisa to Jeremy, then to Fiona. And when he looked at Fiona, he gave her a little smile before turning away.

"I'll lead because I know where we're going," Ace said. "Burke, you stay near me, Suzie behind her, then Lisa and the lawyer. Gibby, you bring up the rear." He looked at the older man. "How well armed are you?"

Fiona looked at Gibby. "Two pistols and a knife in his boot," she said softly.

The old man smiled at her. "And... ?"

"I don't think I'll tell," she said, smiling at him.

Gibby winked at her, then looked at Ace. "I'm armed well enough. Lead on, and, this time, I think you should lead us *all* the right way."

Ace gave him an answering smile before turning away and starting to walk again. Once they were going, Ace said over his shoulder to Fiona, "Get what was left of the papers from her and read them to me."

It took Fiona a second to translate his command, but she understood that he wanted the coffee-soaked papers that contained the story of how the lions got to be where they are. When her father had written her the story of *Raffles*, she had been immobile, so she'd read the story with intense interest. But when he'd sent the story about the golden lions, she'd been in the middle of a soccer tournament and she'd paid little attention to what was on paper, much to the chagrin of her teachers. Therefore, she didn't remember much of the story.

Suzie had heard the "command" and she had the papers out and ready.

"They really are a mess," Fiona said to Ace, doing her best to stay beside him as they walked. If she weren't as tall as he was, she'd never manage, and she was tempted to look back to see how short little Lisa was doing, but she restrained herself. Maybe Ace was trying to get rid of them. And maybe he knew that the two of them were the targets of whoever was out there, so he wanted to separate them from the group. So we can be shot first, she thought with a gulp.

"Well?" Ace snapped when she was silent for so long.

"It's difficult to make out," she said. "There are just phrases, parts of sentences that I can read. But here goes. 'Weather thick and foggy; two days later fog lifted; land straight ahead, black towering cliff face four hundred feet tall. Wind dropped; eerie calm descended; ship drifted toward cliff with everyone knowing it was going to crash. But cliffs seemed to...' I can't read this. 'They... opened up,' I think it says. Yes. 'The cliffs opened up as they approached their doom. *Something, something.* Ship drifted into cavern in rocks until mainmast ground against cave roof and ship wedged. *Something...* Ship sank before dawn.'

"There's a lot of missing text here. Someone, I can't read the name, was planning to seize the ship, but it wrecked before he could take over. After the wreck, he grabbed jewels and took command of the island. This is funny and I remember this. This horrible man dressed in scarlet robes from fabric from the wreck. He was violent and autocratic. Killed one hundred twenty-five survivors, including women and children, and made Lucinda his mistress."

She looked up from the torn, stained papers. "Even in the original there was no explanation of who Lucinda was, but at the time I remember imagining how beautiful she was. I thought..." A look from Ace made her look back at the papers.

"Let's see... Another man on the island, Williams, had forty followers and was able to repulse two attacks. He finally made a surprise attack and took... I can't read the name.

"Anyway, he took the bad guy prisoner. Then there's a lot missing here, but it seems that the captain of the ship and forty-five others had sailed for help and had returned, and when they got back, the bad guy, along with his henchmen, surrendered and were taken back to... wherever the ship came from and hanged." Fiona began to riffle through the pages.

"Let's see... These other pages—oh, I see, they're the middle of the story. Everything is out of order. There's a long description of what the people went through while they were stranded on the island. I can only make out phrases.

" '...drunk off of salvaged bottles of muscatel, ate cheeses and olives... built a camp of huts with palm-leaf roofs, decorated with Flanders tapestries... Apes on island, stole their food. They...' "

Fiona held the papers up and twisted them about. " 'They shot some...' I guess they shot the monkeys, but the flesh was nasty tasting... Oh! This is interesting. The island wasn't uninhabited as some of the sailors seem to have been eaten by natives. What else? 'They... created saws out of swords.' That sounds sensible. And... yes, 'They killed a fifteen-foot crocodile, roasted it and ate it.' I think it says that the meat was very good."

"It is," Ace said succinctly. "What else?"

" 'They... met...' I can't make it out. Oh, yes. 'They met the local king, gave him gifts of textiles, glass goblets, mirrors... and...' No, I can't make it out.

"That's all I can read except..." Fiona smiled. "I think it says that Sophia fell into a succession of fainting fits."

"All that is very interesting," Ace said, "but what about the lions?"

"Either the part about them is on the coffee-soaked pages and I can't read it, or this story doesn't match the map that was sent that year."

"You don't remember anything about golden lions in any of the stories?" he asked, and his tone said that she was a moron for not remembering something so important.

"Don't start on me," she said, narrowing her eyes at him. "You grew up in this swamp, on the site of the map, so why didn't you find the nails and the lions when you were a kid?"

"Actually, I did."

That statement stopped Fiona in her tracks, but Ace reached back, grabbed her arm, and pulled her forward. "Please don't make a scene," he said quietly. "Do you want the others to know?"

"Know what?" she asked, and there was a hysterical tone beginning in her voice. "Know that *you*, not *me*, have known everything all along?"

"If you start playing female on me, I won't tell you anything."

"Me play female?" She pursed her mouth, ready to hit him with something. " 'Oh, Ace, darling, I can't lift this feather, and it's hurting my teeny tiny ankles,' " she mimicked Lisa.

"You're jealous, aren't you?"

"As jealous of her as you are of Jeremy," she snapped back at him.

"Then that's quite a lot," Ace said softly, and looked at her from under his eyelashes.

In spite of herself, Fiona's breath caught in

her throat, and when she nearly tripped over a fallen log, Ace put his hand under her elbow to steady her.

"Still mad at me for not telling you that my family is fabulously wealthy and that I can easily afford to manufacture your swamp doll and set you up in your own toy plant so you can run it the way you want and never again have to worry that some jerk will fire you?"

At that overlong sentence, without a pause in it, Fiona had to laugh. "When you put it that way, it's not such a bad idea. Maybe I could stand it. But..." Hesitating, she looked away for a moment, then back at him. "But what about... about..."

"Lisa?"

"You *are* going to marry her, remember?"

"When you snooped through my house at the park entrance, didn't you wonder why her picture was under the bed?"

"I didn't—Okay, so maybe I did look and maybe I did wonder, but you've confessed undying love for her since I met you."

"I was lonely, I went back to my parents' place for a month-long visit, and Lisa was there. We had a great time, what can I say? I thought I wanted to spend my life with her. But when I got home, back to here..." He motioned his hand to include the swamp and the constant barrage of wildlife around them. "I knew that she wouldn't, couldn't, fit in. I was planning to break it to her gently, but..." He shrugged.

"But I came along and broke your crocodile,

then woke up with a dead man on top of me and—"

"Alligator," he said.

Fiona gave him a brilliant smile. "I know, but does Lisa?"

Ace kept his eyes straight ahead, then lowered his voice. "I think maybe Lisa has found something she likes more than Montgomery money."

When Fiona gave a puzzled frown, Ace nodded over his shoulder and Fiona looked backward. Their little line of people was paired off as though they were entering Noah's ark. Suzie and Gibby were head to head, whispering urgently to each other, while Lisa and Jeremy were...

Fiona looked back at Ace in wonder. "I guess they've spent a lot of time together in the last week or so."

"Seems so," he said, eyes straight ahead, but Fiona saw the tiniest bit of a smile about his lips. His beautiful lips, she thought.

Her heart was beating hard and fast, and she took a deep breath to try to calm herself down. "So it looks like your wedding is off," she said after a while, trying to sound nonchalant.

"And yours too," Ace said with so much little-boy eagerness that Fiona laughed again.

For a moment they walked in silence; then suddenly, Ace tripped over a piece of wet ground and fell against a hard-barked palm tree. And when he fell, he took Fiona with him, so that they landed in a tumble of long legs and arms. And, somehow, his mouth found hers, and he kissed her for several long, delicious seconds before the others came running.

"Are you all right?" Lisa half screamed. "Oh, Ace, darling, I'd just die if anything happened to you."

Sitting on the ground, Fiona looked up, shading her eyes against the sun, and saw that Jeremy's hands were made into fists at his sides. "*We* are fine," she said with emphasis. "Just tripped over a snake."

"At least it wasn't another dead body," Suzie said, standing in the background near Gibby, and Fiona wondered what it was that they had been talking about with so much intensity.

"Now that everyone is stopped, maybe we should camp tonight," Gibby said, looking hard at Ace. "Unless you want us to circle around some more."

"Circle?" Lisa said quickly. "What does he mean, Ace, honey? You aren't leading us in a circle, are you?"

"Of course not," Ace said, but Fiona could see that he wasn't looking anyone in the eye. "Gibby just means to 'circle the wagons,' that sort of thing, don't you, old man?"

"Sure thing," Gibby said, but his eyes never left Ace's.

Ace got up off the ground, then hefted his backpack. "I brought fishing gear. Gibby, you get some bait, and you, lawyer, get the kerosene stove working. Suze, you know how to fish?"

"I can do most anything, including following

a map," she said, looking at Ace with cold eyes.

"I guess we know what they were talking about," Fiona said into Ace's ear as she got up to stand beside him.

"Go away," he said to her, under his breath, and for a moment Fiona thought he meant he wanted her to get away from him. But then she figured out what he wanted.

"Suzie," Fiona said brightly, "I'll help you fish just as soon as I, uh, take a trip into the bushes."

"I'll go with you," Lisa said in that age-old belief that women should go to the powder room together.

Turning to pick up his pack from the ground, Ace looked up at Fiona and gave her a barely perceptible shake of his head.

"'Scuse me," Fiona said, as lightly as she could manage, "but the absence of stalls makes me crave privacy."

Lisa blinked for a moment at that, then gave a little giggle. "Oh, sure. I understand. You aren't going to escape, are you?"

"I didn't know that I was considered a prisoner," Fiona said, aghast. The woman really was *too* much.

"Oh, yes. It's all over the news. The police want you very much. They think you—"

Jeremy took Lisa's arm in his. "She knows that. She just—"

With a swiftness that surprised all of them, Ace knocked Jeremy's hand off Lisa's arm. "If you want to keep that hand, lawyer, keep it off *my* woman!"

When everyone's attention was on Ace, Fiona slipped through the bushes unnoticed.

Ten minutes later she was still hidden from the group and still waiting. Where is he? she thought. Had she misunderstood him? Maybe he hadn't meant for her to meet him alone? Maybe he was... Maybe he'd been so overcome with jealousy over Jeremy's touching "his" woman that Ace was now in a brawl to the death with Jeremy, and maybe Ace would never show up. And maybe Ace had been lying about—

When Ace touched her arm, Fiona nearly jumped out of her skin. To keep her from making a sound, Ace put his mouth on hers.

"Do you always talk to yourself?" he whispered against her lips.

"*Your* woman?" she said with more venom than she meant. In truth, she hadn't meant to say anything about Lisa. Jealousy was unbecoming to a woman of her caliber. "Your *woman?*"

Ace laughed, then grabbed her hand and started pulling her through the brush. "I've given them so much to do that I figure we have thirty minutes before they miss us," he said as he adjusted the heavy pack on his back.

Fiona pulled back on his hand, as though she were reluctant to follow him. "Sure you don't want Lisa to go with you? Wherever we're going, that is."

Ace halted for a second. "To find the lions, of course," he said. "Did you forget that I told you that I know where they are?"

Actually, she had forgotten that; between the kisses and then his declaration of Lisa being "his" woman, lions, gold or otherwise, had skipped her mind.

But right now logic didn't have much to do with anything, and Fiona stood where she was, not moving.

Ace dropped her hand, then took a step toward her and put his hand under her chin to tilt her face up to his. "Would it help if I told you that I only said that to create a diversion? Would it help if I told you that I've come to love you very much and that if we ever get out of here, I plan to marry you?"

"That, uh, yes, that does help a bit," she managed to say.

"Well, then, come on, there isn't much daylight left."

Twenty-one

∽⦿⦿〜

Okay, so a woman gets a proposal from a gorgeous man and she expects to be made love to. You know, champagne and oysters on the half shell, candlelight, that sort of thing.

But what Fiona was receiving was none of that. Instead, she was being pulled through slimy water that was knee-deep (which meant it would be over cute little Lisa's head, she thought, with a smirk), and Ace (the man she loved) was frequently warning her about snakes. And alligators. And other things that she didn't want to inspect too closely.

Needless to say, Fiona's mood wasn't the best. And there was no one to take her bad temper out on but the man slicing through the thick water ahead of her.

"I don't see why you couldn't have figured this out before this," she said petulantly. "If only you'd realized that you knew where the lions were a long time ago, like, say, maybe right after the ol' teddy bear was killed, maybe we could have—"

She paused because Ace had stepped back to allow a snake to slither past them. If Fiona thought she could have closed her eyes and remained living, she would have done so. But she had to keep her eyes open and see everything: dark, murky water, overhanging trees, huge birds flashing by and seeming to laugh at them.

"I only knew what it was that I'd seen when I saw the map my nieces sent. Remember that I grew up on this land. I know it well."

"What a charming childhood playground," she said sarcastically as she hit at an overhanging bit of Spanish moss.

"Beats those concrete-and-steel places they give kids nowadays. Here, watch that, it's a hole."

Turning sideways, Fiona made her way past what looked to be a cavern beneath the water. "How deep is that thing?" she whispered.

"Bottomless, as far as I know." He tugged on her hand, but when she didn't move, Ace grabbed her and picked her up to swing her over some rotting vegetation, then deposited her onto dry land. Sort of dry land. It squished under her feet.

"I will never be clean again," she said, looking down at the wet slime that covered the bottom half of her.

Ace climbed up beside her, then bent his head to kiss her. "Yes you will be," he said softly against her lips, then straightened, turned away, and started walking again. "So where do we want to spend our honeymoon?"

"The Sahara Desert," she said quickly, making Ace laugh.

It was a good thing that Fiona was tall, because otherwise she would never have been able to keep up with his long stride. It was obvious that he knew where he was going, and he meant to get there quickly. She was glad of that because what light there was, was fading quickly.

"Is it too much to hope that at the end of this little walk there's a hotel waiting?"

Ace snorted at that, as though she'd just made a very funny joke.

As the light faded, Fiona moved nearer Ace, not that there was room to slip a dime between them as it was, but she tried to get closer.

As she was looking about her, hearing ominous sounds from every shadow and seeing shadows where there shouldn't be any, Ace said,

"We're almost there," and his voice made her jump.

"It's all right," he said softly, "you're with me."

"Yeah right," she said, "like all the snakes and 'gators know you by name."

"Mostly," he said, amusement in his voice. "Wanta hear how I found the lions?"

She was sure that something huge and hairy had just moved behind that tree. But then, maybe the tree was moving. She was holding on to Ace's hand with both of hers now, and her whole body was plastered against his side. Silently, she nodded.

"I think I was about ten, and I was out walking one day—"

That made her halt. "Ten? And walking in *this?*"

"Come on," he said, tugging on her hands. "You sound like my mother. I was in more danger near traffic than here. Anyway, I was walking and I saw a TV disappear behind some vines. Because of what happened later I don't remember much except that suddenly there they were, staring at me. I think they have emeralds for eyes."

Fiona waited for him to finish the story, but he just kept moving through the swampy land and said nothing else.

"Okay, I'll bite," she said after a while. "You were out slogging through swamp, fighting off snakes, mosquitoes, and man-eating crocs, and you were following a walking television when you came across a couple of golden lions—with emerald eyes, no less—and then what? Years later you didn't *remember* it? Was your childhood so exciting that you found pirate treasure and anthropomorphic machines every day, so you couldn't remember all of it?"

Ace laughed. "A 'TV' is a turkey vulture, and there was a little more to it than that."

"So?" she said impatiently.

"Eager, aren't you?"

She narrowed her eyes at him in threat.

"I had a bit of an accident that day."

She was *not* going to encourage him to go on with his story. She wasn't going to give him the satisfaction of begging him to finish what he was telling her.

"If you use this story with that doll of yours, do I get a cut?"

"You get tourists and me. What else do you want?"

At that Ace turned and pulled her into his arms and kissed her more thoroughly than he ever had before. "Nothing," he said, his lips against her ear. "Just you."

After a moment, he pulled away, and holding her hand securely, he started walking again.

"So what happened that day?" she asked, breaking her vow not to ask. But his kisses seemed to make her forget things.

"Broke my leg, then had to walk back because I knew no one was going to find me where I was, and I ended up with a fever. Later I thought I'd made up the lions, something I'd seen in delirium."

She thought about what he was saying and tried to imagine a little ten-year-old boy hobbling through the swamp with a broken leg. "How long were you in the hospital?" she asked softly.

He squeezed her hand in acknowledgment of her perception. "A couple of weeks."

Just when it got so dark that Fiona could see nothing, Ace pulled her into what seemed to be impenetrable jungle, but he was able to part the curtain of vines and enter into a space of such blackness that the void frightened her. And when Ace released her hand, it was all she could do to keep from crying out in fear.

But she held herself in check and stood silent and motionless as she heard him fumbling about with his backpack; then, after what seemed forever, he turned on a flashlight.

And that made things worse. All around them was dark, creepy-looking vegetation. The silence of the place made her skin crawl.

"Let's get the lions and get out of here," she whispered. "I don't like this place."

"That will be a bit difficult to do," Ace said, amusement in his voice. "We'll have to 'get them' as you say, in the morning."

It took her a moment to understand what he was saying. "Morning?" Her voice was rising in hysteria. "Morning? You want us to spend the *night* here?"

When Ace put his hand on her ankle, she did give a squeal of fear. But his hand moved up her calf, and she looked down at him. While she had been looking about the place in terror, he had unfurled a sort of sleeping-bag tent, a place that one could crawl into and zip the front and be safe from the darkness that was outside.

But, more important, the look in Ace's eyes was unmistakable. She looked into those eyes and she forgot about lions and murders and police trying to find them. Her knees gave way under her, and she sank down slowly to his open arms.

Deftly, easily, Ace pulled her into the little tent and zipped the door shut behind her; then he turned the flashlight off. For one small breath, Fiona seemed to be alone; then, suddenly, Ace was on her, pulling her to him, holding her, caressing her.

She hadn't realized how much pent-up emotion and longing was inside her until she touched him. In an instant, they were tearing at clothes, pulling them over their head; shorts went down over knees and ankles.

And everywhere hands and lips and skin touched. When Ace's mouth found her breast, Fiona moved her head backward, giving him access to the most sensitive spots on her throat.

His hands moved downward, over her hips, over the roundness of her buttocks.

And she explored his body. She touched the shoulders and back that had made her mouth dry with lust many times. She didn't know how long she had wanted him, but at that moment it seemed to be forever.

When he entered her, she cried out in surprise and delight, and Ace's mouth covered hers.

She didn't know what she had expected him to be as a lover, but the fire in him was not what she'd expected. But she had known he was a passionate man, passionate about his birds, passionate about his swamp, so when the fire that was within him came to the surface, she was the willing recipient.

They moved about within the little tent, their long arms and legs pressed against the sides of it, and they pushed and pulled and tried to reach more of each other, tried to get closer than they were.

Fiona wrapped her legs about Ace's strong waist and held on as he drove into her with force. And her body arched to meet each thrust as it hit her inner being, completing her, filling her, unleashing some deep secret within her.

And when he at last came, she was with him; feeling the explosions that rocked her body made every part of her quicken.

"I love you," he said as he collapsed against her sweaty, nude body.

She kept her legs wrapped about him, holding him tightly to her as she caressed his hair. She wanted to know every part of him, know his body as well as her own.

And she wanted to know what was inside of him. She wanted to share herself with him in a way that she had never shared with anyone else.

Maybe it was good that they had come to

know each other under such adverse circumstances, because she knew that in the future she'd never have to pretend with him. She and her women friends had joked that there was a "dating" personality that a woman kept with a man. "Until she lands him," Ashley said. "Then she can be herself."

Fiona had never been past that "dating personality" with a man, not even Jeremy. Not until she'd been accused of murder, that is.

But because of the way she'd met Ace, she had been her worst with him. He'd seen her tired and grumpy. He knew her sarcastic side and her spiteful side. He knew that she could be smart and she could be dumb. He even knew that she could sometimes be calculating and mercenary.

But he still loved her.

"A penny," Ace whispered into her ear as he moved to lie beside her, her head on his shoulder.

She smiled into the darkness. "I..."

"Out with it," he said gently. "Whatever it is, I've heard worse."

"When my father visited me, I tried to be the best little girl in the world," she said quietly, then said no more.

Ace took a moment to consider what she'd said. "In the hopes that he'd like you so much that he'd take you away with him instead of leaving you in boarding school."

"Right," she said, and there was a lump in her throat. "Those newspapers that talked about my lonely childhood weren't too far wrong." Turning, she put her mouth near on his neck. "But you..."

Again Ace hesitated. "But I love you even though I know that you are one bad-tempered lady."

"I am not!" Fiona protested. "At least not unless I'm being hunted for murder."

"And you find yourself with a man you dislike thoroughly."

"Well, you weren't very nice to me," she said in protest. "And, Ace Montgomery, if you tell me again that I broke that damned alligator of yours, I'll... I'll..."

"What?" he said, laughter bubbling in his throat, and his hand was beginning to move over her hip. "You'll set fire to my ticket booth?"

"I thought I just did set fire to your ticket booth," she said throatily, then nibbled on his ear.

"Oh? I don't remember. Why don't you show me again?"

"Okay," Fiona said as she moved her leg over his. "I think I will."

Twenty-two

⌒⊙⊙⌒

"So where are they?" Fiona said at the first sign of daylight the next morning. She had already struggled into her clothes and was on her knees inside the tent.

Still lying down, Ace yawned as he looked up at her. "Don't you want something to eat first? Or drink? Or—"

One look at his eyes and she knew what else he had in his mind besides food. Already his bare foot was running up her calf.

But she moved away from him. "What I want is a bath first and a life second. And I can't have either until we solve this mystery and get out of this swamp."

Still yawning and rubbing his head, Ace sat up in the tent; then when his head hit the ceiling, he lay back down. Fiona was backing out of the nylon.

"Even if you do see the lions, how's that going to tell you who killed Roy and Eric and Rose?" he asked.

"I don't know, but all of it helps. Do you think I have lice in my hair?"

"More likely leeches under your clothes. Why don't you remove them so I can check your skin?"

"Good try, but no. Get dressed and get out

here," she ordered, but there was a soft smile on her lips. Almost over, she kept thinking. Their ordeal was almost over; she could feel it.

Once she was outside the tent, she looked around and instantly knew that she was standing in something that was man-made. Nature hadn't done this. Besides, the Florida swampland was very flat, but this place was... It was like a two-story stone house, but it was hidden and seemed to be almost underground. In the front of the place vines hung down and old vegetation grew, so that it was almost dark inside.

When Ace emerged from the tent, Fiona hadn't moved but was staring about her. "What is this?" she whispered, for the place had an eerie feeling.

"I think it must have once been a burial place for some ancient people. It took a long time to build."

While she stood in one place, Ace took two steps away and picked up something from the ground, something shiny, then held it out to show Fiona. It was a silver pen, corroded and dirty.

"Yours?" she asked.

"My uncle's. I gave it to him." Ace's hand closed over the pen, and he looked about him. "I think maybe my uncle came here often, and I think he knew very well what I had seen when I broke my leg. But he told my parents that he knew every inch of the reserve and that there was no 'stone cave' that I kept describing."

"So how did he keep you from exploring and finding it again?"

Turning, he gave her a crooked smile. "He said this was government land and there were bombs planted over here. When I was older and knew that was a lie, I just assumed there was quicksand or too many 'gators or whatever. And also, when I was older, I wasn't here that often and..." Trailing off, he kept looking. "When you get older, you lose your urge to explore, and besides, whenever I started to walk this way, my leg began to hurt."

"I don't know how you can tell one place from another," Fiona said under her breath.

"You want to see the lions? You want to see what has cost so many lives, my uncle's included?"

Fiona opened her mouth to say yes, but there was part of her that wanted to run back outside into the hot Florida sun and never look at a cave again. But she found herself nodding; then when he reached for her hand, she took a deep breath and followed him.

He turned on the flashlight, then led her behind the tent, then down some stone steps, and she realized that most of the structure must be underground. With each step downward, the hairs on the back of her neck stood up straighter. It was as though a thousand eyes were watching them.

"I don't like this place," she whispered.

"Lots of dead people in here, I'd think," he said cheerfully.

"Very funny. You don't think the guys who had the lions built this, do you?"

Ace gave a snort of laughter. "I think this has been here thousands of years, and I think archaeologists would love this place. The lions are relatively new, only five hundred or so years old I'd guess, but then I don't know much about Chinese art."

"We'll take them back with us and ask someone," Fiona said, clinging to Ace's hand, her eyes searching the stone walls that dripped water under the vines that clung to them. Lizards scurried about, making her jump with their quick movements.

"Great idea," Ace said. "I'll carry one and you get the other one."

Fiona could only nod at his words as they went down two more steps. In front of them was what looked like an iron door. "In the future, I want to *read* about adventures, not have them. I really and truly do not like this place."

"You ought to see it in total darkness with a broken leg. Then you'd really like it."

"If that was a joke, it needs some work. Do you have a key to that lock?"

Reaching out, Ace gave a tug on the huge lock hanging on the metal door, and it came away in his hands, rusted through. When he pushed on the door, Fiona fully expected it to crash on broken hinges, but it swung inward easily.

"As I suspected," Ace said, his voice full of disgust. "Uncle Gil must have come here often enough that he replaced the door hinges. When I was here, they'd barely move. I had to shove against them with all my might, and when they did move, I slipped and pow! One leg crunched."

Fiona wasn't going to think about the pain he must have gone through then. "You don't suppose he installed electric lights, do you?"

Ace stepped into the blackness that was behind the door and disappeared for a few seconds. To Fiona, left behind in the darkness on her side of the door, it was an eternity.

"How about a lantern?" Ace asked, and his voice in the stillness made her jump. "Calm down, will you?" He handed her the lantern while he struck a match from the book he carried in his pocket.

"Now, get behind me and walk slowly. I don't like the look of this floor."

"I don't like the look of the floor or the walls or the ceiling or—"

"*Sssh!*" Holding himself very still, he listened. "Did you hear that?"

"I heard everything: snakes, lizards, spiders, all—"

"There! There it is again. Don't you hear it?"

She didn't know the sounds of the swamp well enough to know when something was unusual or not. "Could we just get these things and get out of here?" she said. "A police station is beginning to seem like a pleasure dome."

Ace listened for a moment longer; then he led the way past the door and into the inner cavern.

It was a small room, with stone walls, ceiling, and floor. But there was no vegetation hanging down these walls, no lizards darting about, and the stones were relatively dry.

And sitting in the middle of the room were two huge stylized lions, the kind that sit in front of Chinese restaurants. Only these were bigger than any she'd seen before, at least five feet tall, and they appeared to be made of solid gold. And they had big green stones for eyes.

"Oh," Fiona said, then sat down on the floor to stare at them. There was something regal about these huge creatures, something that made her feel that she was in the presence of majesty. "Oh."

While Fiona sat and stared in relative silence, Ace went to the first lion and ran his hand over the creature.

"My theory is that these were on the ship that went down and these were what all the murders then and now were about."

"How did they get here?" Fiona whispered. She still couldn't bring herself to do anything but look up at them in awe.

"Winches I'd guess, log rolling. A lot of muscle."

"No, I mean, that ship we read about didn't go down off the coast of Florida, did it?"

"I don't think so. Remember the diver and the men who pulled them out of the sea? The ship could have gone down on the other side of the world."

"And someone made a map," Fiona said softly. "A map that my father had."

"That your father stole and falsified," Ace said as he examined the eyes of the second lion.

Fiona didn't protest. It was a little late to try to believe that her father or anyone else on earth was a saint. "How?" she asked.

"I asked ol' Gibby a few questions about why they never found the lions, and I put two and two together. I don't think your father meant to die when he did; I think he meant for *you* to have these."

Fiona looked at him in disbelief. "They'd look great in my foyer."

Ace smiled at her joke. "I only met your father once, but he helped me and, to me, that says a lot about him. I think he must have felt guilty about leaving you to be raised by strangers, so he wanted to give you something, and I think he meant to go with you on an expedition and find these."

"Ah. Sort of a father-daughter night at the PTA, complete with door prize."

"Smokey wasn't used to the ordinary. He was into some pretty underhanded—" Breaking off, he looked at Fiona. "Anyway, that's my theory. Someone took the original map and made a copy of it, a copy so good, so well aged that Edward King, who had the map originally, couldn't tell it from the real map. Gibby said that King had even put—"

"I know, he put his initials in one corner in disappearing ink, and when the map turned out to lead nowhere, he held the map over a candle flame and there the initials were."

"Smokey was smart. Like his daughter," Ace

said, smiling at her. "And Smokey knew a lot about maps."

"But he didn't know much about people," said a voice from the doorway, making both Fiona and Ace turn sharply.

A man was standing there holding a gun.

Ace started to lunge, but the man instantly turned the gun toward Fiona's head.

"Move and she gets it," the man said.

Fiona was looking at the man, looking at him hard. He wore jeans, but the legs were tight enough that she could see that his left leg was smaller from the knee down.

"Russell," she said under her breath.

At that the man took his eyes off Ace and gave her the tiniest bit of a smile. "Smokey always said that you were the cleverest little thing he ever saw." The words were complimentary, but they were said with such hatred that Fiona had cold chills spring up over her body.

"So now what?" Ace said loudly, as though he wanted to distract the man from Fiona. "You kill us and take the lions? After all, you've already killed three people to get them, so why not two more?"

He was in his late thirties, and Fiona could see that his hair was prematurely gray. Her brain was racing as she tried to remember all that her father had written about this man in *Raffles*. He had been young that year when they were looking for the treasure, eighteen at the most. Her father had liked the boy, and Fiona remembered being jealous when she was reading the letters her father sent. If she'd been a boy, maybe she could have been in one of her father's stories.

Smokey had written with compassion for the boy, telling how he'd had a mother who was a prostitute and how, in a drunken fit, she'd pushed him down a staircase when he was two. The boy had survived, but his left leg had never healed properly, so he always walked with a limp.

"If we're to die, maybe you should tell us why," Ace was saying, and Fiona could see that he had concealed his lower half behind a lion so the man wouldn't see that he was trying to pull a knife out of his pocket. For a horrifying moment Fiona had a vision of the two of them grappling and someone dying.

But suddenly, Fiona's mind was clear, very, very clear.

She looked up at the man, who was just a few years older than she. "You don't want the lions, do you?" she said softly. "You never wanted them."

At that both Ace and Russell turned toward her.

Slowly, so as not to frighten him into movement, Fiona came off the floor and stood but a few feet from him. She was taller than he by at least six inches. "You just want me dead, don't you?"

"Yeah, I want you dead," he said, and there was no life in his voice.

"And him too?" Fiona said softly. "Must he go too? Why don't we let him go back to his fiancée, then you and I—"

The man gave a snort of laughter. "His girlfriend and the lawyer have been having it off for days. That lawyer is after her money. She's loaded, you know, and so is he." With a sneer, the man pointed the gun at Ace.

"That's enough reason to let him go," Fiona said. "This is between you and me, not him."

"Listen, Burke," Ace said loudly, bringing the attention back to himself, "I'm not leaving here without—"

"Don't call her that!" the man shouted, then held the gun out in his trembling hand. "She doesn't deserve that name!"

"All right," Fiona said calmly to the man. "He doesn't know what's going on, so he doesn't understand. He just happened to be related to someone who was in the way. It's not his fault."

"Don't give me that crap. I know what you two were up to last night. I heard all of it." He was a good-looking man except that there was something missing in his eyes, something that might be called sanity. Now, his mouth twisted into a smirk. "I even saw you two."

"As you said," Fiona said with a little smile. "He's rich. I was doing what I could to get him to give me money. I deserve money." Her voice lowered. "Like you do."

Out of the corner of her eye, Fiona saw Ace move, and she knew he had eased his knife out of his pocket. But what good was a four-inch blade against a gun? By now she knew Ace well enough to know he'd try to be a hero, and he was going to end up dead.

In a quick movement, Fiona placed herself between Ace and Russell. Behind her, she heard Ace's sharp intake of breath in annoyance. When she was between them, she turned so she could see both men at once.

"I'd like to introduce my brother," she said to Ace, then looked at Russell and said, "Half or whole?"

"Only half," he said. "I got the bad whore and you got the good one."

"I see," she said, pretending to know more than she did.

"Well, I don't see anything," Ace said loudly; then in one fluid movement he sat down on the rear end of the golden lion nearest the man with the gun. For all the world he looked like a man sitting in the company of friends. "One of you want to tell me what's going on?"

"She's the one that got the education, not me," Russell said, his hostility unmistakable.

"True, but you got to spend time with our father," Fiona said, sounding like a jealous child.

"Whoa now, I think you better start at the beginning," Ace said in a half shout as he put up one hand.

Why is he talking so loud? Fiona wondered; then she heard the tiny noise outside the open door. Someone was coming down the stairs, feeling his way down the old stone steps, using only the light that came from the lantern inside the room. But Fiona had to admit that half a ton of gold made good reflectors.

"What did Rose know?" Ace asked loud enough to make the walls ring.

"She saw you, didn't she?" Fiona said, not quite as loud but loud enough to cover the tiny sounds the person on the stairs was making. "She recognized you." Maybe it was at the mention of Rose, but Fiona suddenly knew who was on the stairs, and, more important, she knew how that person fit into the story.

"Why should I tell you anything?" Russell said petulantly. "Why should I—?"

He didn't say any more because someone hit him on the head with a little nylon backpack, and the gun went off, deafening everyone.

Epilogue

"Tell us again, Aunt Fiona," the little boy said, looking up at her with big eyes filled with curiosity.

"Yeah, tell us the part about the gun and the lions."

Fiona still wasn't used to being called "aunt," and she wasn't used to having a family, at least not one the size of the Montgomerys and Taggerts.

It was four months since that horrible day in the "golden cave," as the Montgomery children called it.

"Leave her alone," Cale Taggert snapped as she juggled identical twin boys on her hips.

Fiona was having trouble remembering names and who went with whom, but she knew that Cale was a famous mystery writer, and Fiona was dying to talk to her. She wanted to ask her where she got her ideas for her fabulous books.

"It's all right," Fiona said, smiling. "I don't mind."

Looking across the heads of the many people in the room, all of whom Ace swore were related to him, Fiona looked at the man she was to marry and smiled. Family was something that she'd always wanted, and it's what she'd got, although not quite in the form that she meant to get it.

"Go on," the little boy urged.

Fiona looked down at him and wondered who his parents were. There were so many children, and half of them seemed to be identical twins. In fact, there were so many twins that she wondered if maybe the baby she was carrying was actually two of them. She hadn't told Ace yet, but she would tonight.

She turned her attention back to the little boy. "Okay, let me see, where do I start?"

"With the lions!"

"No, tell us the story of *Raffles*," said another child. "I want to hear all about the bad men and the one that was your brother."

Raffles was a hit TV show now, much to the chagrin of parents, who universally seemed to hate the characters and the morals, or lack of them, that were represented in the show. It hadn't yet been revealed that the plump creature who lusted after the pretty young man was actually a woman.

The Montgomery money had been able to keep the papers from finding out the whole truth about the murders, so the fact that *Raffles* had actually happened wasn't known to the general public. And just before the show aired nationally, someone looked at Roy Hudson's original script and saw the name "Raffles" in there and changed the name from *Raphael*. "It wasn't a show to name after an angel," someone was quoted as saying.

Any profit that was made by the show that

had been left to Ace and Fiona in Roy's will was going to charity.

And the lions that had been taken from the cave were already in the back room of a museum in Florida that was very near Kendrick Park. At the end of the second TV season of *Raffles*, it was to be revealed that the story was vaguely true and that the lions the despicable characters in the show had been searching for but never found were on display in the museum in a brand-new wing. The new wing was a re-creation of an ancient burial mound, with stone walls and steps down into a room where the lions stood alone. The money to build the room had been donated anonymously.

In the new garden off the new wing of the museum was a gorgeous display of birds put on by neighboring Kendrick Park. And when the wing was opened, there was to go on sale a doll named Octavia, manufactured by the newly formed Burke Toy Company.

On the board of directors of the toy company was Fiona's mother, Suzie. "The good whore," as Suzie said on that day when she stepped through the door and clunked "Russell" on the head with Lisa's little backpack that she'd filled with rocks.

His real name was Kurt Corbin (renamed for the story by Smokey after Kurt Russell, the boy who played Jaimie McPheeters on TV), and he was the product of a liaison between Smokey and an alcoholic prostitute named Lavender. Smokey had been sickened at the way his son had been raised by the woman, so when a second long-term liaison produced a little girl, Smokey was ruthless in taking her away from a woman he viewed as little better than Lavender.

"I loved your father," Suzie said. "Really loved him. But he..."

It had taken Fiona a while to comprehend that she had a living parent, and it was still going to take time for her to forgive her father for keeping Suzie from her all her life.

"He told me that he was turning you over to some rich relatives of his and that you'd have the best of everything," Suzie said, sniffing from crying. "He talked about riding lessons and having your own pony. I didn't know the truth until I read about you in the papers. And I thought that if you were a sociopath, then it was my fault. That's why I wiped up the coffee with those papers. They told all about me but it was too soon for you to know."

Ace said that he only believed half of the story Suzie was telling, since it made her look perfect and Smokey the bad guy. "I don't think we should inquire too closely into where she's been these last years or with whom."

Fiona nodded in agreement. After all, Suzie had been living in a community that seemed to be riddled with people who didn't want to be seen outside their little compound.

But whatever Suzie was, wherever she had been, she had certainly come out the hero in the end. Through her underworld connections she had found out where Ace and Fiona were hiding and had sent them the message that said they'd find what they needed at the Blue Orchid. Neither Ace nor Fiona had asked her where she'd obtained the passports with the fake names.

After Suzie had clobbered Kurt with Lisa's backpack, Ace had wasted no time wrapping a belt around Kurt's hands and making him immobile. He was no more tied than Lisa came pounding down the stairs demanding the return of her pack.

Ace looked up from over Kurt's unconscious body and said, "How did you find us?"

"Him," Lisa said with distaste as she pointed at Gibby.

"Stole your map," Gibby said cheerfully. "I figured you'd know where you were headed and wouldn't realize it was missin'."

"I didn't," Ace said.

It was Jeremy who was awestruck by the lions; he couldn't take his hands off them. "It seems such a shame to put them in a museum," he whispered as he caressed one of the four emerald eyes.

"We could always melt them down and split the money," Ace said loudly; then when Jeremy's face lit up, Ace gave a snort of derision.

As for Fiona, she turned her back on Jeremy without regret.

Two hours later Ace's cousin, Frank Taggert, had a helicopter there and took the lot of them out of the swamp. And later Frank turned an army of investigators loose on finding out the facts of what Kurt had done.

Kurt hadn't bothered to cover up his own trail because he thought that he was safe in his anonymity, so there were hotel records, phone records, and eyewitness accounts. Several people had seen Kurt with Roy Hudson, and most of the patrons of a seaside restaurant had seen Kurt and Eric together the night Roy had been killed. "But I didn't think anything about it because the papers said that those two had killed him," was the reply all the people gave.

By the next morning, when Ace and Fiona faced the police and the press, they were followed by six lawyers armed with enough paper to flood the courtroom. And just to make sure that the judge understood what the three murders had *really* been about, Frank had one of the lions crated, moved, then reopened before the judge.

In the end, "false arrest" was the verdict and Ace and Fiona were free to go.

Of course Frank was being sued by three conservationist groups who said he'd violated "archaeological standards" or some such when he'd removed the lions from their "original" resting place. Frank hired some museum curators to tell how old the lions were and attest that they were originally from China.

The last Fiona heard was that the Chinese government was about to sue for the return of the lions or for billionaire Frank Taggert to pay for them. But Frank said not to worry, that the courts would take so long to decide who owned the lions that...

"We'll all be long dead," Ace said.

But Fiona was happy with the results of everything. In Suzie, she now had a blood relative, and she would soon have an enormous family by marriage. And the wedding had better be very soon because there was already a baby growing inside her. But, from the looks of the size of the families, no one was going to be shocked at her having a baby just seven or eight months after the wedding.

"Happy?" Ace asked, coming to stand beside her and slipping his arm around her waist.

"Very. But..."

"But what?" he asked, a small frown betraying his concern.

"I'd like to go home," she said softly.

"Oh." His voice was flat. "Your apartment. Did the rent ever get paid on it? I thought Frank—"

She put her fingertip to his lips. "Home to Florida."

Ace couldn't have looked more shocked. "You hate the place. You hate the heat and the swamps and the—"

"I know that you want to make it on your own and you don't want to use your inherited money but do you think we could bulldoze that cabin of yours and build something like our house at the Blue Orchid? Something with air-conditioning and a swimming pool? And"—she hesitated, then lowered her voice—"and a nursery."

Ace looked away for a moment. They were surrounded by people, but at that moment they were alone on the planet. He looked back at her. "Yeah, I think I can do that. You... have any idea when the nursery should be finished?"

"In about seven and a half months, I think."

He didn't say anything as, again, he looked away from her, but she could see the big vein in his neck pounding.

" 'Heron' if he's a boy and 'Ibis' if she's a girl," he said at last.

"I was thinking more 'Spoonbill' and 'Gnatcatcher.' But only if they're twins," she shot back at him.

At that Ace laughed so loudly that the whole room stopped and looked at him. But he just smiled, his fingers entwined around Fiona's.